Cover design by Okay Creations
Book layout by Lori Colbeck

ISBN: 978-1-950348-65-7

The world is filled with rays of sunshine if you know where to look. Thank you to all the glimmers of light who help illuminate the darkness for those of us who so often lose our way.

ONE

DARBY ZAMORA LOWERED her pink cat-eye sunglasses as she watched a windsurfer in dark blue swim trunks expertly lean into the breeze pushing him along Chammont Lake. Though she was onshore with her bright red painted toenails buried in the warm sand, she could appreciate the way his body moved with the grace of a dancer.

"I bet he's hot," she muttered.

Jade Kelly didn't even glance up from the book she was reading. "It's not even eighty degrees out yet."

Darby tore her eyes from the muscular figure zigging and zagging in the distance to the woman sitting beside her. Then she leaned forward enough to look around Jade at Taylor O'Shea, the third member of their little circle. The smirk on Taylor's lips confirmed that Darby had heard correctly. She'd shared her admiration of the man's physique, and Jade had responded with commentary on the weather.

"I wasn't talking about the temperature, Jade." Darby snorted with disbelief. "For freak's sake. Get your nose out of that book and check out that fine specimen before us."

Jade blinked at Darby for several seconds before gasping with realization. "Oh! Who?" She whipped her head from side to side, oblivious to the man Darby and Taylor had been watching. "Where?"

Darby sighed as she glanced toward the man who was no more than a distant blur now. "Never mind. What are you reading?" She snagged the paperback and then frowned at the cover of the self-help book. The smiling, well-put-together blonde on the front was surrounded by big colorful text that promised to help the reader heal from unexpected life changes. "Why do you read this crap? There's nothing wrong with you."

"I'm glad you think so." Jade cocked a brow over her sunglasses as she held her hand out in a silent request to have her book returned. When Darby didn't hand it over immediately, Jade wriggled her fingers, gesturing for her to hand it over. Then she sat forward as if to snag it.

Darby pulled it from her reach and flipped through the pages to read the chapter headings.

"There *isn't* anything wrong with you," Taylor confirmed. "You're practically perfect in every way. Just ask Liam."

Jade shook her head as she grabbed the book from Darby. "Don't start."

Darby chuckled as she was tempted to ignore the warning and dive right into the game Taylor had started. Her and Taylor's new favorite pastime these days was teasing Jade about her non-relationship with her non-boyfriend. Liam Cunningham was clearly head over heels for Jade, but as a recent divorcée, Jade wasn't ready for a relationship yet. Liam appeared to be on standby, waiting for the first sign that she was. Darby and Taylor suspected that as soon as Jade gave him the slightest hint she might be interested, he was going to pounce on it. And her.

Before Darby could engage in mocking Jade's inevitable relationship status, her phone dinged. "Saved by the bell," she muttered as she pulled the device from the holder on her chair.

After a moment of turning her phone this way and that to best see the screen in the midday sun, she tapped on the icon that indicated she had a new email. The second her inbox opened and she was able to read the subject line, she gasped and sat taller.

"What is it?" Jade asked, sliding her sunglasses down. Concern filled her voice, but Darby didn't respond other than to lift a finger in the universally known sign to wait.

Darby swallowed, tapped the new message from *The Noah Joplin Show*—her favorite podcast—and read the first paragraph.

Congratulations! The Un-Do Wedding Boutique has been selected as our small business of the week!

The Un-Do Wedding Boutique was Darby's latest attempt at making a living without working too hard. She'd done a million different things—property management, bartending, waitressing—but none of them seemed to stick. Every job she had ended up demanding more effort and time than she wanted to commit to. She preferred to be free with her time and focus. Not that she didn't want to work. She was more than willing to work—however, she refused to be one of those people who let their so-called careers take over their lives.

Jade had been one of those people and ended up divorced. Taylor was that way too. The best way to tell how her business was doing was to test her mood. If things were going well, she was happy and easygoing. When things weren't going well, which was too often, she was miserable and grouchy.

Darby wasn't about to let her entire life be dictated by a job. Nope. Not happening. So she floundered here and there and tried this and that, waiting for the right opportunity to come along. She was certain that had happened several weeks ago when Jade was helping her organize her closet and found the garment bags filled with wedding dresses that Darby had made by hand for brides who had never seen their dream day arrive.

Darby had been in a funk because her latest venture, Mistress of Ceremonies, had turned into a series of unfortunate circumstances where Darby had to explain that her list of party-planning services had *not* been code for sexual favors. Her bills, her coming due, and her party-planning schedule had been empty. Unless she'd wanted to take up some of those gross offers the strange men thought she'd been proposing, she'd had to come up with a new plan. But it had been Jade who'd pointed out selling the unused wedding dresses would be easy peasy. Darby had only had to list the already made dresses for sale as is and take the cash. And she had plenty of dresses too—from extravagant to simplistic bridal and obnoxious to tame bridesmaids' dresses. She even had a few adorable flower girl dresses she could sell.

But sadly, like most of her ventures, The Un-Do Wedding Boutique hadn't gained the traction needed for Darby to stay caught up on her bills. If something didn't turn around soon, she would have to look for an hourly position. The thought made her skin crawl.

There were a lot of things Darby could tolerate. An office job was not one of them.

However, presenting her store on *The Noah Joplin Show* was sure to turn things around!

As she read the email a second time, Darby fanned herself with her other hand. Her adrenaline spiked and caused her body to heat. Her eyes grew larger with every bit of information. Finally, she looked up but didn't see her friend's face. Her mind was elsewhere. "Give me a moment to collect myself." Her voice had come out breathless and trembling.

Taylor leaned forward and pulled her glasses off as well. "Darbs?" she asked, sounding as worried as Jade had. "What's wrong?"

"Nothing. Nothing is wrong. Actually..." Excitement filled Darby's chest and erupted in a high-pitched squeal as she kicked her feet in the sand. "Oh my gosh! This is the best news ever!"

"What is?" Jade demanded.

Pressing her hand to her chest, Darby rolled her head back and looked up at the sky as if she couldn't believe what she was about to say. "Have you ever heard of Noah Joplin?"

"Of course," Jade said hesitantly. "He has like a million followers."

"Well, more like a *quarter* million, which is significantly more than I have." Darby thought about her number of followers for a few seconds. "*Significantly*. He has a new segment where he invites local business owners in to talk about what

5

they do and tries to boost their sales. As soon as I heard him announce the new segment, I filled out the online form. That was two weeks ago. I thought for sure he wasn't interested in my shop, but look at this... I'm in." Darby's voice was unnaturally high, and she nearly started squealing again as she bounced in her chair. "Oh my God. He's so cute. He's so freaking cute."

"Who are you talking about?" Taylor asked, effectively splashing cold water all over Darby's moment.

Darby frowned at Taylor. Of course she didn't know. "Noah Joplin is the biggest Internet star in eastern Virginia. He's going to go all the way. He's going to get a national show someday. I know it. He's the real deal."

Jade nodded. "I have to agree. He's very charismatic."

"Charismatic," Darby said with a dreamy tone as she sank back and put her hands to her chest again. "That's one way to put it. He's an absolute doll. And I get to meet him."

"When?" Taylor's question was flat. Bored. But at least she'd asked. That was progress. Taylor's rough edges were a side effect of being raised by her grandfather and his horde of contractor buddies. However, over the last year of their friendship, she was starting to learn genuine manners.

Of the three, Taylor was probably the most levelheaded, but that also meant she was the biggest stick in the mud. Jade was smart and responsible, but she was also adventurous and willing to try new things. Trying new things scared Taylor. She overthought everything.

Darby tended to not think things through enough.

Jade turned her face so Darby couldn't see whatever unspoken reprimand she was giving. As a mother of two, Jade was really good at that silent communication. One look, one frown, one firm shake of her head was usually all it took to get Darby to stop acting foolish or Taylor to stop spreading her gloom and doom.

True to form, Taylor immediately smiled as if she'd intended to be smiling all along. Jade returned her attention to Darby with the same encouraging grin. Darby nearly called her on her motherly intervention—something she did to ward off the sibling rivalry–level bickering Darby and Taylor often fell into, even though they weren't sisters—but opted to focus on the email instead.

"Thursday." Darby gasped and turned on her phone's camera app. She yanked her sunglasses off and looked at the dark roots bleeding into her fire-engine red hair. She had an appointment for a touch-up, but not until the following week. "*No!* I can't go in like this. My hair is a mess." She held her hand out to look at her nails. "My manicure is a disaster." She dropped her phone and stuck her lip out at Jade because there was no way that Taylor would understand. "I have to see if my hairdresser can get me in. Like now!"

"I have an appointment for tomorrow morning." Jade pulled her phone from her bag and tapped the screen. "At eleven. If you can't get in, I'll reschedule my appointment and you can have my spot. It's not like I have anyone to impress."

Jade *did* have someone to impress, not that Liam needed freshly dyed hair to look at Jade like she'd hung the moon. Again, Darby passed on the opportunity to tease Jade about Liam's unrequited love. "You're the best."

A brilliant smile crossed Jade's sun-kissed face. Jade's obsession with outdoor activities had given her just enough muscle tone to scream sexy. In fact, she looked more like a model out of some high-end clothing magazine than the girl next door Darby always considered her to be. Ever since Jade had relocated to Chammont Point, she'd been finding herself. Which made her self-help book addiction even more annoying. If anyone knew where she belonged in this life, it was the zen-as-hell Jade Kelly.

For a moment, Darby felt a tinge of jealousy. She'd never fit in. She'd never found her place in the world. And she'd certainly never managed to squeeze herself into any kind of mold as comfortably as Jade fit the one she'd been creating for herself since her divorce. Sometimes it seemed like Jade won at everything she did—successful career, happy kids, easily landing on her feet after her divorce—while Darby floundered and fell and then floundered some more.

However, Darby knew that assessment of Jade wasn't exactly true. Jade's life had been a disaster a year ago. *She'd* been a disaster a year ago. She'd worked hard to bounce back as much as she had, and Darby was thrilled for her.

Just because Jade was better at pushing herself through life's ups and downs than Darby didn't mean things came that easily for her. And just because Taylor tended to bottle things up didn't mean she didn't feel things deeply. In fact, she probably felt them more deeply than most, which was why she was so guarded all the time.

Darby could see that even hidden behind what seemed like ten-inch walls of steel, Taylor was excited for her to land this interview. She didn't have to know who Noah Joplin was for her to be proud. And she didn't have to say she was proud for Darby to know she was. Darby had no doubt that Taylor would tell anyone who would listen that her friend was going to be on the show. And not because she was name-dropping—she probably wasn't kidding when she said she didn't know who Noah Joplin was. She'd tell people because she was proud of Darby in a dysfunctional but supportive kind of way, which Darby had decided was Taylor's real role in life.

Darby leaned forward so she could see both of her friends. "I think you guys should go with me. Noah Joplin records his show at a news studio in Fairfax. An *actual* news studio. I've always wanted to see what a real studio looks like."

Taylor's obviously forced smile spread into something genuine. "I've never been inside a studio either. I wonder how they manage all the cords for the lighting."

"Yeah," Darby said lightly, "me too."

Taylor scrunched up her face but didn't let Darby's lighthearted teasing get to her. They liked to pick and poke, but both knew the other was doing so with love and admiration.

Clapping her hands together, Darby bounced in her seat again. "I'm going to be famous!"

Thursday afternoon, Darby, Jade, and Taylor were guided through the big spaces of the TV studio where Noah Joplin's show was recorded. Darby had to fight the urge to do an impression of one of the newscasters she was familiar with. She could see herself sitting there, dressed to the nines and put together like a star with a bright smile on her face as she shared the latest updates and goings-on in her community. She'd sound smart and people would look up to her.

Yeah. She could totally do that. The desire to run up and

play pretend must have been written all over her face, because Taylor nudged her.

"Don't," Taylor warned.

"What?" Darby asked.

"What you're thinking about doing...*don't*," Taylor muttered.

Darby gasped, trying to fake offense. "I'm not thinking about anything."

"Bullshit. You're totally debating if you should run up to the newscaster's desk and sit in a chair."

She wanted to disagree, but she couldn't stop herself from grinning. Taylor knew her too well, and that was a comforting realization. "I would be a good newscaster." Darby lifted her chin higher as if she'd discovered some great truth. "Don't you think?"

Taylor creased her brow. "Do they have a rockabilly station, Darbs?"

Sticking her lip out slightly, she looked down at her red dress with the black polka dots fashioned to mimic the vintage style. Darby had never been comfortable when she'd been so-called normal. She preferred 1950s-style clothing, bright red hair, and the highest possible heels. "They should. It'd be much more interesting. Then I might actually watch the news." She picked up her pace as the gap between her and Taylor widened. "Do you know how lucky Noah is to get studio space for his podcast?"

"You said so," Taylor stated flatly. "Like three times on the way here, and it's only an hour between Chammont Point and Fairfax."

"He's a star," Darby whispered. "A *real* star. Most

podcasters have cheap equipment tucked away in their parents' basement."

Taylor chuckled as Darby glanced at the two people leading them through the studio. Every time Darby looked at him, she had the urge to pinch herself. This felt like a dream to her, but Jade was acting like this was nothing special. She and Noah were chatting like old friends. She didn't seem the least bit fazed by their location or the status of the man next to her.

Once again, Darby felt a twinge of jealousy at how comfortable in her skin Jade always seemed to be. One of the things that Darby and Taylor shared was their social awkwardness. She glanced to her right and confirmed that Taylor, too, looked out of her depth walking through the studio.

Prior to opening her own business, Jade was some kind of bigwig at a marketing firm, so it made sense that she felt at ease talking to a celebrity. Darby hadn't ever considered Jade's job had been commingling with such cool people, but it must have been. Otherwise, how could she be so casual about talking to Noah Joplin?

Darby was much more comfortable than she used to be about putting herself out there. Not *Jade*-comfortable, but she couldn't imagine her old self agreeing to be interviewed on a podcast. The new Darby no longer minded being the outcast and not fitting in. She'd come to find that as an asset.

Even so, she did wish she could feel a bit more laid-back about meeting Noah Joplin. She'd practically passed out when he'd shaken her hand.

"What are you thinking now?" Taylor asked.

"I want to be like Jade when I grow up," Darby whispered.

"She's talking to one of the most handsome men ever to have walked this earth, and she's not even stumbling over her words."

Taylor raised her brows and chuckled. "Yeah, but have you seen her try to make sense when Liam's around?"

"Liam doesn't hold a candle to this dude."

"I guess that all depends on whose candle it is."

Darby started to ask what that meant, but the room opened up even more and she was suddenly too enthralled by their surroundings to worry about Jade, Liam, and mysterious candles.

The high ceilings and big lights were exactly like she'd seen in movies. So were the cameras. And the big green screen where the weather was delivered looked exactly how she'd always imagined. As much as she thought she would be an awesome newscaster, she knew she'd never be a meteorologist. The pointing and aiming and gesturing at nothing on the green screen behind her would definitely trip her up. Even so, she was in awe of the setup.

"This is amazing," Darby whispered. She didn't think she could possibly see all the aspects of the studio she wanted to see, but she was determined to soak up as much as she could. Turning her head this way and that, she tried to memorize everything.

"It's pretty cool," Taylor agreed.

Darby gawked at her. "Pretty cool? What is with you two? We are walking through a television studio."

"In Fairfax, Virginia," Taylor pointed out. "It's cool, but I'd feel more excited if we were in Hollywood."

Blowing out a breath, Darby shook her head. "This is as close to Hollywood as we'll ever get. Make the most of it."

They walked through another door and started down a hallway. There were several smaller spaces that had been allocated for the podcasts hosted through the news station, each with fancy equipment and foam squares on the walls to help with dampening sound. Darby recognized a few names on the signs.

Each studio was barely bigger than Darby's walk-in closet. Then, like a beacon in the night, there it was—Noah *freaking* Joplin's studio. He opened the glass pane door and gestured for the three of them to enter.

"I'll give you a quick tour—really quick since there isn't much in here." Noah smiled and winked at Darby. "Then we'll sit and chat to get you comfortable with the scene before we go live."

As soon as he reminded her why she was there, a knot formed in her chest. Darby Zamora was standing in a studio with Noah Joplin, about to go live with him in front of all his viewers, and...

"Oh, God." Darby pressed her hand to her chest as reality sank in, and like a fire sweeping across a dry forest bed, her nerves came to life, causing her anxiety to flare. "I...I can't do this."

"What?" Taylor asked.

Darby's heart plummeted to the pit of her stomach, and she shook her head as she turned away. "Nope. No way. I gotta go."

Taylor blocked her exit.

"I'm out," Darby said. "I am not doing this."

"Darby," Noah soothed in a deep, calming voice. "It's perfectly normal to be nervous—"

She shook her head harder. "I'm not nervous. I'm dying.

Right now. Death is here. For me."

Noah smiled, and the world nearly stopped spinning.

"And now I'm dead," she muttered.

Putting his hands on her upper arms, he waited until she met his gaze. "Take a few deep breaths." He closed his eyes and inhaled deeply then blew the air from between his lips. The rush of air smelled like mint, which she found oddly soothing. Mint wasn't on the top of the list of soothing scents for her, not usually, but as she inhaled, the smell calmed her.

After his second demonstration of how she should be inhaling and exhaling, Darby closed her eyes and mimicked his technique.

"And one more." Noah repeated the process.

When Darby lifted her eyelids, he was smiling at her. Her stomach fluttered but with a different kind of nervousness.

"How's that?" he asked softly. "Better?"

"I guess," she said, though she wasn't sure if she'd told the truth. She felt like elephants were having a wrestling match inside her stomach—rolling, tumbling, and tearing her apart bit by bit.

"We're going to talk, Darby." Again, he'd used a soothing tone. Like some kind of freaking hypnotherapist or something. "We're going to sit right there at that table, and you're going to tell me about your business. You'll tell me a few nice stories about how you made the dresses, and you'll talk about how you came up with the idea to sell them. We'll talk like you'd talk to your friends."

"You're going to do fine," Jade said.

Darby glanced toward Taylor, who gestured for Darby to move farther into the studio.

"It's like twenty minutes of your life." Taylor casually

tossed out her usual logic and lack of sympathy for Darby's plight. "You can do this."

Darby lifted her hand to her forehead and noticed how much her fingers were trembling. Dropping her hand back to her side, she clenched her fingers into a tight fist. "Yeah. Okay."

She hesitantly moved to the chair where she knew— from watching his show online—guests sat. She only half listened as Noah showed Jade and Taylor the equipment and explained how the foam on the walls absorbed the sound so voices didn't echo and mics wouldn't screech from feedback. Normally, Darby would be enthralled by what he was saying, but her heart was in her throat and her breath was coming too fast and shallow.

Twenty minutes. That was what Taylor had said. Twenty minutes of her life.

As soon as Noah took the seat across from her, Darby looked to her right. Taylor and Jade hovered in a corner of the room behind the man who would be operating the camera. Darby knew his name. Noah introduced him at the beginning of every podcast. Sometimes he even engaged with the guests. *Luke*. That was it. His name was Luke.

Jade and Taylor stood behind Luke as he put on his earphones and got ready for the podcast.

The podcast where she was going to be the guest. Front and center. *Oh boy*.

"Okay." Noah settled in to the chair across from her. "For the first segment, you're going to sit quietly. Your mic won't be on. I'm going to talk, do the opening bit, and then I'll introduce you. I'll ask a few questions. All you have to do is smile and answer. This is going to be straightforward, and it's going to go by really quickly."

Darby nodded, and after he pushed her earphones closer, she put them on. They drowned out much of the noise in the room, and suddenly everything was a blur. Noah was smiling his charming smile and talking as casually as he had with Jade when they'd come into the studio. He was so relaxed, so calm, that Darby actually felt reassured and was able to take a real breath. This couldn't be too bad. If it was, he'd be nervous too.

Twenty minutes. Darby had taken showers longer than that.

She breathed again. Deep, soothing, calming breaths. She slowed her mind, and when Noah started his introduction, she gave herself one last, quick pep talk.

This was going to be easy peasy and over in a jiffy. This was her big break. This was going to put her shop in the spotlight and turn her luck around.

You got this, Darbs, she told herself.

"I'd like to welcome this week's small business owner, *Darby Zamora*." Noah sang out her name in the fun and zany way he always used when introducing guests. Hearing him apply that off-key tune to her name made her giggle and eased her nerves a bit. "She's the owner of The Un-Do Wedding Boutique, which has quite an interesting concept behind it."

She glanced over to where Jade and Taylor were standing. Jade smiled and Taylor gave the thumbs-up. Silent cheers from her personal squad. Swallowing hard, Darby focused on Noah again. A wave of heat washed over her, and she thought she might break out into a sweat, but he winked and smiled, and she was drawn into his charms. As quickly as it had overcome her, the heat subsided, and she almost forgot she was on a live podcast.

"Darby, how did The Un-Do Wedding Boutique come about?"

"Oh," Darby said, and even she heard the tremble in her voice. "You see, I was having a hard time getting my other business, Mistress of Ceremonies, off the ground because everyone thought I was offering sex. I wasn't," she was quick to add when Noah's eyes widened. "I was planning parties. Or trying to, anyway. I was a party planner... A Mistress of Ceremonies. Get it?"

"Got it." His smile widened, clearly amused by the conversation.

"Well, a lot of people—men in particular—thought it was something completely...inappropriate." She rolled her eyes. "I'm not even going to tell you what this one guy thought amuse-bouche meant."

Noah laughed and hesitantly asked, "What *does* it mean?"

"Nothing bad. It's a complimentary hors d'oeuvre." She laughed and pressed her hand to her chest. "Well, trying to explain that only led to more misunderstandings, because he thought he was getting something else altogether. And for *free*!"

Darby glanced around, pleased that not only Noah, but Luke, Taylor, and Jade were laughing at her story. The anxiety left her as she realized she could do this. She could totally sell herself and her boutique. This really was easy!

"Uh, well," Noah said when he stopped laughing. "I can see why you struggled to get that business off the ground. How did that lead to this fun spin on wedding consignment?"

"Oh, well, I had a seamstress business a long time ago. I like to sew my own clothes because"—she gestured down at herself—"curvy girls with unique tastes in fashion can't run to the department store. So, anyway, in between sewing high-waist slacks, short-shorts, and faux vintage swing dresses, I sewed wedding attire to make some cash."

"Faux vintage..." Noah laughed again. "Sorry, you're going to have to spell all that out for me. I don't know nearly enough about women's fashion to understand what you said."

As if the man had flipped a switch, Darby found her groove as she explained her clothes and the vintage style she preferred and how much she loved making the clothing. Suddenly, she was in her element. Her smile was natural, and the words were flowing from her lips without a single stammer, hiccup, or incoherent thought.

Then he turned the topic again. "Okay, so you were up to your eyeballs in polka dot dresses and people misunderstanding what complimentary hors d'oeuvres meant. How did that turn into your hilarious wedding dress consignment shop?"

Oh. Back to Un-Do. She must have gone off on one of her rambling tangents. Jade and Taylor were always pulling her back to topic. They had actually reminded her to stay focused. Easier said than done when she got to talking.

Darby stumbled through her thoughts for a few seconds, trying to regain her footing. "Well, you see, my best friend Jade came over to talk me through the crisis and organize my closet because I tend to clean when I get upset. Anyway, there were all these garment bags stuck way in the back of my closet, and she asked what was in them. I told her those were dresses from cancelled weddings that I'd never charged the brides for, so I got to keep them, even though I had no idea what I was going to do with them. That's when she had this total light bulb moment and suggested I sell those while trying to figure out my next business venture. And here we are."

"Here we are," Noah agreed. "Now, part of the reason we chose The Un-Do Wedding Boutique is because you have these hilarious stories to go with each dress. Are those true stories?"

Darby giggled, thinking of the fun she'd had sharing the background of the dresses. "Mostly. Some are *slightly* embellished for entertainment purposes. But don't ask which ones," she quickly added. "I'll never tell."

"Fair enough. How did you come up with the name The Un-Do Wedding Boutique?"

"Well, it's like a play on words," she said. "I do, but...not. Un-Do. I do. *Un*-Do. Get it?"

He laughed again. Damn. She was nailing this interview! This was awesome. She wanted to give herself a high five for being so damn good at this. Darby glanced toward the corner. Jade gave her an enthusiastic thumbs-up, and Taylor smiled a real, genuine smile. Even Luke, the camera guy, seemed to be having a good time watching the interview.

When Luke noticed Darby looking his way, he asked, "How many weddings get cancelled? Like, how many wedding dresses can one seamstress have?"

She waved her hand. "Man, you don't want to know how many women find out their men are snakes *after* getting engaged. It's like they think they have us snagged and can finally reveal their true colors. No offense to the men in the room."

"Tell us," Noah encouraged, "what is the craziest story you were ever told about why a wedding was cancelled?"

Darby paused, only for a few heartbeats, before laughing. "Well," she said teasingly before breaking into a story about a groom, two bridesmaids, and what *apparently* took place on a secluded beach somewhere on the west side of Chammont Lake. The bride only discovered the groom's betrayal because she found three pairs of underwear in her canoe the next morning and recognized her fiancé's as one of them.

"No way." Noah gasped and then broke into a fit of laughter. "How did she find out who the other two pairs belonged to?"

"That," Darby said, "I don't know. But..." She told another tale of a bride who did tell her how she found out her groom was cheating. He called out her sister's name in bed!

Noah gasped dramatically as Darby confirmed the story was true. A hundred and ten percent.

"Well, we are about out of time," Noah announced, "but I have to say this is easily my favorite small business highlight we've done so far. I don't know if we can top this one. Thank you for visiting us, Darby, and for all of you out there, be sure to visit The Un-Do Wedding Boutique." He rambled off the website information, and then her ears filled with the sounds of a commercial.

"We're out." Luke turned his focus to buttons and screens and whatever it was he did to get them ready for the rest of the show.

Noah's smile never faltered as he pulled his earphones from his head. Darby pulled hers off too. As she did, she glanced at Taylor and Jade. They didn't seem nearly as amused as she thought they would be. Taylor forced a quick smile when she caught her gaze and Jade gave her a slight nod, but they weren't laughing like they had been minutes before.

"That was fantastic, Darby," he said.

"Really?" she asked, soaking up his praise since her friends seemed less excited. She wished she could sit there and dissect everything she'd said and relive the interview, but she didn't have time. He stood and all but ushered her and her friends from the studio.

"We only have a short break," he explained. All of Noah Joplin's shows went out with only a few seconds of delay. He never prerecorded. If he had, he wouldn't have had to bring Darby in at this particular time on this particular day. Even so, knowing that he'd be back on the air in thirty seconds or so, she was hesitant to leave.

Noah stood and gestured toward the door, but Darby couldn't make herself stand. This had been the most epic moment of her life, and she wanted it to last.

"Thanks so much," Taylor said to Noah as she gripped Darby's hand and practically yanked her from the chair and toward the door.

Though she didn't want to go, she was glad Taylor had jerked her from her daze. She probably would have sat there staring and smiling like a fool for the entire hour of Noah's show. But now that the spell was broken, a new kind of euphoria washed over her.

That. Had. Been. Awesome!

As soon as the three of them were outside, Darby rolled her head back and let out a squeal. Her smile spread so wide her cheeks ached. "So?" she asked, eying them. "What'd you think?"

"I think you did great," Jade said.

Darby's smile faltered when she noticed Taylor doing that forced smile thing that Jade always encouraged her to do. "What? What's wrong?"

Taylor let her smile fade as she shrugged and glanced at Jade, who shook her head almost imperceptibly, but Taylor said, "It's just... Do you think you should have told Noah all that stuff about the cancelled weddings?"

"What stuff?" Darby asked, trying to remember what could have possibly upset her friends.

"Those were some pretty private stories you shared," Jade said, sounding equally as hesitant. "Maybe we should have talked about that before you went on the air."

Darby waved her hand to dismiss their concerns. "I never shared anyone's name. Nobody could possibly know who I was talking about."

"Chammont Point isn't that big," Taylor reminded her. "People know more than you think."

"I had clients from all over the region," Darby stated, slightly offended that Taylor didn't understand that her work was sought after. Or at least a few people outside of Chammont Point had reached out to her. "You guys." She gave a slight laugh, surprised by their behavior. "Relax. Nobody could possibly know who I was talking about. *Nobody.*"

She turned on her heels and headed toward the exit, practically walking on air.

TWO

THE NEXT MORNING, Darby dropped onto her sofa and clicked the icon on her phone to check her online store sales. She was ready to print labels, ship boxes, and collect the windfall from her interview the day before. Closing her eyes, she took one last moment to manifest success as the app opened. Her smile and her spirits sank when she noticed she didn't have a single new sale.

"That can't be right," she mumbled.

Scrolling through her analytics, she could see that visits to her site had increased by the thousands. She'd had so many notifications about new comments on her products that she'd had to turn off the beeping sound on her phone so she could get some sleep. How could there not be a single new sale?

Opening the site, she selected one of the dresses and scrolled through the comments.

Beautiful work.
Funny stories.
This is cool.

That was the sum of what she read. Until...

I don't think it's funny at all. She's making money off people's broken hearts.

Darby's stomach knotted. That wasn't true. That wasn't what she was doing at all. She was just selling dresses.

Seriously, a commenter responded to the broken hearts assessment, *this is cold.*

A sick feeling washed over Darby. Why would anyone say that?

She went back to the product details and read the description of the dress and the sidenote.

This bride dodged a bullet. Literally. Her groom ended up in jail after pulling a gun during a drunken argument with his neighbor.

Darby chuckled. That was funny. Not mean. She didn't say anything derogatory about the bride. Why would anyone say this was cold?

Jade walked into Darby's house without hesitation. "Hey." She used to knock but gave up the habit some time ago, especially since Darby never knocked when entering Jade's place. Knocking was for strangers and salesmen. "Taylor and I are headed out onto the water. Want to come?"

Darby was tempted to say no. She did *not* have a love of the water like Jade. Nor did she have the athletic build like Taylor. So why in the hell would she want to sit in a kayak trying to keep up with her friends as they playfully raced across Chammont Lake?

Her idea of being on the lake was a raft lightly floating on the waves created by the adventurous people on personal water crafts and in boats. Or even better, sitting on the shore and watching other people enjoy the water. On the rare occasion she did go swimming, she liked to stay in the cove where she and Jade lived so they were the only ones in the water. On the nicer stretches of beach of Chammont Lake, the water could be crowded.

Darby's favorite water activity was to find a spot in the sand and stay put until they had to go back to work, which was whenever they chose since they all worked for themselves. Jade was steadily growing her new marketing business, and Taylor was trying to establish herself as a contractor but wasn't having much luck. Darby much preferred when they were sitting together, soaking up the sun.

Yet, every time Taylor and Jade planned an afternoon kayaking, paddleboarding, or canoeing, Darby went along.

She never told them how much she hated it. If she did, they'd stop inviting her, and while Darby knew she should be okay with that, she really wasn't. She hated when Jade and Taylor spent time together without her. She'd never had real friendships before these two, and old insecurities revealed themselves when her friends planned time without her.

So despite knowing that her arms would ache and she'd end up overheated with sweat rolling down her back and brow, she nodded. "Yeah. Okay."

Jade tilted her head and eyed Darby. "Everything okay?"

Darby held out her phone. "People are being kind of mean." She lifted her face and creased her brow as Jade crossed the room to her.

Jade took the phone and dropped onto the sofa as she looked at the screen. She was silently scrolling when Taylor came in.

"You two coming or what?" Taylor asked.

Darby looked down at her bright yellow dress. "I need to change." She pushed herself up and headed to the bedroom while Jade stared at her phone. She heard Taylor ask what was going on but didn't listen for Jade's response. However, as soon as she was in shorts and a light T-shirt, she rejoined them. "What is that all about?" she asked, gesturing toward her phone.

Taylor furrowed her brow and pressed her lips together as if she didn't want to answer. The words came out of her anyway. "We told you yesterday. Not everyone is going to find those stories amusing."

Jade looked up with a sympathetic smile. "Maybe you need to reconsider your sales pitches, sweetie. The dresses speak for themselves without all that stuff about the wedding cancellations."

Darby accepted her phone and read a few more of the comments. After reading a few funny responses, she shrugged. Though there were a few who didn't seem to get that the stories were for fun, most of the comments were upbeat and supportive of the listings.

"I don't know," she muttered. "Just because a few people are overly sensitive doesn't mean everyone is. Right?"

Jade and Taylor glanced at each other, but Darby locked the screen on her phone and stuffed it into her pocket.

"You can't please everyone," she said. "I learned that a long time ago. I won't let the naysayers get to me. They surprise me, that's all. Now that I know the trolls are coming, I can ignore them. It's fine." She shrugged off the sense that she'd been attacked and marched into the kitchen and pulled out a water bottle. "Okay, here's the deal. I'm going kayaking with you, but you have to remember I'm slower. Don't go darting off and leaving me alone. Got it?"

"One race," Taylor all but begged. She smiled wide as she looked at Jade. "One race so I can reclaim my title."

"No," Darby moaned, but her protest fell on deaf ears. Her friends were already taunting each other. Part of her wanted to back out, but then she watched them head for the door without seeming to notice she was hesitating, and the part of her that needed to belong pushed her to follow.

Rolling her head back, she silently pouted as they walked toward the shore. Once there, they pushed their kayaks into the water and climbed in as they'd done dozens of times before. The trip started out fine, a nice slow and relaxing pace, but soon they were picking up speed, and then as always, Taylor shouted, "Last one to the buoy has to make dinner," and they were off.

Darby tried to keep up. "Why are you going so fast?" she called, but they were too far ahead to hear her.

However, she wasn't so far behind she couldn't hear them taunting each other as they cut through the water like it was offering them no resistance. Setting her paddle across her lap, Darby swiped at her brow and took a few deep breaths, trying to restore her oxygen levels. In the distance, Taylor lifted her paddle up and hooted out in victory as she neared the buoy. Jade yelled something about a redo, and they both laughed.

Suddenly, defeat settled over Darby. She hated moments like this. Far too often, she felt like the third, and flat, wheel in the trio. She didn't like it. Jade and Taylor didn't do it intentionally. In fact, Taylor often insisted *she* was the one who didn't fit into their group. But sometimes, Darby's old sense of not belonging was too strong for her to ignore, even when she was with her best friends.

Darby had never fit in. She'd never been a part of a group. She'd always been on the outside looking in. After years of feeling like that, she'd learned to embrace being different when, a few years prior, while waiting tables, she had served a table of loud, confident, and amazing women. As she'd refilled margarita glasses and chip baskets, she'd overheard them talking about the beauty contest they were entered into. Darby usually ignored the conversations of her customers, but these women looked like her. Curvy, boring, and about as far from glamorous as one could get. They did not look like beauty queens.

That night, when her shift ended, she went to the club her customers had been discussing. There, strutting the runway, the women had changed from ordinary to out of this world. Witnessing her first Pinup Contest had changed Darby's life. She'd been enamored by the women who'd walked the stage in vintage rockabilly dresses paired with bold hair and makeup. What captured her even more was that none of them seemed self-conscious about their bodies. Not a single one shrank back when the spotlight fell on her. They were brave and feisty and had inspired the hell out of Darby.

As soon as she'd gone home, she'd scoured the Internet for patterns and made clothes to adopt the classic look. The victory rolls, bright lipstick, and colorful dresses suited her. She'd dyed her hair fire-engine red and learned how to draw her eyeliner into exaggerated wings. For the first time in her life, Darby Zamora felt at home in her skin. She was no longer ashamed of her pear shape or shorter than average height.

The clothes became her armor against the self-doubt that had always plagued her, and she'd learned to disregard what other people thought. She was free. Her confidence had quadrupled overnight. She no longer felt the need to hide inside herself. Something about the heavy makeup, fun clothing, and deliberate desire to be seen had shaken her out of her wallflower persona. She was awake for the first time in her life. And she loved it!

But that didn't mean her old insecurities were gone. They were there, and they tended to nag at her whenever Jade and Taylor seemed to be able to get along without including her. That was trivial, petty, and not a great way to feel about her friends, but the nagging was undeniable.

Jade and Taylor circled each other, tossing out more teasing words, before paddling back to Darby.

"You okay?" Taylor asked, still smiling from the race she'd won.

Darby groaned miserably. "It's hot. I have sweat in unsexy places, and I'm starting to smell like an unsexy man."

Jade chuckled as she came to Darby's side. "Drink some water, and then we'll go around the island."

"No," Darby whined. "You know I can't keep up. Can we go home now? There are margaritas there. An entire pitcher. Waiting for me to drink it all."

"Why do you come with us?" Taylor asked. "We all know you hate kayaking."

"I don't..." Darby sighed as she struggled to get her kayak turned around. "Okay, I do. I hate this damn thing with the passion of a thousand burning suns, but it's fun being with you guys."

"We do plenty of other things together," Jade said. "You don't have to do this to spend time with us."

Taylor cast a glance at Darby. "She's afraid she's going to miss something."

Darby didn't deny the accusation. She couldn't. Being insecure in her friendship might be silly, but the doubt, the fear, the worry that someday they would realize she wasn't good enough to be their friend was real.

Jade offered her a sweet smile. "Come on. Let's go home. But no margaritas. It's not even noon yet."

Darby blew out a raspberry to show her discontent but secretly was happy they were headed back to shore. By the time Darby made it to the sand, Jade had pulled her kayak onto the beach and Taylor was a few seconds behind her.

As soon as the three of them were standing together, Jade quietly said, "I wish you wouldn't let your insecurities get to you, Darbs. We're your friends. We're not going to ditch you."

"I know." Darby felt heat flood her cheeks. "It's silly, but..."

Silence hung over them for a few seconds before Taylor asked, "Are you ever going to open up about whatever?"

Darby lifted her brows. "Whatever?"

"My mom ditched me when I was a kid. Jade's ex-husband is a lying cheat who broke her heart. You've hinted at being an outcast, but you never talk about it."

"I was a nerd. That's all."

"You know, you expect us to be all open and honest," Taylor said, "but when it comes to talking about your issues, you always blow us off. That's bullshit, Darby. Jade told me a while ago that we had to be gentle with you because of whatever you've been through, but you've never told us *what* you've been through."

Darby screwed up her face as she looked at Jade, who simply shrugged, which was all but admitting she'd said that. "Fine, you want to hear my sad story? We were poor. I never fit in. People picked on me for being Mexican in a predominately white school. The usual high school growing pains bullshit. Nothing as dramatic as maternal abandonment or a broken marriage. Normal life *bullshit*."

Taylor's stare implied she didn't believe Darby.

"I..." Darby glanced back out at the water. "I didn't have friends. I was an outcast, which made me an easy target. The other kids were mean. More than mean. They were cruel. They made me hate school." She looked down and sighed. "They made me hate myself. I hated myself for a long time because of the things they made me believe. You may not like this"—she gestured toward her red hair, navy blue fitted shirt, and high-waisted black shorts—"but for the first time in forever, I feel good about who I am. I feel good about myself. I know my style doesn't suit you, but dressing like this means I get to control how people see me. They don't get to tell me how I should be seen. This gave me my power back. Power that I let other people take away from me."

"Hey," Jade said soothingly, "you have us now. We're going to be right here, and we aren't going anywhere, Darby."

"Thank you." Her smile faded, and she shrugged as embarrassment tugged at her. "I guess that's why I hate it when you guys do stuff without me. I know you aren't leaving me out, but I was always the last one chosen in gym class or for group projects. It's silly to feel like this as an adult, but I don't like being left out. It reminds me of sitting alone every day in the cafeteria in high school with my nose shoved in a book so people thought I *wanted* to be alone."

"I get it, Darbs," Taylor said. "You don't have to explain to me. I mean, look at me. I wasn't exactly prom queen. People steered clear of me because I was awkward and...maybe a little mean."

"*No*," Jade gasped with faux shock, "not you."

"Only to those who tried to cross me," Taylor clarified. "I never fit either. And I don't have to tell you how damaged I am from my mom's so-called parenting. She was in prison before my eighth birthday. Trust me, that screws a kid up. But things are different now. Things are better. We have each other. You also don't have to do things you don't want to do to fit in with Jade and me. It's okay if we do things without everyone included sometimes. You can always hang out here and make us lunch and drinks so we can veg out when we get back."

She smiled in a way to let Darby know she was teasing, but Darby thought that might actually be an okay idea. She'd be doing something *for* her friends, even if she wasn't trailing behind them across the lake. Maybe she'd try that next time. They would appreciate that. Jade would make a big deal about how much she liked whatever Darby had done. Taylor would even smile and say thanks.

That was the best thing about their friendship. They were all intuitively aware of what the others needed. Jade needed to take care of them because she felt she'd been a bad mother to her two kids when they were growing up. Taylor needed to be accepted despite her lack of polishing because people tended to give up on her. And Darby needed her cup filled with love and appreciation because she'd never really had that before.

They all found a way to do those things for the others in small but important ways.

Darby was also really glad her friends understood her insecurities and didn't judge her. Feeling like she was being ignored might seem foolish to some, but Taylor had a lot of the same problems. Jade had that sense of rejection too, only hers came from her ex-husband. They both understood where Darby was coming from, and she knew they would never abandon her.

And that was why they were such good friends.

The feeling washing over Darby later that evening was far too reminiscent of what she'd felt that morning when she'd first seen the posts people had made about her shop being mean. The comments on her page were mostly positive, but the negative ones were increasing in volume and viciousness. Not only were people saying that The Un-Do Wedding Boutique was mean, but a few had even commented that someone who looked like Darby wasn't capable of understanding what she was doing. That thread had spiraled into borderline cruelty.

Darby deleted the comments and blocked a few of the people who had engaged, but that didn't erase what she'd read from her mind. The unease that settled over her was also familiar. She'd felt that way for four long years of high school.

And now she felt that way from her website and the hundreds of messages.

Hundreds of messages. On her website. Waiting for her to read and reply.

She closed her eyes when her phone dinged, indicating someone else had commented on her page. A squeal of protest rose from her throat as she frantically tossed the freaking device aside. She didn't want to see it or hear it ever again...or at least for the next hour or so.

After pulling the faux fur blanket from the back of the couch, she tucked it around her shoulders and over her head as if a blanket fort could hide her from her responsibilities. Even under the cozy covering, she felt the weight of the world crushing down on her.

Damn it.

That now familiar sickness filled Darby because of people on the Internet. Hugging a pillow to her chest, she heaved a big sigh. Tossing the blanket aside, Darby grabbed her phone and texted Taylor and Jade to gather at Harper's if they were able. Darby needed a bourbon caramel sundae with candied pecans and an extra maraschino cherry on top of a cloud of Harper's homemade whipped cream. Then, and only then, could she muster up the strength to get her inbox and her life under control. She could do this. She *had* to do this.

Darby drove to her favorite ice cream shop to order the dessert that was intended to put a little sunshine back into her day. As soon as she parked, she checked her texts to see if either of her friends would be joining her.

On my way, Taylor had messaged. *Get me a hot fudge sundae with nuts.*

"Hey," Jade called, walking up the sidewalk. Even though Jade lived next door, they usually drove separately because Darby tended to dawdle and Jade liked to get right back to work. She'd given up fighting with Darby about hurrying up long ago. As Darby climbed from her car, Jade pulled her sunglasses from her face and tucked them on top of her head. "You okay?"

Darby shook her head. "I can't be a grown-up today, Jade. I just can't."

"Come on." Jade laughed gently and pulled her toward the door. "You find us a table, and I'll stand in line."

As soon as they were inside, Jade asked what Darby and Taylor wanted and then headed toward the end of the line while Darby sank down at a sticky table in the corner. Within moments, Taylor straddled the chair across from her. She looked around the little ice cream shop as if assessing the situation. She always liked to scan the area around her before settling in. Jade thought it was because Taylor was naturally suspicious of everyone, but Darby thought Taylor wanted to make sure nobody was paying too much attention to her. Not that she could be missed when they were in Harper's. Sitting against the pink, mint, and turquoise décor, she stood out like an undertaker at a circus.

"What happened?" Taylor asked.

Darby didn't use the same pouty face and voice she did with Jade. Taylor didn't have the same maternal sympathy. She'd tell Darby to knock it off and spit it out. "Un-Do is getting so many comments."

"And?"

"And my phone keeps dinging. *Constantly*. I can't get any peace."

Taylor widened her eyes. "Well...I can see how that would get to you. Have you tried, oh *maybe*...turning off the notifications for a while?" she asked sarcastically. "Because you can do that, Darby. With the press of a button."

"I know," Darby muttered as she took note of where Jade was in line. Darby needed sympathy, not logic. Taylor wasn't good at sympathy.

"Why do you need notifications on your phone anyway?" Taylor continued with her annoying sensibility. "Take the app off your phone and only deal with customers during your work hours...which you can set because it's your business."

"Yeah, I could do that," Darby said flatly. Part of her wanted to stomp her stiletto and tell Taylor to stop trying to fix everything and feel sorry for her, but like pouting, tantrums wouldn't work with Taylor, either.

Taylor lifted her dark brows and waited for several seconds. "So. Why don't you do that now so you can enjoy your ice cream instead of sitting there looking like you're going to break down?"

"Because."

"*Because*?" Taylor drawled out.

Darby's eyes lit when a teenager dressed in a pastel uniform and paper hat called Jade's name and she accepted a tray being slid across the counter. With Jade at the table, Darby might get a little support for her emotional distress rather than Taylor's attempt at solving the problem. She needed pity and ice cream.

As Jade was doling out their orders, Darby's phone chimed with the annoying ding to notify her of a new comment.

"Do you see?" Darby asked Jade because Taylor would simply tell her to ignore it. Darby pulled the glitter-covered device from her bag and pressed her fingertip to the sensor to unlock the screen. "This never stops."

"Turn it off," Taylor repeated, pulling her sundae closer to her.

Darby ignored her as she opened the administrative page to her online shops. As soon as she saw the notification had been a sale at Un-Do, she checked the shop app and gasped. Okay. Having a sale rather than another comment about her or her shop made things a little bit better.

"What's wrong?" Taylor asked.

"Nothing. I mean." She stared unbelieving at the unexpected number of sales on her site, taking a few seconds to process the information. After a day of nothing but comments—some funny and some malicious—she had actually made a sale. "Someone bought five dresses."

Jade sat next to Darby and leaned over to peek at her screen. "*Really*? That's great."

"Holy shit." Taylor sounded genuine in her excitement. "That's amazing."

"It is," Darby said. "It really is." Suddenly, her gloomy mood faded and the weight that had been pushing her spirits down lifted. She'd made a sale. And a really good one too. Just like that, with that one notification, she felt vindicated in her shop *and* her sales pitch. "What did I tell you?" She beamed across the table at Taylor. "What did I tell you? Noah Joplin saved my life. I should send him flowers."

"Enough," Taylor stated. "Put the phone away and eat your ice cream."

"But..." Darby started.

"Ice cream," Taylor stated.

Before Darby could dig into the bowl filled with a whipped cream and syrup–covered treat, her phone dinged again, and she opened the app. "Do you see that? I made another sale."

Jade stopped lifting a bite of frozen yogurt to her mouth. Jade's battle with cancer had turned her into a health nut, and she only ate frozen vanilla yogurt with almond slivers. However, Darby was certain Jade would add one of the shop's sweet syrups someday. Maybe even colorful sprinkles. "Honey, I never thought I'd say this, but you need to stop working for a few minutes. Your ice cream is melting."

"Speaking of melting," Taylor said in that singsong voice she used right before teasing someone—it was a toss-up who it might be. "I drove by Liam's shop earlier and noticed someone's car there."

Jade rolled her eyes. "I was buying a snack."

"And you couldn't pick that up at the grocery store like a normal person?" Darby asked. "You *had* to go to Liam's store?"

"He has the kind of juice I like."

"I bet he does," Darby muttered, causing Jade to gasp.

Taylor laughed and then winked at Darby. "Wonder why he keeps her favorite juice in stock. Think he's using that to lure her into his sexy little web?"

"Stop," Jade stated firmly. "I am still—"

Taylor cut Jade off as she repeated the overused excuse. "—finding your footing—"

Darby slipped in to finish. "—as a single woman."

Jade gave each of them a quick side-eye, making the point that she wasn't amused. Jade's kids were in college. She had years of practice with that side-eye thing, and she used it like a master. Darby's mom had used that same warning for years.

Darby's mom had passed away weeks after Darby's eighteenth birthday. Though she was an adult, she still had a lot of growing to do that her mom should have been there to see her through. She hadn't realized how much she missed those subtle acts until Jade had come into her life. Sure, Darby was an adult and didn't need maternal reproach, but coming from Jade, the slight shade made Darby feel loved. Even though Jade was only a few years older than Darby, whenever she did that maternal thing, Darby felt warmth in her heart. She felt loved. And she loved that about her friend.

"In other news," Jade said, "look at us. In a few weeks, it will be one year since we met."

Darby's eyes lit. Jade and Taylor really had become Darby's best friends. They spent so much time together that Darby almost had forgotten what life was like before them.

Soon after she'd changed her look, Darby had quit waiting tables and worked up the courage to leave her hometown of Chammont Point for the first time. With her newfound confidence, she thought she'd see the world, but every time life tripped her up—which happened way too often—Darby ended up back in the little town where she'd grown up. She never planned to stay here for long, but the previous summer had once again changed her. The three of them had instantly become an unbreakable trio. Their friendship was something Darby had never experienced before, and she couldn't imagine ever leaving them.

Now that she had two amazing friends, she didn't mind the little lake town nearly as much. In fact, she'd come to find the same comfort living in the tiny cove as she'd found in her clothing.

"Can we go out on a date?" Darby asked. "Like a friendship anniversary date?"

"I was thinking we should do something fun to celebrate," Jade said. "We can dress up and go someplace fancy for dinner. Maybe a nice steakhouse or something."

"No," Taylor stated. "I'm not dressing up. I don't even have anything to wear to a nice burger joint, let alone someplace *fancy*. We'll have a cookout or something."

"We always have cookouts," Darby challenged. "This is special."

"*No*," Taylor stated more firmly. She heaved a loud breath before following up with a softer tone, "I don't want to, Darby. That's not fun for me. I don't like doing stuff like that."

"You don't have to dress up, then." Darby looked to Jade for backup. "Please. We need to do something to celebrate our friendiversary. This is important."

"We should at least have dinner at La Cocina," Jade said.

Darby frowned. "We eat at La Cocina at least once a week."

"Which makes it *our* place," Taylor pointed out. "Where better to celebrate our friendship than at *our* place?"

"Well, I'm dressing up," Darby announced. "This is probably the only relationship I'll ever have that lasts long enough to celebrate anniversaries. You could at least wear slacks or something other than cargo pants."

"I like cargo pants," Taylor said. "Gives me lots of places to hide weapons."

"Why do you need to hide weapons when you can simply pull the stick out of your ass?" Jade asked with a straight face.

Darby rolled her head back and let out a whooping laugh.

This. This was exactly what she needed to take her mind off her businesses.

"Oh my gosh," someone said, approaching the table. "Are you the Un-Do lady?"

Darby stopped laughing, shocked at being recognized. "Uh, yeah."

The woman held her hand up as if waiting for a high five, which Darby hesitantly gave her. "I thought so! I saw you on Noah Joplin's show. You are so funny, and your site is awesome. I love it!"

"Oh," Darby said and sat taller. Holy crap! Someone had recognized her? From her online shop? Her spirits lifted as she smiled more widely. This must have been what it was like to be Julia Roberts! "Thank you so much," Darby said, adding extra sweetness to her words. She didn't want to get a reputation for being cold to her fans.

"I sat up laughing my ass off half the night," the woman continued, talking fast around her big grin. "I think I read every single description you listed. The little tidbits you share about why the weddings were cancelled are hilarious."

"I'm glad you like them," Darby said with that extra superstar effort. "You are so sweet."

"Hey, don't listen to the haters," the woman said before backing up a step. "Your shop is amazing. I wanted you to know that."

Darby waved at the woman before she walked away. However, her smile faltered when she looked at Jade and Taylor. Neither of them seemed at all impressed that Darby had experienced her first genuine moment of being a celebrity. "What?"

Taylor narrowed her eyes at Darby, looking as angry as Darby had ever seen. Her heart dropped as she thought her friend was about to cuss her out for something.

"Can I help you?" Taylor demanded.

Darby opened her mouth but before she could speak, Taylor pushed her ice cream aside, looking like she was about to fight. Finally, Darby realized Taylor wasn't talking to her. She turned and spotted several people staring at her. They didn't look thrilled about seeing Darby there. They didn't seem excited to meet her. However, with Taylor staring them down, they looked away.

Only then did Darby glance around Harper's and notice there were several people staring her way. The woman who had all but announced to the world who Darby was had brought attention to her... A lot of attention to her.

Suddenly Darby recalled the comments on the page. The "haters" that the woman had mentioned. People mocking her clothes, her hair, her makeup. Suddenly, she didn't feel like a celebrity. She felt like a pariah. An outcast. Like she didn't belong.

Like the nerd sitting alone at the lunch table in the high school cafeteria.

Swallowing hard, she pushed her ice cream away too. "I should go."

"Don't," Jade said.

Darby barely heard her. She was on her feet and out the door in a heartbeat.

THREE

DARBY WAS STARING out at the cove the next morning doing her best to not let the hateful comments on her website and hard stares from customers at Harper's get to her. However, ugly thoughts, recollections of what had been said, had kept her up most of the night and woken her in the morning, only for her to find even more nasty comments.

A dark cloud was forming over her spirits, blocking out the rays of light she'd been basking in ever since Noah Joplin's interview. Darby was no stranger to depression.

Her mom used to call it self-pity, but Darby knew it was something darker. Her mom had been great at pulling Darby from these bouts of turning in on herself, but after she'd died, Darby had a really hard time overcoming the episode. Some called it grief, but if Darby were honest, she had slipped into a depression that had taken her almost two years to get through.

If she were honest, that feeling was creeping up on her again. Not the full-on depressive episode that she'd faced when her mother died, but the haunting need to withdraw and disappear was growing.

For a few minutes, Darby had felt like a success. A real success. She'd been walking on air. She was certain The Un-Do Wedding Boutique was going to spring her into a new direction—a career she would love. But now...everything felt like it was on the cusp of collapsing around her, as things tended to do.

She never seemed to find her balance for long, but she'd hoped things were turning around for her.

Her shoulders slumped as the sun disappeared behind a literal cloud. The forecast was calling for rain, and she thought that couldn't possibly be more fitting for her mood. And her life.

Sunny one minute, storming the next.

She didn't know why she was so surprised. This tended to be the rhythm of her life. Things never seemed to work out for long. Disaster was always right around the corner. She should have known this was coming. Even so, she was blindsided by the negativity coming toward her from all directions.

When her phone rang, she ignored it. She wasn't in the mood to chat. With anyone. She'd already sent Jade back to her cabin and replied to Taylor's texts that no, she didn't want company. When she was in a funk like this, she was better left alone.

Another day had brought another round of nasty comments on her boutique and left her in a foul mood. She didn't need to spread that around. There was enough ugliness in the world without her barking and picking fights with her friends—which she feared she might do if they lingered in her space for too long. If they saw how down she was feeling, they would try to fix it. They'd tease her and make her smile or drag her out of the cove and into the world she was desperate to avoid. They'd try to cheer her up.

And that was the last thing she wanted.

However, after a second set of ringing, she glanced at the screen of her phone to see who was trying to break into her gloom. The number on the screen was one she didn't know, so she again ignored the call.

But then the phone rang a third time.

Cursing, she answered by slapping her fingertip to the screen and dramatically swiping to connect. "For God's sake, what do you want?"

"Darby?" an annoyingly cheerful voice asked.

The happy sound was like a cheese grater scraping across her nerves. She closed her eyes and cringed. "Yeah," she answered with a flat and uninterested tone that was intentionally the exact opposite of what she'd heard.

"Oh my gosh!" The cheese grater turned into a coffee grinder. "I found you."

Something about the voice coming through the phone was familiar, but Darby couldn't place it. She scoured the recesses of her mind, trying to figure out where she'd heard it before, but nothing came to the forefront of her foggy brain. Running her fingers between her eyes, she felt a headache starting to throb, and she exhaled.

Between the stress and the impending change in the weather, the pressure was getting to her. Usually, she enjoyed a good guessing game. Not today. This was one of the rare times when a potential surprise annoyed rather than amused her.

As she dropped her hand, Darby furrowed her brow. "So it seems. Who *is* this?"

"This is Jennifer Williams," the woman practically squealed out, "from high school. You remember me. Right?" The way she made her voice nasally and stretched out the words made her sound like a bad rendition of a 1980s Valley Girl. "Oh, you probably remember me as Jennifer Crosby, but it's Williams now."

The picture that formed in Darby's mind didn't match anyone she could recall from high school, not that she spent a lot of time reminiscing about those days.

"We had chemistry together with old Mr. Hall," Jennifer said with that odd cooing tone again. Darby immediately assumed she had a horde of children who only responded to the unnatural pitch that giving birth seemed to produce in women. "Remember? He always smelled like bologna?"

Chemistry class had been a nightmare for Darby. One of the cooler kids had unhooked Darby's bra in the midst of an experiment. Darby had squealed and jumped, knocking her beaker over and nearly starting a fire. The entire class had laughed, and Mr. Hall had made Darby pair up with someone "more responsible." For the rest of the semester, Darby had to work with a partner because Mr. Hall didn't trust her, even though the accident hadn't been her fault. Worse than that, she had to listen to jokes about the incident from almost everyone at Chammont Point High.

That one moment had set off years of torment, with Darby as the target.

Seconds passed as recognition forced its way through the remaining daze lingering in Darby's brain. She had worked hard to put those horrible years behind her, but they came rushing back like repeated punches to the gut as Jennifer rambled on. Every snide comment, every joke made at her expense, and the overwhelming dread she faced every morning as she walked into the high school. Those years had been hell for Darby. Those years had broken her. If she were honest, she still hadn't fully recovered from the pain inflicted by her teenaged bullies. Their words still haunted her like ghostly whispers trying to scare her back into the social obscurity they had forced her into.

When Darby finally remembered a nerdy little thing named Jennifer Crosby, she sat taller. Jennifer had been an outcast like Darby, but not quite as far on the outside looking in. Jennifer had friends, one or two at least, but Darby wouldn't have counted herself as one of them. Jennifer had been a band nerd, a science geek, and socially awkward.

Which meant despite her level of geekiness, she had still been higher on the social ladder than Darby. Not that being more socially accepted than Darby Zamora was some kind of feat back then.

"Oh my gosh," Jennifer continued. "I can't believe we haven't spoken since high school."

Darby could. She'd cut ties with everyone she'd gone to school with the day she'd graduated. She hadn't looked back, and that had been intentional. She hadn't seen or heard from Jennifer since that day, and she wasn't certain why she was now. They certainly had no common thread holding them together, and Darby certainly wasn't expecting a personal invite to any kind of reunion.

Last summer, Jade had invited some of her old classmates to the cove. Darby had enjoyed helping her plan and play hostess as they caught up. She had felt a twinge of jealousy as they'd laughed and shared old stories. Not because Jade had other friends, but because Darby knew she'd never experience anything like that. She didn't have funny tales to tell or old friends to share them with. Not that she suspected that was the reason for Jennifer's call.

"Yeah," Darby said. "It's been a long time. What's new?"

"In case you don't know this, I'm a *totally* successful influencer now," Jennifer said, going on to explain that she had a podcast with a *huge* audience, and it just kept growing. The forced energy oozing from her words was enough to made Darby close her eyes to resist the urge to hang up. She wasn't friends with this person. They'd never been friends. Why the hell did she care about Jennifer's podcast?

Darby shoved those bad feelings away and focused on Jennifer touting her online success. She had a video channel with over a hundred thousand subscribers. Her podcasts varied from vacation spots to new restaurants and even fashion fads. She covered all the up-and-coming people, places, and things. She simply couldn't believe how her little website had turned into something so amazing.

Darby couldn't believe that the Jennifer she remembered from high school had turned into an influencer. Then again, Darby was nothing like the old version of herself either. Time and experiences changed people, so she shook the image of the old Jennifer from her mind and built a new one.

"Nice" was the only word Darby managed to push out, from fear she'd reveal the bitterness she felt. Not that she wished anything bad for Jennifer, but she didn't need her nose rubbed in someone else's success right now.

"So I couldn't help but wonder," Jennifer continued, drawing out the words and reminding Darby of one of those life coaches hyped up on caffeine; not only was she far too chipper, but no sane person sounded that excited, "if you're the same Darby Zamora who owns The Un-Do Wedding Boutique, that *awesome* new online shop."

"Yes. That's my store."

"Great!" Jennifer's enthusiasm was obviously forced. Nobody could be that excited to find out Darby owned a virtual store, no matter what she was selling. "I thought that was you when I watched *The Noah Joplin Show*, but you've...*changed*." She said the last word like she wasn't sure if she was giving a compliment or not. Darby considered pointing out that Jennifer had obviously changed as well, but then Jennifer picked up her speech in that far too happy tone again. "I'd love to talk to you about your shop for my show. I live in Fairfax now, but I can be in Chammont Point in about an hour. Where can we meet?"

Not *are you interested* or *do you want to*. Just *Where can we meet?*

Darby was offended by the pushiness, but she bit back the snarky words threatening to spill from her. This was why she'd wanted to be alone. Because she knew she'd say something mean, and then she'd have to find a way to make up for her bad behavior.

The self-deprecating cycle was one she'd been trapped in for years. Irritation grew low in her gut as the old and new parts of herself battled over how to respond. She should say no. Tell Jennifer thanks for the opportunity, but she'd pass. But then she felt bad because Jennifer had taken the time to find her and call. She'd invited Darby to her show, and turning her down would be rude.

Darby closed her eyes and silently cursed herself. She'd

never been able to stand up for herself or tell someone no without feeling bad for doing so. That was what had led her to being the perfect target for the crap she'd had to deal with for four long years at Chammont Point High.

All the times she failed to stand up for herself came rushing back like one of those flashy old-time movies where the scenes were chopped together and running into one another in a way that didn't make sense. Something strange washed over her in that moment. She narrowed her eyes as she cursed her past self for being so damn weak and scared all the time. She again chastised her past self for being the victim of circumstance instead of trying to find a way to overcome.

"Darby?" Silence hung on the phone for a few seconds. "People all over the Internet are talking about your shop," Jennifer said, sounding a little less confident. "Your approach is so unique. You're hilarious."

Darby didn't respond as she tried to process the feelings brewing inside her.

"I am so totally impressed by your success," Jennifer continued. "I really want to share it with my viewers. Imagine how much traffic your site will get after I tell them about it. They're going to go *crazy* for your wedding boutique."

Darby didn't need anyone to go crazy for her wedding boutique. Her wedding boutique was making *her* crazy with all the messages she was getting. Even though the positive feedback still outweighed the negative, the sardonic comments were overwhelming.

Had she known that some people would take her sales descriptions so personally, she would have clarified on Noah's show that they were funny little snippets meant to gain interest. She'd never meant for anyone to take the stories as mean-spirited or as her mocking the brides. She would have explained...

Darby sat a bit taller as serendipity slapped her across the face with a gigantic wake-up call screaming, *Hello!* She had missed that opportunity on Noah's show, but she was being handed the opportunity to change that. With Jennifer's podcast. Jennifer didn't have nearly the following that Noah did, but she still had a larger platform than Darby. And she was inviting Darby to talk about the site...giving her the chance to tell people to calm the hell down.

"If I highlight your virtual shop on my site," Jennifer continued, "over a hundred thousand people are going to know about it. That could really help your sales. However, if you aren't up for it—"

"No," Darby said, cutting her off. This was her chance to set things right. She was taking it. Her depression and resentment over Jennifer's call fizzled out, and a renewed purpose filled her. This was her chance to make things right. She was taking it! "I'm up for doing your interview. Come to my house as soon as you get to town." Darby rambled off her address and a thank-you to Jennifer for reaching out.

When she hung up, she glanced at Jade's cabin, debating if she should ask for some of her friend's marketing expertise this time. Instead, she rushed back to her cabin and did a quick cleanup. She'd invited Jennifer to her home. She couldn't have empty glasses and wadded-up tissues sitting around. Darby wasn't a slob by any means, but the last twelve hours had been rough on her, and she'd let things pile up.

Within half an hour, her little cabin was spotless, and she was digging through her closet for the perfect outfit. She chose her favorite halter dress—a bright red that matched her hair—and a pair of killer black heels. She finished the ensemble with a chunky black necklace and matching earrings. As she styled her hair into victory rolls and a low bun, she kept one eye on the clock, making certain to leave herself enough time for her makeup.

By the time Jennifer showed up at her door, Darby looked like she was ready to strut down the catwalk. She smiled a big fake smile and invited Jennifer into her cabin. Though the living room was small, the bright colors and open blinds made the cheerful space seem larger. Jennifer lifted her brows as she took in the living room. Darby was used to people doing a double take when they first saw her colorful home.

Yellows, blues, and reds were her chosen colors, which made for a cheerful space, but one that some people found to be too much. Darby didn't. She thought it was perfect. The colors were uplifting and bold. Taylor had once told her that her home looked like it'd been decorated out of children's building blocks. Darby liked that comparison. She hadn't taken offense. She thought that was fitting, actually. She liked the happy feeling the vivid colors created.

But she knew that style wasn't for everyone, and looking at Jennifer's white capris and baby pink blouse all but confirmed she was one of those people. She probably would have loved Jade's cool and subtle style much more than what she was faced with walking into Darby's cabin.

"This is...unique," Jennifer said, looking around. "Not quite what I was expecting."

Darby grinned. "I'm not the little mousy girl you remember from all those years ago."

Jennifer's smile softened. "Neither am I. It's good to be grown up, isn't it?"

Darby sighed as she let some of her defenses slip. She'd been in a shit mood all day. It was time to let go of the clouds she'd allowed to form over her head. She needed to shake it off and take the steps she needed to move forward. She had invited Jennifer here to help clear the air, and she couldn't do that if she let her grumpy mood continue.

Smile, she told herself. *Really smile.*

Taking a breath, she let it out slowly and forced away some of the gloomy aura that had been hovering around her all morning. "Yes. It is."

Moving farther into Darby's cabin, Jennifer gestured toward a cloth mannequin in the corner. The curvy bust was on a pole that was steady enough for Darby to pin dresses as she worked on them. Most of the clothes she designed were in larger sizes because thin women found vintage-styled clothing in stores much easier than women like Darby, who had curves. She made the occasional single-digit-sized outfit, but most of her clients wore larger clothing, hence the larger-sized mannequin.

"Darby, can you sit so the mannequin is over your shoulder?" Jennifer asked, though it sounded more like direction. Since she was the one with the successful podcast, Darby didn't think she should argue about where she sat, though the light was better by the window.

"Oh, sure." Darby moved a yellow straight-backed chair to the desired location and then perched on the edge of the seat, tall and proper. "How's this?"

"Perfect," Jennifer said with a smile.

She took a few minutes to set up her camera and portable

light on a tripod—which made Darby feel better. She didn't want shadows falling across her face. She needed to be bright and perky on the video when she nicely told people to simmer down.

Several minutes later, Jennifer finished fussing and sat on the couch. "Are you ready to start?" she asked.

Darby filled her lungs, straightened her spine, smiled brightly, and then nodded.

"Tell me," Jennifer said, jumping right in, "how did The Un-Do Wedding Boutique come to be?"

"Well..." With a smile plastered on her face, Darby explained her catering business and how trying to get it off the ground had become overwhelming. She explained how her best friend suggested she sell things she'd already created until she decided what to do next. She even explained how she'd made the dresses for brides but had kept the dresses rather than charging them for weddings that weren't going to happen.

Then she slipped in how she had decided on the sales tactics. "I'm trying to recoup the money I'd invested in the time and materials for these dresses," Darby explained, getting the part where she was going to soothe all the naysayers and let them know she meant no harm. "The little stories I tell online are a sales tactic. They're there to get attention."

A flicker of something lit in Jennifer's eyes but faded away before Darby could identify it. "So they aren't true?" Jennifer asked.

"Well...they're true, but..." Darby stumbled over her words. She hadn't expected to be challenged, or she would have had a response on hand. "They're not... I mean..." Shit.

Maybe she should have consulted with Jade first. Jade could have helped her put the words together so they came out faster. Smoother. More genuine.

She glanced in the general direction of Jade's house, but it was too late to call for backup now. Returning her focus to Jennifer, Darby smiled. "I don't tell anyone who those things happened to. My former clients' names are never revealed."

"So," Jennifer said, "because you keep the real names anonymous, you think it's okay to share their stories?"

Darby sat back a bit and blinked long and slow to process whether that had been a real question or a subtle attack. "They're *just* stories."

Jennifer leaned close, and the sparkle in her eye returned, reminding Darby of a vampire in a movie closing in on its prey. She beamed in a way that made Darby feel like Jennifer was setting a trap. "Tell me, how does it feel to capitalize on someone's broken dreams?"

Darby hadn't been expecting the sudden turn. "Excuse me?"

"That *is* what you're doing," Jennifer pressed. "Don't you think?"

"No," Darby stated. "I didn't cancel the weddings."

"But your business is called The Un-Do Wedding Boutique. Your tagline is 'Her bad luck is your great deal.' Don't you think that's a little...*insensitive*?"

Darby froze. Insensitive? No. Maybe. *No*. "It's... It might be a little...tacky," Darby said.

"A little?"

Sitting taller, Darby jutted her chin out ever so defiantly. The pissy mood that had plagued her all morning returned threefold, and thunder rumbled through her brain. "It's bridal consignment. I'm *selling* things that people no longer need. I'm not breaking up weddings. Let me remind you," she stated, "I didn't even charge the brides for the work on those dresses. That's why I'm selling them. To finally get paid for my time and effort."

Jennifer's pensive look faded and her smile returned. "Well, you've certainly been successful...getting paid."

Not nearly as confident as she'd been a few seconds prior but equally as angry, Darby nodded. "Yes, I have. I made those dresses. I deserved to get paid for my work, even if the weddings were cancelled. I did the brides favors by not charging them. Selling the dresses now is simply my way of getting compensated on the work and materials."

"Of course," Jennifer said with a sickeningly sweet voice. "I'm not trying to upset you."

"I'm not upset," Darby said, though she was more than upset—she was offended. "I don't like what you seem to be implying."

"And what is that?"

"That I'm peddling in heartbreak and enjoying it."

"Oh, no, that's not what I'm implying at all."

Darby didn't believe her. Her instincts were sending up warning flares that she could no longer ignore. This had been a terrible idea. Unlike when she was sitting in Noah's studio, enthralled with his brilliant smile, Darby was getting an icky feeling off Jennifer. Something about this wasn't right. Something stunk like rotten deviled eggs at a summer picnic.

"I think you should go," Darby muttered.

Jennifer tilted her head to one side and grinned. For a moment, Darby thought she was going to protest, apologize, or maybe ask to stay. However, all she said was, "Okay." She hopped up, packed up her camera and tripod, and disappeared so fast, Darby's head nearly spun.

Even when she was sitting alone in her living room, the fire in the pit of her stomach grew. This was bad. Really bad. She'd made a stupid, stupid mistake by allowing that interview to happen. Though she hadn't fully grasped what Jennifer had been up to, Darby knew she'd been up to something.

"Oh, shit," she muttered as she jumped to her feet and rushed out the door. She was in tears before she reached Jade's house.

Darby sat slouched on Jade's firm sofa while Taylor paced before her. As soon as she'd walked into Jade's and rambled about what had happened, Jade had gone into her small but practical kitchen to fix them a pot of tea. Apparently in between heating water and stuffing the infuser with something call oolong, Jade had texted Taylor, who barged in minutes later looking like she was ready for a fight. Then again, Taylor almost always looked like she was ready for a fight. She rarely let her defenses down.

Rather than drink the tea Jade had poured for her, Darby dabbed her nose with a tissue and told them how Jennifer Williams had tricked her. *Maybe*. She thought, after it was all over, that she'd been tricked. However, she didn't *really* know. Either way, the interview left her feeling queasy, and she was certain she'd made a bigger mess of things.

"I think she was trying to get me to say things that made me look bad," Darby said.

Jade held up her hands as Taylor made another pass across the small living room. "Can you stop before you wear a hole in my rug?" she asked softly.

Taylor froze in her tracks and then spun and faced them. The anger on her face was almost enough to make Darby cringe. She had an evil eye that rarely went challenged. Her dark hair, sharp features, and dark eyes gave her a raven-like appearance that worked in her favor when she was trying to scare people off. She'd tried using it on Jade and Darby early in their friendship, but she'd underestimated how much her new friends needed her cynicism to balance them out.

However, in that moment, Darby felt the harsh stare all the way down to her bones. She understood Taylor wasn't angry at her; even so, she cringed. Taylor was definitely the protector of the group. There were plenty of times when people made fun of Darby for her outlandish appearance, only to snap their mouths shut and dart off after one hard, brutish stare from Taylor.

Taylor must have seen Darby's reaction because she rolled her head back and counted to five in the way she did when she was trying to control her temper. When she looked at Darby again, she had a softer stare—not gentle like Jade's, but definitely lacking the someone's-gonna-die fire.

"Why didn't you call us? *Before* you did the interview." Taylor dropped into a chair and shook her head. "We would have been there."

Darby sniffed. "I don't know. I thought... I don't know what I thought. I wanted to make things right. I wanted a chance to explain to the world that I'm not being vicious on my boutique. I'm being...clever." Her lip trembled, and she dabbed her eyes.

"I'm sure it wasn't as bad as you think," Jade said as she handed Darby another tissue. As much as Jade tried and as many times as she reassured her, Darby didn't agree. This was bad. She felt it in her bones. She'd made a horrible mistake.

Big tears rolled down Darby's cheeks. "I think it was, Jade. I really do think she set me up to make me look bad."

"Why would she do that?" Jade asked.

"To take advantage of her," Taylor stated as if that was the most obvious thing in the entire universe.

Jade shook her head. "No, Taylor. You're being suspicious. As always."

Taylor scowled. "Being suspicious saves me a hell of a lot of time, Jade."

"Don't fight," Darby said quietly before Jade could respond.

Darby's father had disappeared before she ever knew him, but she still felt like a kid watching her parents brawl whenever Jade and Taylor butted heads. She'd usually wither into the background and wait for them to stop. This time, however, she couldn't do that. She needed them to help her sort through the mess she'd made.

"We're not fighting," Taylor barked and then let out another of her big sighs. Dropping back into the chair, she sagged like she carried the weight the world. Her shoulders always drooped like that when she felt uncertain about something.

Despite her troubles, Darby tried to find the words to reassure Taylor. She wanted to tell her that she wasn't responsible for defending Darby against the world, but that was futile. As soon as they'd become friends, Taylor had stepped into the role of guardian. Little did she know what she was getting into. Darby had a way of getting into hot messes—and not just online.

Taylor hadn't even been around for the bigger disasters Darby had created, like that time she'd inadvertently had an affair with a married man. That was totally not Darby's fault. He hadn't told her he was married—if he had, she would have kicked him to the curb—but his wife had blamed Darby. She'd stormed into the bar where Darby was working and tossed a drink in her face before calling her a long list of unsavory names.

Darby had gotten fired over that mess. She'd hate to think what Taylor would have done to the man if she'd been around then. She probably would have strung him up and beat him with a barbed wire–covered bat. Okay, nothing quite that violent, but it wouldn't have been good.

Jade, on the other hand, probably would have talked to Darby about her feelings and gently encouraged her to do a bit more digging into the next guy who came along.

Though their approaches would have been different, they both would have come from the same place. Frustration that Darby had made a mess of things, but not necessarily frustration *with* Darby.

"Why would you do an interview like this without preparing first?" Taylor asked pointedly but without the angry undertones. Taylor didn't always know how to express her concern and her protectiveness, but she felt both for her friends. She was angry, and since she couldn't take her frustration out on a situation, she directed it toward Darby and Jade.

"I told you. I thought it would help," Darby said with a grimace. "I wanted to explain to the people leaving all those atrocious comments that they're taking the dress descriptions out of context."

"Darby," Taylor stated firmly, "they aren't taking them out of context. That's the problem."

Darby swallowed at the attack. "They're stories to get attention on the website, Taylor. I'm not telling people *who* they're about."

"You don't get it," Taylor said in a hushed tone as she pushed herself up and paced again.

Sitting taller, Darby narrowed her eyes. Taylor wasn't the only one who could give nasty glares. "They are *just* stories."

"Look," Jade said calmly, acting as the mediator, "until Jennifer has uploaded the interview, we have no idea what her intentions are or how Darby is going to come across."

"No, Jade, *you* look," Taylor stated flatly. "I know you're all into living this new 'forgive and forget and move on' mantra, but you need to take your rose-colored glasses off for a minute and take a good look at what happened."

Jade gawked at her for several beats before volleying the attitude right back at her. "And you need to stop looking for a reason to be pissed off at the world. And stop snapping at Darby about her website. What the hell is wrong with you? She's upset enough without you being a jerk to her."

Taylor gestured toward Darby. "She's not listening. People are telling her what she's doing isn't okay, and she isn't listening. *We* told her that it was a bad idea, and she *didn't* listen."

"I am listening," Darby stated. "I'm allowed to disagree. And I do disagree. Venomously."

"*Vehemently*," Jade muttered.

"Whatever," Darby stated with the same amount of snark Taylor had been using. "I didn't say Jade Kelly was all set to marry Liam Cunningham until he called her sister's name in bed. Did I?"

Jade held up her hand. "I'd like to clarify, using Liam and me as an example is not okay, and I don't have a sister."

"Exactly," Darby stated. "That's my point."

Taylor creased her brow and shook her head. "How is that the point?"

"*Nobody* knows who those stories are about," Darby said. "They could as easily be about Jade as much as they could be about you. Nobody knows."

"The brides know," Taylor stated. "Their friends and family know."

Darby groaned with her own growing irritations. "Okay. So a handful of people *might* be able to connect some dots and come to a conclusion, but unless they say something to someone else..." She threw her hands up and looked at Jade. "Make her stop attacking me."

Jade looked at Taylor. "Darby can run her site how she sees fit."

Scoffing, Taylor dropped into a chair and shook her head.

"She's right," Jade continued. "She isn't naming names or pointing fingers."

"Thank you," Darby said, sitting taller.

"However," Jade continued, "that doesn't mean *you're* right, Darby. Those stories were likely shared with you in confidence. Anonymous or not, you're sharing what were possibly the worst times of someone's life to sell your products. That's not the best sales practice, and I really think you should think about if this is what you want to continue doing."

"I sold three more dresses yesterday," Darby said.

"That's great," Taylor said, but she clearly didn't mean it. "Congratulations."

Jade cut her that motherly side-eye she was so good at. Using that maternal tone Darby loved and Taylor loathed, Jade said, "You want to protect your friend, I get that, but you can't behave like this."

"Like what?"

"A teenage punk who isn't getting her way," Jade pointed out.

Taylor narrowed her eyes and lifted her chin a notch. "I'd rather be a teenage punk than a pushover, Jade."

"Oh man." Darby clutched her hands together, dreading whatever was about to come next, but the tense moment was interrupted.

Parker Alonso, a friend of Jade's, opened the door, and her bright smile fell a bit as she looked from Jade to Darby to Taylor. "Hey, ladies," she said tentatively.

Jade pushed herself up as if the heated exchange hadn't even happened. "Hey you," she cooed and opened her arms to take Marie from her mother. Whenever Parker and her nine-month-old came around, Jade turned into a big cooing mess. This was one of the rare times Darby was thankful for that. The rage that had been on the verge of erupting in the cabin instantly dissolved.

Parker worked with Liam at his shop, and her visits

usually gave Darby and Taylor reason to tease Jade. However, none of them were in the mood at the moment.

"Everything okay?" Parker asked as she handed her little one to Jade.

"I guess we'll see," Taylor said before turning to leave. She stopped and shook her head at Jade. "I hope you're right. But I don't think you are. I think this is bad, Jade, and Darby needs to do something before it gets worse."

As Jade settled Marie on her hip, Taylor huffed out a sigh and left. Pushing herself up, Darby muttered a soft farewell to Parker and then started toward the door too.

"Darby," Jade called. "I want you to think about why some people might not find what you're saying amusing. That's all. Think about it."

A fresh round of tears stung the backs of Darby's eyes. She had expected more out of her friends. She had expected them to jump to her defenses and help her fix this. Not turn on her too.

"Okay," she said.

"You can stay," Jade said softly.

Darby gave her a weak smile and shook her head. "I need to go."

"Where?"

"To think."

"Darby," she called, but Darby didn't acknowledge her as she walked out, feeling even worse than she had before.

FOUR

LATER THAT EVENING, Darby jolted with surprise when a loud shriek burst through her open living room window. The needle she'd been using to hem a pair of lime green shorts slipped through the material and jabbed the tip of her pointer finger. Gasping, she dropped the shorts and pinched right above her knuckle, causing a little bead of blood to form.

Putting her finger to her mouth, she attempted to ignore the sounds coming from outside. As she suckled the wound, her neighbor squealed merrily again. Frustrated, Darby stood and peered between the teal faux wood blinds in time to see Jade stumble out of her kayak. As Jade dragged the raft to shore, Liam splashed her and called her a slowpoke. Another scream from Jade disrupted the calm of the little cove the women shared.

Their cabins were the only ones nestled in the small tree-shrouded inlet, which was usually peaceful. Not many people ventured toward the cove since there wasn't much to it, so when Jade and Liam started their flirty playing in the water, it was nearly impossible for Darby to ignore.

Jade had been through a lot over the last couple of years and deserved all the happiness she could find. Darby was proud of her best friend for all she'd overcome and wanted her to be happy. But she was also a little irritated that Jade's happiness was so loud when Darby was having such a bad week.

She frowned as Liam caught Jade around the waist and spun her, causing yet another of her loud yelps to echo through Darby's ears. Which was the last yelp and flirty laugh Darby could handle. If having Liam chase her through the cove and kick water at her as she squealed in false protest made Jade happy, then more power to her. But that didn't mean Darby had to witness it firsthand.

After flipping the blinds closed, she turned and scanned the contents of the small living area of her lakefront cabin. Though she'd chosen bright colors and fun retro patterns, her home suddenly felt sad. She could barely look at her bright blue sofa and not see Jennifer Williams sitting there luring Darby into a trap.

Darby glowered at the funky belongings that used to bring her so much joy. Everything was falling apart. The world was turning on her. Even her best friends didn't seem supportive of her new venture.

This was the first bit of success—real success—Darby had ever tasted, and people were dumping all over it. All over *her*. She deserved happiness too. Didn't she? She deserved to have success too. But here she was. Her dresses were selling, she had money coming in, and the very people who should have been happy for her weren't.

"That's it!" Darby whirled on her high-heeled Mary Janes, marched across the room, and flipped on her record player. After placing the needle on a vintage Etta James album, she turned the volume up to drown out Jade's and Liam's laughter. The last thing Darby needed to hear was someone else being so damn happy.

Storming to her kitchen, she yanked the fridge door with the flair of a teenage drama queen. Darby stared at the contents. Limes. A bottle of queso. Perfect.

She grabbed those two items and kicked the door closed as she put them on the counter. Her frown deepened when she looked at the empty dish where she'd expected to find ripening avocados.

"It's okay," she told herself. "It's fine. That's fine."

Grabbing a bag of chips from the top of the fridge, she carelessly tossed them next to the queso and grabbed a plastic bowl from the cabinet. After emptying the cheese into the bowl, she popped it into the microwave and pressed a button to warm the contents.

Then she opened another cabinet and grabbed her bottles of tequila and triple sec. She slammed the cabinet door and yanked open a drawer to find her manual juicer. Three limes should do it. No, four. This was definitely a four-lime margarita day.

After rinsing her hands and the limes in the sink, she easily sliced them in half and squeezed each half vigorously over her blender, poured in a guesstimate on how much triple sec and tequila to add, and topped the mixture with ice.

She fiercely pressed the button to blend the mixture and then tore open the bag of chips. As she yanked the two sides apart, the plastic tore more than she'd intended, and tortilla chips scattered across the counter and floor, causing Darby to squeal. About that time, the bowl in her microwave emitted a loud pop before the contents exploded and covered the see-through door.

As soon as it did, the smell of burned cheese started to seep out of the microwave. She pulled the door open, wincing when cheese slid from the inside and dripped onto the counter below. The moment Darby touched the bowl, she realized the depth of her mistake. The heat seared her fingers, and she dropped the bowl and jumped back. Swinging her hand to ease the burn, she hit the blender and knocked it off the base, sending the ice, liquor, and lime juice across the counter and onto the floor.

Tears instantly filled her eyes. So much for margaritas and chips.

Could anything else possibly go wrong?

As soon as she thought that, she noticed a glob of melted cheese oozing down her dress.

"Darby?" Jade asked from the living room. "Oh my God. Honey."

Darby blew a strand of red hair from her eyes as she turned on her heels to face Jade. Sometime during her ongoing disaster, one of her victory rolls had come undone and dangled limply over her left eye. Jade's pale skin was red, likely from her time out in the sun, and her gray eyes widened. Her auburn hair was tousled, and Darby stopped short of asking her friend if she'd been doing tawdry things with Liam. However, Jade was still in denial about when she and Liam were going to end up together. Sooner rather than later, if their daily giggle sessions were any indication.

Jade stared at her, wide-eyed. "What the hell happened?"

"I don't know. I just..." In an instant, the world crumbled in on her. "I can't do anything right."

"Oh, babe," Jade cooed as she walked toward the kitchen. She looked down at the floor before holding her hand out and gesturing for Darby to join her. Darby took her hand and stepped over a puddle of chips soaking up margarita and right into Jade's hug.

"I have cheese on me," Darby sniffled.

"It's okay. I don't mind." Jade soothed her for a few moments before leaning back and wiping Darby's cheek. "Wanna tell me what happened?"

Snuffling her emotions up, Darby shrugged. "Everything is falling apart. My life is like a disaster." She gestured toward the kitchen. "Like tortilla chips without the guacamole. Burned queso. A margarita spilled on the kitchen floor."

"Okay," Jade said as she lifted her hands and widened her eyes. "I get it, Darbs."

"No, you don't. While you're off frolicking with Liam, my life is falling apart."

A deep furrow creased Jade's brow. "*Frolicking*?"

Though Darby was tempted to explain to Jade that she was, indeed, a frolicker where Liam was concerned, this wasn't about them. Darby's spirits were wilting like a hydrangea getting too much sun. "I can't go on like this." Though she prided herself on her straight posture, she deliberately slouched as the weight of her discontent settled on her shoulders. "I can't be a chip with no guacamole, Jade."

Jade turned Darby's face toward the sunburst-style mirror hanging on Darby's living room wall, and they looked at their reflections. Jade offered a sweet maternal smile, to which

Darby responded with an exaggerated pout. She pressed her bottom lip out and batted her long false lashes. Those displays always earned Darby a little extra affection from her friend.

"Look at you," Jade said with a sweet, supportive tone. "You're not a chip without guacamole, honey. You *are* guacamole. You're not even average guacamole. You're loaded guac with jalapenos and onions."

Darby pushed her bottom lip out a bit more. "You think I'm loaded?"

"You're totally loaded *and* spicy." Jade gave Darby another sweet smile before tucking her fallen victory roll back into place. Darby snagged one of the extra bobby pins she always kept nearby and held it up for Jade to secure the style. "There," Jade said sweetly. "There's my girl."

Darby felt better for about two seconds, but then that mashed potatoes without gravy feeling came over her again. "My life has turned into a disaster, Jade. Nothing is right. Everything is wrong." The panic in her chest swelled again. Darby collapsed onto her couch as a lump formed in her throat and tears tugged the backs of her eyes. "What has happened to me?"

Jade did her best to hide her amusement, but Darby saw the grin twitching at her lips.

"Don't laugh, Jade," Darby warned. "I'm in the midst of a real crisis here."

"I'm not laughing."

"You want to. Your mouth is spasming like a fish out of water." Darby pointed toward Jade's face and noticed a little dot of a wound on the tip of her finger. "Look at that. I stabbed myself while sewing. I never stab myself. And look at my kitchen. The world has upended and is crumbling around me."

"Oh, baby," Jade said with a patronizing tone. "You're having an off day. That's all. You know what you need?"

"A tornado to whisk me away. A fairy godmother to turn me into a princess. A new life in a land far, far away."

"Ice cream at Harper's. I'll call Taylor. We'll have sundaes for lunch," Jade said with a singsong voice as if that would tempt Darby.

Damn it. The idea of an ice cream sundae covered in gooey hot fudge, crumbled cookies, and whipped cream did make her feel better. With a forced sulk, Darby held her hands out.

"Fine," she said as soon as Jade pulled her to her feet, "but what about my kitchen?"

Jade looked her over and smiled. "Go change into something less...cheesy..."

"Ha-ha," Darby muttered.

"And I'll call Taylor to pick up some ice cream and come over."

Darby pouted. "No. She was mean."

Jade lifted her brows. "She was concerned. Not mean."

"She was *mean*."

"Well then, let her make it up to you by bringing ice cream to you." She pointed toward the bedroom. "Go."

"Fine. But I want extra whipped cream. And nuts. And Taylor is buying." She spun and marched off as if that made her demand more valid.

As soon as Darby walked out of her bedroom in a fresh dress, she realized why Jade had been so concerned. She really had made a mess. Even though Darby had taken her time to change and wash the cheese out of her clothing, Jade was still mopping the floor and Taylor was staring up at the ceiling. Darby followed her gaze. Somehow there was a stain of what must have been margarita on the ceiling.

"How in the hell..." Darby started, squinting at the stain as if that would help her figure out how that had happened.

"What happened, Darby?" Taylor asked.

"I had a moment." Darby opened the paper bag on the counter with the Harper's logo across the front. She pulled out three containers and smiled at the one with the whipped cream oozing from the edges. "Yum."

Taylor cleared her throat as she looked at Darby.

Darby stopped licking her thumb long enough to cock an eyebrow.

"Say thank you for getting you ice cream," Taylor instructed.

"Say you're sorry for being a ginormous bitch earlier."

Taylor stared. So did Darby.

"Okay," Jade said, setting the mop aside, "now that that's settled..." Redirecting was her go-to tactic to defuse a spat between Darby and Taylor before one could begin. Though Taylor was one of Darby's closest friends, they tended to butt heads like siblings. Even so, Darby wouldn't trade Taylor for the world. Butting heads or not, she cherished the bond they'd formed in the last year.

"Tell Jade thank you for cleaning up your mess," Taylor stated.

Darby smiled at Jade. "Thank you, Jade." Then she returned her stare to Taylor and smiled. "Now, tell me you're sorry."

Taylor stared for several more seconds. "I'm sorry the truth hurt your feelings."

Jade sighed, and Taylor conceded.

Lifting her hands, Taylor added, "And that I was a bitch about it."

Darby accepted the apology. "Thank you for getting me ice cream."

"You two are freakin' impossible," Jade muttered as she pushed a sundae toward Taylor. "Eat your damn ice cream. It's melting."

Taylor dug into her treat. "I am sorry, Darby," she said more gently after a few bites. Taylor wasn't good at apologizing or being humble or anything that made her appear vulnerable, so those words meant a lot to Darby.

"Un-Do is *your* business," Taylor continued. "And Jade's right. You are allowed to operate in a way that suits *you*. As long as you don't break the law," she added with a grin.

Darby wanted to be offended by that caveat, but then she considered some of her past antics, like that one time she let some guy pay her to take a suitcase to Mexico City when she was visiting her *abuela*. She'd been so excited about earning a wad of cash, she hadn't considered she'd probably done something illegal until her grandmother chastised her for doing the dirty work for a local criminal and warned that she could have gotten herself killed.

Guilt and worry had weighed on Darby for weeks after

that. Fear that the FBI or some drug cartel would be watching her had her running from shadows long after she'd returned from Mexico City. Even now, years later, Darby couldn't bring herself to visit her grandmother. She was too scared of doing something stupid like that again. Instead, they had video chats and regular phone calls.

So yeah, given Darby's history of transferring unknown substances across the border and possibly getting mixed up with criminals, Taylor's advice about working within the confines of the law was warranted.

Rather than admitting that, Darby shrugged. "Thanks. I really don't think the descriptions are that bad. They're getting attention. That's what they're there for. Right?"

Jade smiled in the way she always did right before reassuring Darby she wasn't as screwed up as she thought. "Honey, we don't like seeing people come after you. That's all. We want to protect you like you'd protect one of us if the tides were turned. But we can't do that when you won't remove the thing that's causing the hurtful comments. We aren't attacking you," Jade pressed. "We are trying to protect you. You get that, right?"

Darby frowned as she poked at the pile of whipped cream covering her ice cream. Everything from Harper's was made in the store with fresh ingredients. Their whipped cream had always been Darby's favorite thing on the menu, but in that moment, she couldn't bring herself to taste the sweet topping. Her stomach was too busy twisting around itself to crave the sweetness of the cream and sugar mixture.

"I didn't express that well," Taylor admitted and gave Darby a half grin. "Big surprise there. But Jade's right. *Again*. I don't want to see people picking on you. It makes me want to protect you. But I can't."

"Because they're online," Darby said.

"Because you're leaving the door open and inviting them in," Taylor said. "Your descriptions—"

"Are selling points," Darby insisted.

Taylor glanced at Jade, clearly seeking backup since her kindness always made more headway with Darby than Taylor's wrecking ball of reality did.

Though Darby reminded herself that her friends were trying to look out for her like Jade had said, part of her felt like they were ganging up on her. Clearly they'd been talking about this issue. They'd obviously discussed how to get Darby to see things their way. And if they'd been talking about that behind her back, part of her had to wonder what else they talked about without her. What other things had she done that they debated when she wasn't around?

"Darby," Jade said, pulling her attention to her. "Have you considered how you'd feel if someone shared your secrets online? Even if no one knew it was you, *you* would know. People close to you would know. And it would be embarrassing. Maybe even hurtful. I know you don't want to hurt anybody, Darby. You're better than that."

Darby's heart dropped to her stomach, and she shook her head slightly. She hadn't considered that her site could be hurtful. Embarrassing, maybe. A little tacky, sure. But hurtful? "No," she said softly. "I wouldn't want to hurt someone."

"But you have to consider that someone might be hurt by having their story shared on Un-Do's site. They might find it hurtful to see the comments people are making about why their weddings were cancelled. Some of these women might not have recovered from the betrayals that destroyed their lives." Jade put her hand to her heart. "I'd be devastated if I found out people—even strangers—were laughing at how my husband ditched me right after I recovered from cancer. That would be awful, Darby."

Putting her ice cream on the counter, Darby swallowed hard. "I was trying to make my store more appealing. I didn't intend to hurt anyone." She frowned as she realized Taylor was toying with a tube of eyebrow gel Darby had set out to remind herself to replace. The tube was all but empty, and Darby kept forgetting to buy a new one. Taylor probably didn't even know what that was for, and Darby didn't have the energy to explain. Besides, she wasn't messing with it out of curiosity. Things had gotten intense. Jade's attempt at turning things in a way for Darby to understand had brought an emotional surge to the room that had made Taylor uncomfortable.

Emotions always did.

"Using humor is a great way to increase traffic and sales," Jade said, drawing Darby's attention back to her.

"But you can't do it at someone else's expense." Taylor tossed the tube back onto the counter and stood upright. "You need to take that part of the description off, Darbs. No big deal."

"What will I do if my sales drop off?" Darby asked.

"We can find a new way to make the dresses sell," Taylor suggested. "That's literally what Jade does, right?"

"Right." Jade gestured toward the laptop sitting on Darby's coffee table. "We'll come up with something great."

Taylor gave her a softer, more encouraging smile. "Jade isn't going to let you fail if she can help you."

Darby pushed her sundae aside and shrugged. "Okay. Fine. I'll take the stories down."

"Good. Let's do that now," Jade said, as if she didn't trust Darby to do it on her own.

That wasn't her intent. Knowing Jade, she was doing her best to be supportive, but Darby didn't want Jade's maternal instinct to go that far. Having her sweet and supportive was wonderful. Having her helicopter to make sure Darby did her homework was too much.

She was perfectly capable of updating her website without supervision. However, when the urge to defy her friends flared, Darby tamped it down with the reminder that Jade and Taylor were only trying to help.

They followed her to the couch and sat on either side of her as her laptop loaded. She again had to remind herself not to snap and point out that she was perfectly capable of handling this on her own.

As soon as her laptop booted up, she clicked on the Internet icon and opened the window for Un-Do. She gasped at the number of new comments she had. Closing in on two thousand since she'd last checked.

"Whoa," Taylor muttered.

Darby caught the wide-eyed glance Jade gave Taylor but wasn't sure if it was to hush her or to share her shock. Darby only had to click on a few new comments to realize the surge was due to Jennifer Williams posting a video about the store. Darby's heart thudded, and her stomach tightened.

You heartless bitch was one of the first things she read, followed by *How fucking dare you?*

"Oh, no," Darby whined.

"Shit," Jade cursed harshly. "Find the video."

"I don't want to," Darby said as her already tense stomach knotted even more tightly. "I don't want to see it."

"We have to know what we're dealing with," Jade said softly.

Taylor reached over as if she was going to take the laptop, but Darby pulled it closer to her. If this was going to happen, she was going to be the one in charge. That at least gave her some sense of comfort. Having Taylor take over would make her feel like she had no control. That wasn't okay at the moment. She didn't want to do this. She didn't want to see the next disaster unfold, but if she had to, she was going to be in control of clicking Play.

Darby opened on the link to Jennifer Williams's website and her anxiety tripled so fast her head grew light. There, on the top of the page, was a picture of Darby with the words *The Woman Behind The Un-Do Wedding Boutique: Comedian or Coldhearted Snake?*

Now that she'd clicked, her first instinct of not wanting to know kicked in again. The need to be in control faded and the urge to run nearly overcame her.

"I can't watch," Darby said, putting her hand over her eyes. But as soon as she heard Jennifer's voice filtering from her laptop, she parted her fingers enough to see.

There, with a bright smile and perfect hair, Jennifer shared with her viewers that today she would be talking with Darby Zamora, owner and operator of The Un-Do Wedding Boutique. However, the way she said Darby's name and the name of her shop sounded angry and bitter. She wasn't going to be sharing with her viewers how Darby was only trying to make back the money she'd lost. Or that she hadn't meant for people to take the tales about the weddings so seriously.

"I hate her already," Taylor muttered from where she sat next to Darby.

On Darby's other side, Jade sighed. "Can we watch this before we decide we hate anyone?"

"No," Taylor and Darby said in unison.

Darby lowered her hand when she heard her voice coming from the laptop. At least she looked pretty. Her hair was amazing in the lighting and her prim posture made her look perky. "Hey, maybe I should start doing a podcast."

"I think you have enough on your plate," Taylor said.

As soon as Jennifer finished explaining who her special guest was, she cut to Darby rambling on about how her catering business had failed, so she'd decided to sell some of the dresses she'd previously made.

All was well, until Jennifer explained with a perfectly saddened face how those were discarded wedding and bridesmaids dresses from broken weddings and undoubtedly broken hearts. Her sad explanation cut to jarring footage of Darby on Noah Joplin's show laughing about the bride who had discovered two of her bridesmaids had slept with her fiancé—at the same time!

Rather than the moment of lighthearted giggling that Darby remembered, she came across as cold and...mean. In that moment, Darby sounded *mean*. And heartless. In *that* moment, she understood why people were leaving such shitty comments on her page. Hell, if she didn't know better, she might have been tempted to tell herself to go to hell for what she'd done.

Jennifer certainly knew how to edit a video together. And that wasn't necessarily a compliment.

Darby swallowed hard and sank back onto the sofa as Taylor cast a glance at Jade.

Jennifer reappeared, but her friendly smile was gone. Instead, she looked sad and shocked and innocent. Compared to the hard stare Darby had been caught giving, Jennifer looked like a doe in the woods staring down a hunter. "I couldn't believe what I was hearing either," she said. She pouted ever so slightly. "I simply couldn't believe this woman was so happy to be humiliating her former clients. So I spoke with some people who could give me a bit more insight into the woman behind The Un-Do Wedding Boutique."

"Oh, no," Darby muttered. Her stomach dropped when one of her ex-boyfriends appeared on the screen. Mark Penn had been her first real boyfriend. The first so-called relationship she'd ever had. They'd had fun, but Darby was introverted and awkward. She was still growing. Mark wasn't. He was content being Mark—watching racing on the weekends, drinking a lot of beer, and not cleaning up after himself.

When he'd started spending more time at Darby's tiny Fairfax apartment than she wanted, she hadn't had courage to tell him he was overstepping her boundaries. Instead, she'd waited until he'd gone to visit his brother and then packed up all her belongings. By the time he'd returned, she'd moved out and the apartment was being cleaned for the next tenant.

Yeah, she knew now that had been a shitty thing to do,

but at the time, disappearing without a word had seemed like the best option.

Hearing him tell the story made her understand how immature that particular decision had been. She didn't believe for a minute that Mark was still heartbroken after all these years, but she still felt bad for her actions.

"Oh my God. How did Jennifer find *him*?" Darby asked with a whiney tone. Panic was grabbing hold of her. She'd certainly made a much bigger mess of things than she'd realized.

"You'd be amazed what people can dig up on social media," Jade said. "I can tell you far more about my ex-husband's new wife than I ever wanted to know."

Taylor leaned to look at Jade. "You cyberstalked his new wife?"

"Of course I did. Why wouldn't I?"

"Shh," Darby said. "Jennifer isn't done destroying my life yet."

Next up, more than ready to tell the tale of Darby's misdeeds, was Ted Woodfield.

"Okay," Darby stated firmly, "this guy doesn't get to trash me. He was thirty-four when we dated and still lived in his mom's basement. He still had a toy car collection for frick's sake. No. He does not get to trash me."

But he did trash Darby. He said she was high-maintenance —which Darby wouldn't deny. He was the first boyfriend she'd had post–retro Darby era. She was still learning how to exist in her new skin and had been a little wild and demanding.

She frowned. Fine. He had a valid complaint, but he still lived with his mother.

"But that's not even the worst of it," Jennifer said and shook her head sadly. "Darby Zamora really isn't what she seems. Just ask poor Sue Berdynski. She's one of the brides whose story Darby shared with the world."

When Darby saw the face of a teary-eyed woman fill the screen, bile rose up her throat and burned. The ice cream in her stomach churned and instantly soured.

"Sue, how did it feel to have the tale of your broken engagement shared so publicly?"

Sue sniffled, wiped her eyes, let her lip quiver, and said, "I'm so humiliated. That was the worst day of my life, and I was finally starting to recover, and now..." Her chin trembled as if she could barely contain her crying. "Now everyone knows."

Darby gasped. "Everyone knows because *she* came right out and told them it was her!"

"Shh," Taylor hushed.

When the camera cut back to Jennifer, she shook her head sadly. "I asked Darby how she felt about what she'd done. This is what she had to say."

Darby looked furious in the footage that popped up. "I'm peddling in heartbreak and enjoying it."

"Your business is called The Un-Do Wedding Boutique," Jennifer said. "Your tagline is 'Her bad luck is your great deal.' Don't you think that's a little...*insensitive*?"

"I'm getting paid," Darby said, sounding aloof.

Again, the video cut to Jennifer. "Well, you've certainly been successful...getting paid."

"Yes," Darby said, "I have."

When Jennifer returned, she shrugged and shook her

head. "There you have it. The owner of the incredibly popular Un-Do Wedding Boutique. In her own words."

Darby gasped. "That's not... That's not..." She turned to Jade with wide eyes. "She spliced my words together to make me look bad."

"Surprise, surprise," Taylor said flatly and pushed herself up. "I'm burning that bitch's house down."

"No, you're not," Jade said. "For God's sake, how will that help Darby?"

"It might make me feel better," Darby said and then swallowed hard. "I feel sick. Like, I could barf sick. She made me look really bad, guys. Like...*really* bad."

"I'm going to take care of this," Taylor said.

Jade's lips dipped into a deep frown. "Sit down, Taylor."

Taylor crossed her arms and huffed.

"No," Jade pressed, "you cannot burn down her house."

"Fine. But I will scare the shit out of her."

"No, you won't," Jade said.

Darby choked out a sob, causing her friends to look at her. "Guys. This is a disaster."

"You need to post an apology," Jade said.

Gasping, Darby sat back. "No. Why should I... She lied. She edited that footage together, Jade. I didn't say those things. Well... I did, but not the way she made them look."

"Darby," Taylor stated firmly.

Darby slammed her laptop closed and then jumped up. "No. I will not be bullied by her lies."

She marched back to the kitchen where she'd left her sundae, which had turned into a melty mess. Grasping her spoon, she lifted her chin a notch as she stared at Jade and Taylor. "I'm not changing one damn thing."

FIVE

DARBY WISHED she could go back to that moment when she and her best friends were sitting on the beach just a week ago. Back before Noah Joplin told the world about her website. Instead, she sat by herself on her sofa the next afternoon, staring at the comments on Un-Do's website.

Two days ago, the majority of messages had been telling her how awesome her shop was. Several women even expressed interest in having Darby design and make a dress for a wedding. People loved the styles and the uniqueness she'd brought to the gowns. Her site had been filled with praise. Sure, a few people had made comments about the site being inconsiderate to the would-have-been brides and some thought the stories shouldn't have been shared, but for the most part, the posts had been positive.

Now, less than twenty-four hours after Jennifer's video was posted, Darby's wedding boutique *had* turned into something vicious. And the malice was aimed at her!

Before, *cool* had been the main adjective used on her shop. That had been replaced in far too many posts using words like *ugly* and *cruel*, and there were even a few instances of *money-hungry bitch*.

Though part of Darby told her to let it roll off her back—she didn't even know those people—the words still cut at her. She didn't like people thinking bad things about her, and it didn't matter if they were strangers. She wasn't mean. Or cruel. Or money hungry.

She'd simply been trying to pay her bills and keep her head above water. Like everyone else in the world. Why'd they have to turn it into something else? Why had *Jennifer* had to turn it into something else?

Darby sniffed as she blindly deleted all the comments rather than sort through looking for the posts that were defending her and had something nice and supportive to say about her appearance and her business. As soon as the comments were deleted, she turned off all commenting and access to her inbox so no one could message her.

Jade would likely tell her that was the wrong approach, but Darby didn't care. As long as messages were coming in, nice or not, she'd be too tempted to read them. And those not-so-nice messages were getting meaner by the minute. Sure, some people were coming to her defense, but that didn't take the sting out of what people were saying.

Some people had the ability to let cruelty bounce off them, but Darby had always soaked up the negativity like a sponge. Those words would worm their way into her mind and take over. She'd roll them around until that was all she heard and all she felt, and then they'd consume her.

She'd try to hide, try to disappear, but they'd find her and convince her that all the bad things people were saying were true.

She'd been through this before too many times in her life. She didn't want to go through it now, so turning off the comments now was the best approach to save what was left of her peace of mind.

Sue Berdynski had made Darby sound like a heartless wench who hadn't given a damn about anybody else. And those jerk faces Mark and Ted had no right to tell the world about their breakups. They had thrown her under the bus to have five seconds of fame on Jennifer's podcast. Darby would kick them both in the shins if she ever saw them again.

But even worse than what her ex-boyfriends had done... people were mocking her appearance. Yes, she was used to that to some extent. People often looked at her when she was out and about. Some even snickered or made rude comments. Darby had learned to let those things roll off her back. In fact, she wore them as badges of honor because the teenage version of herself would have crumpled. She'd learned to use those disapproving looks and sarcastic takes on her appearance to build herself up rather than to tear herself down.

However. This was different. This *felt* different. Their attacks weren't curious glances or whispered comments followed by a round of giggles. These were direct. These were well-aimed and intended to hit her where it hurt. These weren't simply passersby taking a second look. People had sought her out, made a concerted effort to find her website, with the intention of trashing her.

Darby had once again become an easy target for people who had nothing better to do with their time than cut someone down. She felt vulnerable. Singled out. Weak. And worst of all, she felt like she was alone—the same kind of scared loneliness that had followed her down the halls of Chammont Point High School for four long years.

She was the sole owner of The Un-Do Wedding Boutique. She was the only person responsible for the failure and success. She was the only one there to take the angry words being tossed her way.

Closing her eyes as big tears rolled down her cheeks, Darby pulled the blanket from the back of the couch and wrapped herself into a bright yellow faux fur cocoon. As she hid herself into a makeshift burrow, she tried to calm the anxiety gripping her chest. Her heart thumped hard, and breathing became more and more difficult as old fears resurfaced.

All she'd ever wanted was to be free to be herself. To live her life without being harassed or bullied. And maybe have a few really good friends.

Though she was in her thirties now, she'd finally gotten exactly what she'd always been seeking. It had taken years, but Darby had found the courage to be herself *and* she had two amazing friends. But she felt like she was on the verge of losing everything.

The sound of Darby's phone dinging made her nerves sizzle like bacon on a hot griddle. The dark clouds were closing in on her, and the idea of someone from outside this storm reaching out made her stomach roll with the instant expectation that it was another ugly comment. Another rude assessment of her clothes. Another cruel joke about her weight.

She didn't want to see who had texted her and why, but despite the anxiety the notification had caused, she couldn't resist. Sliding her hand from the blanket shelter she'd created, she snagged her cell phone and looked at the screen.

Taylor had texted her. Knowing it was a friend—someone who wouldn't tell her that she weighed too much to dress like that or that she should take herself more seriously—was a relief.

Doing okay?

Darby stared at the text for a few moments. Her natural instinct was to say she was fine. That lie was one she'd told so many times in her life. So many times someone—her mom or a teacher—would ask if she was doing okay, and rather than tell them she felt like she was dying inside, she'd fake a smile and say she was fine.

Society had a way of making people feel like admitting they weren't okay made them weak. People weren't supposed to burden others with their problems, so "fine" became the go-to answer, when the reality was that Darby wasn't fine. She wasn't even close to fine.

But still, though Taylor was one of her closest friends, she hesitated to say so. A voice in her head told to toss the phone aside with the text unanswered. Another told her to tell the truth and admit that she needed help. And yet another, that one so many people listened to, told her to type out the words *I'm fine* and turn away from the help she knew Taylor was offering.

That voice was winning out, but then Darby considered who she was talking to. Taylor wouldn't take "fine" as an answer. Taylor would see through the lie and call her on it.

Telling Taylor she was fine in the midst of this mess would have been like telling her the grass was purple. She'd know it was a lie.

Darby texted back a simple, straightforward response. *No. Harper's?*

Darby almost laughed. The way they were buying up Harper's ice cream to make Darby feel better, the store might run out of stock soon. They hadn't even spent this much time eating treats when Jade was going through her divorce. Darby hiccupped a breath as she realized that was because Jade was like a gazillion times stronger.

Darby didn't want to crawl off the sofa and face the world. She wanted to stay there, hidden, unseen, until all this blew over and she could once again show her face without fear.

But she knew from years of experience that if she allowed herself to hide away, time would pass by without her noticing. If she didn't push herself to keep going, days would pass by with her barely moving from this spot. She'd never gotten so deep into her depression that she'd go without bathing or changing, but she'd heard that could happen. And it didn't surprise her.

The weight of sadness was too much to carry sometimes. She could see how some people wouldn't be able to push themselves to keep going—even if that mean a hot bath or a solid meal. There had been times when she'd get so caught up in feeling bad that she wouldn't let herself feel good, even for a minute.

She'd developed bad coping habits thanks to being such an outcast. Sometimes it was just a nagging sadness she couldn't name and wouldn't go away.

However, when her mom had passed away, Darby had embraced those old ways she'd discovered in high school. The blending in, keeping quiet, going days without speaking.

She didn't want to do that again. She didn't want to find

herself so far beneath the weight of this that she couldn't find her way out. Not that she thought Jade and Taylor would allow it. That was one of the many benefits of finally having friends. Real friends. They knew she struggled with depression and had a tendency to withdraw.

She knew they were going to take care of her. She knew that. Even though she was feeling beat up and worn out, she knew they'd take care of her.

Darby swallowed hard and sniffed before responding. *Yeah. I'll meet you there in 15.*

I'll text Jade.

Huffing out a big sigh, Darby fought the urge to retract her answer. She had to get up. She had to keep moving. That was what her mom would have told her.

Turning her wrist up, Darby looked at the tattoo she'd put there twelve years ago. *Love, Mom* had been copied off the last birthday card her mom had ever given her. She traced the letters and remembered her mom's voice, and then another round of tears trickled over her cheeks. She really could use her mom's hugs and words of encouragement right now, but she would have to settle for Jade and Taylor reminding her they were there for her.

Darby stuck her lip out in defiance as she shoved the blanket from around her. She went to the bedroom to get ready to go. No doubt she had black mascara trails down her cheeks. She walked into the bedroom, dropped onto the chair at her vanity, and looked at her reflection.

As she did, words she'd read on Un-Do's site rolled through her mind. People picking on her style, her hair, her makeup. She hadn't been able to let those go. Those pierced her armor and made her soul bleed. Those hurt.

The same way the high school bullies had found a way to hurt her all those years ago.

And like all those years ago, Darby shrivelled. The need to hide returned, and she snagged a facial cloth from the dispenser on her vanity. She wiped her makeup away and then tugged the hairpins in her perfectly primped rolls free. Her bright red hair fell around her face.

Fifteen minutes later, she realized she was running late, but she didn't care. Jade and Taylor would wait for her. She needed a few minutes to get used to what she'd done to herself.

A pair of dark denim capris hugged her curves, but rather than a halter top in some outlandish color, Darby had paired the pants with a white button-down blouse that she usually wore with puffy skirts or short shorts. She'd brushed out her hair so the red strands hung down around her shoulders. Not a victory roll or barrel curl was to be seen.

And her makeup? She'd toned that down so her usual eyeliner wings only swooshed enough to accent her dark brown eyes. Opting to pass on her false lashes, she'd added black mascara to the natural hairs, but the effect barely stood out in comparison.

After sliding on a pair of flats, Darby looked at her reflection again. She looked so...normal. Other than the bright red hair, of course, but even that seemed tame without her usual style. Taking in her reflection made her feel a bit sad.

She'd stared at herself for a long time wondering why she needed to look what so many had called "clownish" to feel good about herself. Maybe she was the fake they all had accused her of being. Maybe she *was* desperate for attention.

Without her usual flair, she felt vulnerable. She felt average. She didn't feel like herself. Then again, maybe she didn't even know what that was supposed to feel like.

Picking up her phone, she debated texting Jade and Taylor and letting them know she'd changed her mind. She wasn't up for having ice cream right now. She stopped, though. She needed this time with her friends. The reminder that she wasn't alone would be a huge comfort with all she was feeling inside.

Grabbing her purse, Darby left the house, but the gloom followed her all the way to Harper's Ice Cream Shop. When she walked toward it, she noticed Jade and Taylor sitting next to each other on a bench but not speaking. They were both looking at their phones. The sight wasn't that unusual, considering everyone in today's society was more caught up in their own world than sharing another's, but the scene made Darby's fears and insecurities spike. She wondered if they were reading the same comments she'd read. If they were, would they agree? Would they think she was fake? Clownish? An attention-seeking joke?

The knot that formed in Darby's gut was irrational. She knew that, but her lip trembled a bit as the idea of losing their trio took hold of her heart.

Jade glanced up and noticed Darby first. A loud gasp caused Taylor to focus on Darby too. They both stared with slack jaws as Darby approached the ice cream shop.

"What are you wearing?" Taylor asked, which Darby thought was amusing considering Taylor was the one who had told her a thousand times she needed to tone down her look.

She looked at herself and shrugged. "Thought I'd try something new."

The concern in Jade's eyes was undeniable. "Honey..."

"It's something new," Darby stated, blowing off their concerns. She didn't want to dwell on them, because she would break down and cry. The feeling of being lost inside her own body was one she was far too used to but hadn't experienced in a long time. It was creeping up on her now, and she didn't want to stare it down. Not yet. "You guys ready for ice cream?"

She yanked open the door and walked in. As she skimmed over the menu the three of them had memorized long ago, she felt the weight of stares on her. She ignored them and the stress that embraced her. When she approached the counter, she smiled at the girl behind the register.

"Whoa. You're the Un-Do lady."

Darby's smile faltered as she noticed several of the people behind the counter looking at her and whispering. Great. They were probably going to spit in her ice cream. "Yeah. I guess." She considered not ordering but decided she really needed the treat. She'd keep an extra close eye on whoever made her order.

After asking for a banana split with extra nuts, she stepped to the side so Jade and Taylor could get theirs as well. As her dish was filled, she kept an eagle eye on the teenager scooping different flavors and drizzling sauces.

Once they were sitting around a table, Darby sent up a silent prayer of thanks that her order hadn't been violated by teen mischief.

"What's up with your hair?" Taylor asked.

"I wanted to change things up," Darby said, hoping her friends would stop staring at her. As she glanced around, she realized far too many people were watching them. Not everyone seemed to have noticed her or recognized her from Jennifer's video, but she suspected a few did from the way they were leaning close and lowering their voices before glancing her way, much like they had done the last time they were at Harper's and a woman had called out to Darby. And like that day, Darby suddenly felt uncomfortable. While she'd taken big strides in recovering her confidence, having all these people glancing her way was causing her to shrivel inside like she'd done for four long years at Chammont Point High School.

"Why now?" Jade asked, distracting Darby.

Darby shrugged. "Why not now?"

Jade tilted her head in that mom-knows-best way. "Because changing things up now, *tonight*, makes it seem like this change is a direct reaction to Jennifer Williams and her shitty video of lies."

Darby swallowed. "I thought maybe...maybe now isn't the best time to be standing out."

"You're not changing because of her," Taylor said.

Darby poked at a strawberry sitting atop a big scoop of vanilla ice cream. "You guys don't get it."

"I get it," Taylor stated. "And you're not changing because of *her*."

"It's not because of her. It's because...a bunch of people on my website called me fake. They're right. I *am* fake." Tears burned Darby's eyes as she looked from Taylor to Jade and then back to her ice cream. "All this is a facade. A big fat act to...to keep people away. I'm fun to gawk at and snap a picture with and admire from afar, but this"—she gestured toward her red hair—"is like armor. When people look at me because of my hair or my clothes, I know they're looking at me because of things I can change. I can't change my ethnicity or my body shape, but I can control what they see. But it's fake. It's a facade so they don't see me. What she did today... She broke through my armor and exposed me in a way that... She made me look bad on the inside. I'm not bad on the inside."

"No," Jade said grasping her hand, "you are beautiful, Darby. Inside and out."

"You guys are my best friends. You have to say that."

"We're your best friends *because* of that. We wouldn't be your friends if you were ugly on the inside."

"You're friends with me, and I'm dead and rotting inside." Taylor smiled when Darby chuckled. Clearly that was her intent.

"Don't let her make you feel bad about yourself. Or your appearance. Or your intentions," Jade continued.

Darby sniffled as she looked at Taylor.

"I'm still up for burning down her house."

After wiping her cheeks, Darby dragged her palms over her pants. "I'm back in high school again."

"You're not," Taylor said. "And you're not fake. We're going to fix this."

"What do I do in the meantime?" Darby asked. "Maybe you haven't noticed how people are looking at me, but I have. They hate me."

"Nobody hates you," Taylor said.

"You're going to apologize," Jade said. "Take off the descriptions and apologize."

"I think she should take her shop down altogether," Taylor said. "Delete it and be done."

Jade shook her head before Taylor finished. "That's admitting guilt without saying a word."

"She should at least turn off the messages."

"I already did," Darby said before Jade could argue. "They were getting too mean."

"You can turn off your messages," Jade said, "turn off comments, but you cannot close your shop. You can't run and hide."

"She should at least post a video of her own," Taylor said. "Clarify what Jennifer said."

Jade shook her head, but before she could argue, Darby dropped her spoon, clinking it against her dish.

"Stop," she spat, tired of hearing them snip at each other over how to handle her problems. "Look, I think Taylor's right. I should take down my shop and donate what I have left. Thrift stores will take those dresses. I need to bow out before I'm completely cancelled. Then I can try to make a comeback under a different name later."

"You're not going to run," Jade insisted.

"You don't know how ugly this is going to get," Darby said as tears burned her eyes. "People are going to start being savage toward me because it's trendy. I'm about to get obliterated online. I've seen this happen a thousand times. It's going to get bad."

"No," Jade insisted. "We're not going to let that happen."

Taylor scoffed. "And how are you going to stop it, Jade? You can't control the Internet."

"Stop fighting," Darby said quietly. "Not over this. Not over me."

"We're not fighting," Jade said.

"Nobody's even thrown a punch yet," Taylor said and then grinned again. "I'm kidding. We're not fighting. We're disagreeing because we want to do what's best for you."

Pushing her ice cream away, Darby frowned. "I think... I think I have to disappear."

"Darby," Jade begged. "We can fix this. Don't abandon all your hard work."

Darby considered the suggestions. Even if Jade thought she could fix this and Taylor thought she could help Darby barrel through, she had seen this before. She knew how bad this was going to get before it got better. She never thought she'd be on the receiving end of it, though.

"Fine. I won't shut down the shop. Yet," Darby said to Jade as she stood. "But if things don't get better, and *fast*, Darby Zamora is going dark. Poof. Gone."

And with that, she turned and walked out of Harper's for effect. And because she didn't want to cry in front of strangers.

As she'd done earlier in the day, Darby stared at her reflection for a long time, this time to adjust to the new hair color. Her signature bright red hair was now a few shades darker than her natural near-black strands. She hadn't seen her hair like this for years. She wasn't really digging it, but the hair and her clothes—black capris and a white fitted shirt—blended in. And she'd decided that was a good thing.

For now. This seemed like a good time to go back to blending into the background.

Names like *freak*, *dork*, and *nerd* might roll off others, but they were like spears to Darby's sensitive heart. She'd become an ace at avoiding those kinds of attacks back in high school. The first step was to blend into the background as much as possible. Something Darby had come to loathe was her best chance at survival. Turning herself back into a nobody, becoming like everyone else, hiding her true self away in an isolated tower somewhere like freaking Rapunzel.

Darby assessed the large supply of makeup and hair care products on her vanity. When she'd first decided to change up her look, she'd spent her entire paycheck—which wasn't as much as some—on new makeup. She'd watched video after video until she'd mastered fake lashes, eyeliner wings, and lip liner. She'd learned the importance of a good foundation and finishing spray. Those things might have seemed silly to others, but they had saved her.

Grabbing her trash can, she made a sweeping motion, knocking the bottles, tubes, and sprays into the bin. Her soul ached as she thought about how much she loved each and every one of them. Maybe she should keep them. Just in case.

"No," she muttered to herself.

She set the can down and pushed herself up. However, she didn't even make it to the bedroom door before turning around. "I'll save them for later," she said and set the trash can inside her closet so the products were still there but she wouldn't have to see them all the time.

"Hello," Jade called from the other room.

When Jade had first moved to Chammont Point, she'd constantly lectured Darby about knocking before entering. Darby had countered that if Jade didn't want her best friend walking in, she should lock the door. At first Jade insisted that didn't make sense; however, now Jade walked into Darby's house as freely as Darby walked into hers.

That was a good thing most of the time. That made them feel more like family.

But this was one time when Darby wished she'd remembered to lock the door.

She wasn't up for company. She needed more time to get used to this new version of herself before sharing the changes with her friends. No doubt Jade and Taylor wouldn't understand Darby's need to camouflage herself while under attack. They wouldn't understand that this was the best way.

Jade popped into the bedroom and her smile fell. "Darby," she whispered.

Darby swallowed hard and then smiled. Without her thick application of bright red lipstick, her lips felt odd. Her smile felt fake. It *was* fake.

"What have you done?" Jade whispered as she came into the room. She gingerly touched Darby's much darker hair, and concern filled her eyes. "Honey, this isn't—"

"It's okay," Darby said, stepping around her. "I like it."

"Do you?" Jade asked, following behind her.

Darby yanked her fridge door open and scanned the contents. She really could go for some of her mom's comfort food right now. Her mom had been the best cook. A heaviness settled over Darby's chest as she remembered all the times her mom would hug her close and remind her that even if Darby didn't have the best clothes or the nicest house, she had a really good heart. And then she'd serve up some barbacoa and all would feel right in the world.

Tears welled in Darby's eyes as she stared at her near-bare fridge. She should have learned to cook like her mom.

She shouldn't have acted like she was above cooking. In Darby's mind, her mom's dreams of owning a restaurant had undermined her ability to provide more for them. Her mom had worked in a restaurant, hoping to learn what she needed to know. Instead, she'd spent her life working a minimum wage job for someone else.

After she'd died of a heart attack, Darby had been lost. In fact, she still was.

She sniffled as Jade walked into the kitchen. Closing the fridge, she turned, and her resolve shattered at the sympathy on Jade's face. Darby's hope and happiness crumbled into a million pieces.

"I want my mom," she whispered.

Jade enveloped her in a big hug as Darby let her tears go. Although Jade was the so-called maternal one of the group, her embrace wasn't nearly as comforting as Darby's mom's had been. Even so, Darby couldn't deny the sense of love and belonging. She clung harder. Cried harder.

"I'm sorry Taylor and I made things worse for you," Jade said.

"You didn't."

"We did, but we weren't trying to."

"Taylor isn't really going to hurt someone. She doesn't express her anger well, that's all." Leaning back, Darby looked at Jade's face. "You know this."

"Yeah," Jade said. "I do. But this is a serious situation, and her threats of violence are distractions that don't help."

"She's trying in her own way. You know she won't act on them."

"That's not the point. The point is, we don't need that right now."

"Are you okay?" Darby asked after a few seconds. "You're usually the one defending Taylor."

Jade nodded. "I know. But today, right now, we need to focus on real solutions to what's going on with you. It's going to be okay," Jade said softly. She stroked Darby's hair and kissed her head. "I promise. It's going to be okay."

"You don't understand." Darby moved around Jade and dropped onto her sofa. After snagging a tissue, she blew her nose twice and then slumped down into a slouchy, miserable mess. "I thought I'd finally outgrown feeling like such a loser, Jade."

Easing down, Jade brushed a few now-black strands from Darby's face. "You aren't a loser. Babe, this is a ripple in your life. Nothing is ruined. And we aren't going to let people come after you."

"This is a game to them, you know? Ruining lives is a joke to people like that. They don't understand how much hurt they cause when they do this."

"I know. But you aren't alone in this, Darby. You have friends—friends who are going to help you. Taylor and I are right here, ready to fight for you. *With* you. We are going to do everything we can to defend you and your boutique from this attack."

Darby leaned over enough to rest her head on Jade's shoulder. "I love you."

"I love you too." Jade rested her head on Darby's. "Is there anything I can do to make today better?"

"Make me some barbacoa and tell me I have a good heart."

Jade was quiet for a moment before saying, "How about if I order you some from La Cocina and tell you that you have a beautiful heart? The most beautiful heart I've ever known."

Darby blinked and smiled slightly. "Can I have extra tortillas?"

"Of course," Jade agreed.

With her mood marginally lifted, Darby pushed herself up. "I'm going to make a big pitcher of margaritas, nonalcoholic for you, and set the table outside. I think we should eat in the sunshine, don't you?"

"Sounds good," Jade said.

Darby glanced back when Jade rambled into the phone. After only a few seconds, she realized Jade was inviting Taylor, and Darby's spirits felt even lighter. The thought of sharing her favorite comfort food with her best friends as they sat in their cove made all her problems fade away. There were few things Darby loved more than planning little moments like this. She wasn't much of a cook, but she had so much fun setting the scene.

By the time Taylor arrived with the order from La Cocina that Jade had called in, there were three perfectly salt-rimmed margarita glasses on the table. Darby's favorite funky dishes had been set out, and her speaker was playing salsa music from a streaming service. This felt like a party for three, ready to roll.

Despite the cloud hanging over her, Darby rushed toward Taylor to help with the bags of food.

"What happened to your hair?" Taylor asked as Darby neared her.

"I decided to change the color," Darby answered flatly. "Did they add extra tortillas?"

"I hope so. Jade paid for them."

"I'll pay her back."

"No you won't," Jade said, joining them as set their dinner on the table. "This is my treat." She reached into a bag and pulled out something rolled in foil. "Extra tortillas."

Darby clapped with glee before reaching for them. She smelled the foil and closed her eyes. "Yes! They are still warm." Darby opened the container with barbacoa in it, inhaled deeply, and moaned her appreciation. "I love you, Jade."

Jade smiled and blew her a kiss before settling into a chair to eat her salad. "How was your day?" she asked Taylor.

"Long. I put up some kitchen cabinets in this old lady's house. I had to yell at her all day because she refused to put in her hearing aids. My helper for the day smelled like he hadn't showered in weeks. I really need to find a steady crew, but I can't justify it when my projects are still so random. Darby, why did you do that to your hair?" Taylor's tone came across as genuinely confused and concerned. "You like your hair red."

Darby shrugged. "Like I said yesterday, I shouldn't stand out so much right now."

She ignored the concerned glances that passed between her friends. Though she adored Jade and Taylor, the truth was, they had only been friends for a year. They didn't know Darby well enough to understand that she needed to slink into a corner right now. She needed to withdraw and assess. She needed to not be in the midst of the chaos she usually thrived in.

She needed peace. She needed to be invisible.

SIX

THE GROCERY STORE was about to close when Darby ducked inside. She had waited until late in the evening to go shopping, hoping to avoid the crowd. The last thing she wanted to do was run into someone who might be willing to confront her. She'd pulled a fedora down low on her forehead and added sunglasses to hide her face. The look was straight out of a trashy tabloid magazine, but Darby was determined to not be recognized.

She ignored the stares and an associate who asked if she needed help as she snagged a basket. Clutching the bright blue basket like it could save her life, she rushed straight to the veggie section and grabbed three avocados, two tomatoes, and a handful of jalapenos without checking the ripeness. Like a woman on a mission, she headed for the snack aisle, where she nabbed two bags of tortilla chips without seeing which ones were on sale. She didn't have time for that. She knew what brand she liked and was willing to pay a few extra cents for them if it saved her time.

Next, she rushed toward the cookies and grabbed a pack

of chocolate chip soft bake and a bag of the shortbread ones she liked to dunk her in her tea. Ignoring the calorie count of the contents of her basket, she grabbed a box of premade cupcakes for good measure.

That would be enough to get her through a day or two of emotional eating. The last thing on her list was replacing the tube of near-empty eyebrow gel, which she seriously debated leaving without.

She was almost done. Almost home free. Did she really need cosmetics? *Really*?

The debate wasn't really one she needed to have. She rushed toward the familiar corner of the store. She knew exactly what she needed and exactly where to find it. The detour would only add a few minutes to her trip.

However, as she turned the corner, her breath caught. She hadn't wanted anyone confronting her, but that didn't mean she wasn't up for confronting someone else.

Jennifer Williams stood in front of the display of eye shadows, holding palettes in each hand as if she couldn't decide which one to go with. Usually when Darby saw someone being indecisive in the makeup aisle, she rushed forth to help them with their debate. She especially loved when the target of her assistance was a teenager who seemed to be starting out in the wonderful world of colors. She could talk forever to those girls about skin tone, blending, and contrast.

Back when she was in high school, Darby would have given anything to have someone teach her about those things. She would have eaten up every word, and Darby found that most of the girls she found in these aisles did when she offered advice. Every now and then, she considered offering lessons to young ladies who needed that extra boost of confidence makeup often offered.

However, when Darby saw Jennifer standing there, offering makeup tips was the last thing on her mind. And boosting her confidence? Not even on the list. However, suggestions on where to shove the eye shadow palettes came to mind. The idea brought a little sunshine to Darby's cloudy mood.

As she stood at the end of the aisle, she ground her teeth together and debated what Jade would do. Turn and walk away, no doubt. Take the higher road. Avoid conflict. And she would have been perfectly at peace with that decision. Jade's ability to contain her anger was a mystery to Darby at times.

However, Taylor wouldn't hesitate to call Jennifer out for what she'd done. She'd march right up to her and put her in her place. And *she* would have been perfectly at peace as well. Taylor's anger wasn't a mystery to anyone. She never hesitated in sharing it. Darby couldn't say she admired that trait, but she could definitely say she understood it.

After watching Jennifer put one package back and lean closer to examine another, Darby chose to channel Taylor and marched forward. She held her chin up and pushed her shoulders back with all the righteous indignation she'd been feeling ever since that video was posted.

"You intentionally made me look bad," Darby accused without any sort of greeting.

Jennifer nearly dropped the eye shadows from the start she'd received at Darby's harsh words. For several satisfying seconds she fumbled, clearly unsettled. She recovered quickly, though, and quirked an eyebrow at Darby. Any signs of the band geek were gone. Standing there with a smirk on her face and cocked brow, Jennifer looked more like one of the teenage tyrants who used to mock them. The glimmer of amusement in her eyes was far too similar to that of the girl who had unhooked Darby's bra during chemistry class.

Cruel. Savage. Remorseless.

"I didn't have to make you look bad," Jennifer said with an evil smirk. "You did that to yourself."

"You spliced my words together."

"No. I *edited* the interview that you willingly took part in."

Darby narrowed her eyes. This wasn't a game of semantics. This was her life, and Jennifer had intentionally tried to ruin it. Darby hadn't figured out why, but she was smart enough to know that Jennifer had used her. "You *edited* it to make me come off as mean and heartless."

Putting the packages of eye shadow back on the shelf, Jennifer tilted her head in a way that was clearly meant to be condescending. Her highlights caught the incandescent glow coming down from above them, and her ponytail swayed. The image was a perfect representation of the patronizing scorn the cheerleaders in high school had always displayed right before tossing cruelty Darby's way.

For a moment, Darby felt like a nobody standing in the crowded hallway as everyone rushed from one class to another, stopping only long enough to see if this was the day when the biggest outcast finally got her ass kicked. That day had never come. Darby had never been in a fight, but she'd walked with that fear every day for nearly four years. And that panic came rushing back to her as Jennifer narrowed her eyes and smirked wickedly.

"I wouldn't be able to make you look mean, Darby," Jennifer said with a soft voice, as if that would disguise the sharp edge of what she was saying, "if you hadn't *done* something mean."

Darby shook her head slightly as she tightened her grip on her basket. "You cut that bit about me making a profit on heartbreak to make it look like I was bragging about doing so, instead of pointing out that you were all but accusing me of—"

"Of what?" Jennifer pressed. "Of doing exactly what you *are* doing." The sarcastic sweetness disappeared as she stood straighter and scoffed with a slight shake of her head. She looked over Darby from head to toe as if trying to determine if she was worth the trouble. When she met her gaze again, she glared. "You are using the pain of others to market your website. You are heartless."

Darby gasped and leaned back. Of all the things people had ever said about her, that was not one she was used to. According to Jade, Darby's heart was too big. Too vulnerable. After the shock of the accusation wore off, Darby said, "And you're a fraud. You pretend to be some sweet, innocent little Internet star who happened to find success, but in reality, you're a manipulator and a liar." The moment the words left her, a weight dropped off her chest. She'd been holding on to that statement for days. Giving it life was invigorating. She straightened her spine with a newfound confidence and pushed on. "You wormed your way into my home under the pretense of helping me grow my business, when in reality you were there to trick me into saying things you could use to twist the truth into something ugly. You're a big, stinking fake."

Once again, Jennifer sneered and raised a brow as she gave that holier-than-thou look she'd damn near perfected.

"You're one to talk about fake. Look at you standing in a grocery store at ten o'clock at night in a fedora and pink sunglasses like you're a freaking Kardashian hiding from the paparazzi. You look like a fool. A week ago, you looked like an extra from a Dean Martin movie."

Darby furrowed her brow as she tried to connect the dots on Jennifer's intended insult. Calling her a Kardashian? Okay. Calling her a fool? Whatever. But an extra in a Dean Martin movie? What did that mean? She yanked her sunglasses off and squinted at her foe. "Are you saying that I looked like a martini?"

"What?" Jennifer asked. "No. What? You looked like...you know, like...an out-of-date bombshell."

Darby rolled her eyes as she scanned her memory. "Dean Martin was mostly in westerns and comedies. I think you meant James Dean."

"Whatever."

"No, really, there's a big difference between James Dean and Dean Martin. James Dean was—"

"That doesn't matter," Jennifer insisted. "None of that matters. What matters is that you're fake too. You're just fake in a different way. You'll probably look like a bad 1980s era Madonna next. Don't tell me I'm fake when you're standing here like this."

Darby stood taller. "I might put on fancy makeup and clothes, but I would never dress like a bad version of Madonna, and I would never hurt anyone with the intent of getting views on a video. That was wrong and you know it. There is a difference between putting on an act to protect yourself and putting on an act to dupe people so you can make a buck off them."

Jennifer widened her eyes like a doe in a spotlight. "Are you kidding me? Are you freaking kidding me? You... *You* are going to lecture *me* about monopolizing off other people? When your entire website is about mocking women who had to cancel their weddings?"

"I'm not mocking anyone!"

"The hell you aren't."

Darby pressed her lips together. She wasn't going to let Jennifer distract her from the point she was trying to make. "You edited my words and made me come across like a heartless, money-hungry vulture," Darby said. "You made me seem malicious, and you did it on purpose to get hits on your site and make money off your advertisers." Darby glared.

Jennifer snorted as if she couldn't believe those words had been used to describe her. "What about you? You're selling people's broken dreams."

"I'm selling dresses I made with my own two hands. When those weddings fell apart, I did what I could to make things easier for the brokenhearted brides by not charging them for wedding dresses they would never wear. Instead of telling them 'tough shit, pay me anyway,' I swallowed the cost. I was kind and understanding when I didn't have to be. I took a financial hit to help those women, and *you* made me look greedy and shallow to get people to come to your website. You... You're the one who's greedy and shallow and mean."

"Oh my God," Jennifer said with an exaggerated roll of her eyes. When she looked at Darby again, she pushed her head forward and creased her brow as if she couldn't believe what she was seeing. "You seriously don't think there's anything wrong with what you're doing? The way you're making jokes about those poor women and their cancelled weddings?"

"I *never* said anyone's name," Darby stated in what was beginning to feel like her new life mantra.

Jennifer shook her head as if she was trying to understand the words Darby had tossed at her. She looked like she was putting together a puzzle and realizing the pieces didn't fit. "That doesn't matter, Darby. Why can't you understand that *doesn't* matter? They know. Other people know. And you're dredging up what could possibly have been the worst day of someone's life and making a profit off their pain."

"That's not true," Darby insisted quietly.

"It *is* true," Jennifer said. "And it's disgusting. I didn't edit Sue Berdynksi's video together to make her cry, Darby. She *was* crying. And she was crying because she was devastated you'd told the world about her breakup."

"*She* told the world she was the canoe bride," Darby said. "I didn't."

Jennifer's shoulders sagged slightly, barely enough for Darby to notice, and she looked down for several long seconds. When she looked up again, the sarcasm and bitter edge was gone. Her face was sad, like she was giving up. "You don't get it. What you're doing is mean-spirited. More than mean-spirited. It's cruel. Whether you want to believe it or not. It is. You can't tell other people how to feel. If they feel hurt by your actions, you need to reconsider what you're doing. And there are people who are hurting because of your website. Rather than reconsider or even take a moment to think how they might be feeling, you're attacking me in a grocery store for exposing the truth of what you've done. You need to take a step back, Darby. You need to put yourself in someone else's shoes for one minute instead of digging your heels in to prove a point."

A huge breath left Darby—loud and forceful—and took with it a big part of the confidence and determination she'd been holding on to.

Jennifer's words had struck a nerve. A raw one.

Darby could be stubborn, she was well aware of that, but only on things that mattered to her. Being stubborn wasn't a bad thing, not when it was used to protect things, like her work or her website. Not when it was used to stand up for herself against someone who had used her social media platform to bully her.

Rather than stand there and continue to sort through this disaster, Darby shook her head. "Even if you think what I did was wrong, what you did was worse. You intentionally edited that interview. And you know it." Turning on her heels, she stormed off, groceries and eyebrow gel forgotten.

Darby didn't stop angrily marching until she climbed into her old car and pulled away. She ground her teeth hard as she headed home. Rage boiled in her chest until she let out a frustrated scream and slapped her hand on the steering wheel.

The road turned and the little gravel road she'd usually take to the cove appeared, but Darby didn't slow down. She drove by the cove and followed the road around the lake. As she did, she sped up until her car matched her racing thoughts.

From that day on the beach when she was so excited to promote her boutique on *The Noah Joplin Show* to Taylor and Jade pointing out that she should change the sales pitches.

From the initial onslaught of supportive posts to people calling her names and picking on her style. From Jade saying Darby should consider how the brides feel to Jennifer pointing out that Darby was incapable of seeing the truth of her actions.

She pulled her car over at Chammont Lake Lookout Point and turned off the ignition. Leaning her head against the headrest, she stared up at the waning moon and the stars sparkling against the dark sky.

Other memories flooded her as she sat there looking up at the universe. Her mom had been one of those read-the-stars types. Whenever Darby got overwhelmed, they went out into the backyard and sat on the broken and crumbling cement steps of their rental.

The answers are in the stars, little one, her mom would say. *All you have to do is look up and listen with your heart.*

"Okay," Darby whispered. "I'm listening."

She sat, staring, but no words of wisdom filtered down to her. No ah-ha moments hit her. Not a single light bulb went off to show her the way.

Something built low in her gut, though. She tried to ignore the sensation, but it grew heavier and heavier by the moment.

She pictured Jade sitting out by the cove early in the spring. Her divorce had been finalized for like five minutes when her ex-husband had announced he was engaged to someone else.

Darby was trying to cheer her up. With the saddest eyes Darby had ever seen, Jade softly explained that it wasn't only being left that hurt. It was the embarrassment of knowing that all her friends, neighbors, and family members knew that he'd been cheating. They knew she hadn't been good enough. And that was humiliating. She'd told Darby that simply trying to hold her head up felt much too exhausting at times.

Darby had tried to reassure her that she was more than enough, but Jade sniffled and shook her head and said clearly she hadn't been.

That conversation had broken Darby's heart. It hadn't been fair that Jade was hurting so much over someone else's actions.

That memory bled into the image of Sue Berdynski sniffling on Jennifer's video as she talked about how humiliating the experience had been and how cruel it was to hear someone talking about it as nonchalantly as Darby had. Sue had said that Darby hadn't seemed to care that she was sharing the most devastating thing that had ever happened to Sue—in fact, she'd said, it seemed like Darby had enjoyed sharing her pain.

Darby deepened her frown as she recalled sitting in Noah's studio. She had been...excited...to share the stories. Too excited, perhaps. Now that she thought about it, she could see how Sue would think she'd enjoyed sharing someone's pain.

Furrowing her brow as tears filled her eyes, Darby sighed. Oh, damn. She *had* enjoyed it. Not causing someone pain— she hadn't realized she'd been doing that. But she had enjoyed being in the limelight, and she'd dragged Sue's broken heart out there with her like it was some kind of show-and-tell.

Darby hadn't done that to be cruel or to inflict pain like

Jennifer had been insinuating, but she definitely hadn't been as thoughtful as she'd pretended to be.

Wiping her eyes, she scanned the surface of the lake and the reflection of the moon warped by the waves.

The answers are in the stars.

Lifting her gaze, Darby watched the twinkling for several more minutes as she, as Jennifer had suggested, put herself into someone else's shoes. Sitting there, imagining how she'd felt when Mark and Ted had talked about their breakups. She hadn't even been engaged to either of them, and she still hadn't appreciated them sharing their so-called heartbreak. Those moments had been private, but they'd shared them, and Darby hadn't been pleased.

Yet hadn't Darby done the exact same thing? And on a much larger scale.

Closing her eyes against the twinkling stars, Darby sighed and then whispered to the stars, "Oh, Mama. I think I screwed up."

As soon as Darby got home from the lookout, she started the shower and then stood under the hot water until it ran cool. Her mind was on repeat, playing the last week over and over, despite her intention to let the water cleanse her mood so she could focus on the situation with a clear mind.

She slowly dried off and dressed in her favorite cheetah print pajama set. Then she took her time drying her hair and going through her bedtime ritual. She was procrastinating because there was another feeling coming over her that she was desperate to ignore.

Shame.

And it was taking over her mind.

She considered calling her friends and asking for an impromptu support session, but she'd already heard all she wanted from them on this topic. She knew where they stood. They had already given their input, and she didn't want to hear it again. They both thought she was wrong, and neither seemed interested in hearing why she disagreed.

And she wasn't quite ready to admit she was starting to think they had been right all along. The hesitation wasn't pride, at least not all of it. It was the fear that she'd said and done things to cause pain and then stuck her head in the sand to ignore the fallout.

Ignoring the consequences of her actions wasn't too far from the norm for Darby, but the other part? The hurting people part? She couldn't stomach the growing realization that she had done exactly that.

She'd been too stubborn to allow herself to think she could have done something that others would consider atrocious. Having spent years feeling like she was an outcast, she'd always considered herself overly sensitive to others. More than one person in her past had told her she had to stop trying so hard to tiptoe around everyone's feelings.

She hadn't tiptoed this time, had she? She'd donned her favorite black patent leather Mary Janes and stomped all over her former clients without even considering that was what she'd been doing. Then she kicked a few of them in the shins for good measure.

At least that was what Jennifer and her legions of fans seemed to think.

Were they right?

Heaving a big sigh, Darby walked into her closet and frowned at the totes of keepsakes she really didn't have the room to store. One day, she didn't know when, she'd make herself go through them all and thin down the old stuff she didn't really need.

She found the box with old books and pulled the top off, sorting through the contents until she found the yearbook that had been calling out to her since she'd gotten home. She hadn't wanted one, but her mom had bought it anyway. This was from her senior year, and her mom had insisted Darby would want it someday. She never had. This was the first time she'd pulled it out since sticking it in the box years ago.

Running her fingers over the cover, she felt the embossing that was made to look like Chammont Point High School—right down to the trees scattered along the school property. The gold lettering proudly spelled out the school's name and the years the contents memorialized.

Darby didn't need to look at the photos to remember that year. Her senior year was burned into her mind. From the first day when someone had commented on how much weight she'd gained over the summer to the last day when she walked out, knowing she'd never have to step foot into that building ever again.

That was what freedom felt like. Darby had never forgotten that.

Tracing the raised design again, she remembered how the kids had carried their books around asking for signatures and excitedly exchanged notes in the pages. Darby had stuffed hers into her backpack and pretended it wasn't there. She might have been able to get one or two people to sign something, but she had been too shy to ask.

The pages intentionally left blank for friends to leave each other notes and promises for forever friendship were still blank.

Darby opened the cover, and it creaked with resistance. Had she ever even opened this back then? She didn't think so. This was probably the first time she'd ever even considered looking through the memory book.

She wasn't in any of the pictures anyway. She hadn't belonged to clubs or joined in activities. The one and only photo of her would be the headshot the school had provided. Her mom hadn't been able to afford a senior photo shoot, and Darby hadn't wanted one anyway. By her senior year, she had zero self-esteem, and the last thing she wanted was someone focusing a camera on her.

Besides, other than her family, who she barely knew since most of them were still in Mexico City, she didn't have anyone to share the photos with. Even if her mom had been able to afford a photographer and a big photo package like most of the other seniors, it would have been a huge waste of money.

Darby flipped through the images in the book, skimming familiar faces of people who had never taken notice of her. They were all smiling and goofing off, happy to have their lives captured. Their friendships were evident in the photos. Most of them probably only communicated via social media these days—that was how those high school friendships went—but it must have been nice, on some level, to have someone from the past remember them.

Unlike the people selected to grace the pages of the yearbook, Darby had been a ghost in the hallways of her school. She'd moved through crowds and classrooms like an apparition. She'd liked it that way. Or so she thought.

Looking back now, she was sad she hadn't tried to push out of that cage some of her peers had put her into. Maybe if she'd tried a few activities or joined a club, she would have found friends like the ones she had now. Maybe there'd be one or two pictures of her with her group hamming it up for the photographer. Maybe she would be able to look back without bitterness filling her heart.

She flipped through the pages one at a time, skimming and remembering until a photo caught her attention. There, far in the background of a photo taken in the cafeteria, sat a teenage Darby Zamora. Her nose was in a book as life went on around her. Her head down, her eyes focused on anything but the people around her.

Tears burned the back of her eyes as her heart ached for that girl she used to be. Lonely. Sad. Isolated. Her mom and her books had been her closest confidants. Her only friends. Darby traced the black-and-white image of herself blurry in the background.

That was so fitting. The colors were dull and her image was vague, almost indistinguishable from the surroundings. She'd become so adept at blending in, most people probably never even noticed her in the background.

Flipping through more photos, she scanned the blurry images instead of the students who'd been the focus to see if there was more of her. She hadn't seen another image of herself until she stopped on the last page of senior pictures. Darby flipped back to look at Jennifer's photo. The contrast between their images was as stark as Darby remembered.

Pale-skinned, blonde-haired, plain Jennifer was just as

geeky, but somehow she wore it better. Clearly, she had been far more comfortable with her place in the world than Darby had been with hers.

Jennifer's smile was perfect from the braces and headgear she'd worn in middle school. Her hair had been slicked back into a perfect ponytail. She'd clearly been posed as a photographer snapped the photo with the lake in the background. Unlike Darby's school-issued headshot, Jennifer had chosen one of those fun senior portraits to share in the book.

Next to Jennifer's bright, shining face was olive-skinned, dark-haired, and nerdy as could be Darby, in a plain T-shirt with her frizzy hair pulled into a lumpy ponytail and a flat smile on her lips. Her acne had flared up the week before school photos were taken, so her picture highlighted her shiny forehead and purple marks from the barely healed breakout. Her cheeks were rounded, and her eyes were haunted.

Considering they had similar social statuses, they should have had similar hurt in their eyes, they should have been bearing similar scars, but somehow they were the complete opposite of each other. Seeing how much made Darby's soul ache. She wished she could go back and talk to her high school self. She wished she could tell Wallflower Darby that everything was going to work out.

"Don't look so sad," she'd tell her teenage self. "You're going to find yourself and have the best friends you could ever ask for. It's going to be okay." Then she'd give herself a hug because she remembered all too well how much she could have used hugs back then.

She closed the book and tossed it aside. She didn't want

to dwell on the past any longer. She couldn't change how people—including herself—saw her back then. Changing the past was impossible.

All she could do was focus on the present. And the present wasn't going so well.

Darby snagged a tissue and wiped her eyes before tears could roll down her cheeks. She never meant to be a bully— she was bullied and knew far too well what that felt like. Never in a million years would she ever want to be that person.

Falling back on her bed, Darby stared up at the ceiling. She had to figure this out. She had to figure out how to right this ship that was sinking.

In her mind, she heard Jade and Taylor all but begging her to remove the descriptions. And she heard Jade telling her she needed to post an apology. She heard Taylor suggesting she take the site down altogether.

For the first time since this began, Darby seriously considered that she had been seeing this entire situation through the wrong lenses.

Was she wrong? As much as Darby didn't want to admit it, Jennifer had a point. Even if Darby hadn't meant for people to take her website personally, some had, and she couldn't tell them feeling like that was wrong.

She couldn't tell them that feeling hurt was wrong.

Sure, she'd posted stories about anonymous people. But they were still about *people*. People who'd had their hearts broken.

Closing her eyes, Darby dropped her hand onto her forehead to slow her mind from spinning as she questioned everything.

SEVEN

DARBY SPENT PRETTY MUCH the entire next morning on her couch staring at her ceiling as the events of the last eight days rolled through her mind on repeat. From Noah's show, the tense exchanges between Jade and Taylor, to sitting alone the night before fighting the urge to let the past consume her.

The feeling that she had been wrong all along was gaining strength and, with it, the shame and guilt that had gnawed at her after her confrontation with Jennifer. And as those sensations grew, so did the urge to hide away from the world and blend into the background like she'd done in that photo of her in the high school yearbook.

Being invisible was a safety net—and not necessarily a good one, but it was a comfortable one. One she was familiar with and knew she could do well. However, she didn't want to feel like that miserable version of herself. She didn't want Wallflower Darby to win again. She'd been struggling with that urge since this began. Sadly, her resolve was fading, and the reality of what her life had become was beginning to overwhelm her.

The part of her that had grown up and realized these feelings weren't normal was screaming out to her. She needed help. She recognized the signs. Depression was creeping up on her, and if she wasn't careful, it would win.

Reaching out to Jade and Taylor, however, didn't seem like the best idea. They had been pushing her to come to terms with what was now staring her right in the eye. She didn't want to deal with any kind of I-told-you-so looks. They wouldn't rub her nose in it—they were better than that. But they certainly weren't above casting knowing glances at each other.

Darby didn't think she could stomach that. She simply didn't have the strength for anyone to make her feel even worse, whether they did so intentionally or not.

So, instead, she'd burrowed deeper into her cocoon of self-pity.

When her phone dinged, letting her know she had a new text, her heart did a funny flip in her chest. It was the same anxious reaction she'd have whenever she was at school and someone noticed her. It didn't matter if it was a teacher, a peer, or a coach. Being noticed caused her to shrink back like she'd been kicked with a cleat.

Dread. The feeling was dread.

Anxiety coming in waves and knocking her off-balance.

Fear of what was to come encompassing her and drowning out the light.

Though her fingers itched to answer, she ignored the text. She suspected it to be either Taylor or Jade, but there was a chance it could be someone else. Someone she didn't want to hear from.

She didn't want to know who was reaching out to her. She

didn't want to know what had gone wrong now. Sticking her head in the sand, or faux fur blankets as it were, was a much better option in her opinion.

She was perfectly content with her decision to let the world go on without her for a little bit longer until a breeze blew through her open window, carrying the scent of burning wood with it. Darby pulled her head from the covers, put her nose up higher, and sniffed to confirm what she'd smelled.

There was definitely a pile of wood burning. And accelerant. That combination could only mean one thing.

"Bonfire," Darby whispered and then rolled off her couch to rush across the room. She peeked through the blinds to confirm.

Though it was the middle of the day, a fire was roaring in the outdoor space she and Jade shared. Sitting by the fire was one of their favorite things to do, but they usually wrapped up their days by the pit, not spent the afternoon out there.

Darby rolled her eyes back as she considered the date. It wasn't anyone's birthday. Not their friendiversary. As far as she could remember, it wasn't a holiday.

Why were they having a fire in the middle of the afternoon? Why weren't they at work like normal people?

As she continued pondering the reason they'd be out there like it was a Saturday evening instead of a workday afternoon, Taylor added another log to the fire while Jade pecked away on her phone. Moments later, Darby's phone dinged again.

This time, she looked at the screen.

Come outside! Jade had texted the first time.

This time, she'd added, *Tay brought lunch and stuff for s'mores.*

Darby gasped. S'mores? *Yes!* Though Jade didn't eat the sugary snacks, she was the absolute best at roasting the marshmallows. Darby tended to burn them, but Jade's were always perfectly golden and gooey inside. Other than margaritas and ice cream from Harper's, the fastest way to cheer Darby up was a perfectly made s'more.

"Yum," Darby said as she clapped her hands together and started for the door, but then she stopped.

Only moments before, she'd been determined to not lean on Jade and Taylor to get through this. She'd been determined to sort this out on her own. The reminder made her hesitate. If she went out there, they would ask how things were going, and she would dump her problems on them, and then they would be determined to solve them.

That was the exact opposite of what she wanted or needed right now.

Maybe she should pass. Maybe she should tell them she was too busy. Or sleeping. Or suffocating in misery.

Come on! Jade texted. *Please!*

Darby twisted her lips as she considered if she should. The temptation of food, especially melted marshmallows and gooey chocolate, was too much to resist. She texted back, *I don't want to talk about Un-Do.*

Okay, Jade replied.

I mean it!

Okay!

With that settled, Darby shoved her feet into a pair of fluffy pink flamingo slippers before rushing out the front door. As she headed toward the common area between hers and Jade's cabins, Darby realized it wasn't only the worries about what they'd say about Un-Do that had her unsettled. She had a lingering concern that Taylor and Jade were angry at each other because of their disagreements over Darby's situation. If they started bickering again, Darby would probably have a complete breakdown right then. She couldn't handle any more animosity than she was already dealing with.

Taylor had reassured her more than once via texts that she wasn't mad at Jade. She was frustrated with the circumstances, but she wasn't mad at anyone. She and Jade were fine. When Darby asked Jade, she'd told her the same thing. Jade had insisted that nobody was mad at anyone... They were all simply concerned.

Even so, Darby had been worried things would be tense between them because of her. Though she had been hesitant to join them, she realized now she needed to get out to the fire and make sure they spent plenty of time together to smooth over any hurt feelings caused by her decision to stand by her website. It was bad enough she had activated a ticking time bomb in her own life. She didn't want to be the reason their friendship blew up too.

Darby hurried toward the fire, and as she neared the impromptu lunch, she noticed a pile of boxes from her favorite pizza place piled on the table. Her smiled widened as excitement filled her. She hadn't even realized how hungry she was until she saw the logo on the box. Had she had breakfast? She couldn't remember, so probably not. Which meant, this...this was her breakfast, and if her friends really loved her, there would be boneless buffalo wings and cheesy bread somewhere in that stack. As well as a deep-dish supreme pizza.

As she neared the sitting area, Taylor picked up a box and flipped the lid back.

Darby widened her eyes at the chicken wings covered in red sauce. "Oh, you're the best." She picked one up and shoved it into her mouth, doing a little jig as the spice coated her tongue. "Pizza?" she asked around the mouthful.

Jade held out a plate to her. "Just how you like it."

A smile spread across Darby's face, and warmth filled her heart. For the first time in almost twenty-four hours, the icky feeling in her stomach eased, like maybe she wasn't the worst person in the world. Her smile softened as she realized that even if she wasn't the worst person in the world, she'd likely moved a few spots closer in the last week.

She silently thanked whatever forces brought these women into her life, as she'd done so many times since they'd become friends. They were all so in tune with one another that it was frightening and amazing at the same time. She had needed them but hadn't wanted to ask for help, yet here they were without even needing to be asked.

The three of them were the friendship version of soulmates. She'd have to ask Jade if there was such a thing. If she asked that in front of Taylor, she'd get uncomfortable like she did whenever feelings became the subject. Darby didn't want to make Taylor uncomfortable when she'd gone out of her way to bring all this yummy food.

"I love you guys so much. I want you both to know how much I appreciate you. I know I've been a little hard to handle lately. I don't mean to be. I'm sorry."

"We're all a little hard to handle sometimes," Taylor acknowledged.

Jade blew her a kiss. "We love you, Darby. We understand you too. You're forgiven."

Taking her plate, Darby dropped into a seat and watched with a full heart as the other two women served themselves. Darby didn't understand how Jade could possibly resist the delicious smells coming from the boxes, but she pried the top off a salad and squeezed an oil-based dressing over it. Taylor, on the other hand, was more like Darby and didn't hesitate to add pizza, wings, and a slice of bread to her plate.

As Darby sank her teeth into the thick pizza with all its glorious toppings, she moaned with appreciation. This was perfect. Jade and Taylor weren't fighting. The table was piled high with some of Darby's favorite foods. The sun was shining, the birds were chirping, and the water in the cove was calm. This was perfect.

Her mood had lightened significantly, but then she saw Taylor frown, and warning flares fired into the sky. Darby's happiness crashed like the Hindenburg. Instantly, she assumed there was bad news. Another lecture. More pointing out how wrong Darby had been to add heartbreak to her dress descriptions. Or maybe, just maybe, Taylor's good-natured picking about Darby's style was about to take a darker turn and she was going to call her out for looking foolish like so many people on the website had done.

"Tay," she hesitantly said after swallowing the food in her mouth. "What... What's wrong?"

Jade stopped fussing with her salad to look up. One glance at Jade, at the way she furrowed her brow and tilted her head, confirmed she saw the stress on Taylor's face too.

"Nothing," Taylor said and stuffed her mouth with a buffalo wing. She faked a quick smile, but the corners of her mouth fell and the effort never reached her eyes, which looked sad. She was terrible at faking. She always had been.

"I don't think so," Jade stated. "If you frown any deeper, your face will implode."

"I'm fine," Taylor insisted again and licked her fingers as she looked out at the water. The short, aloof answer was her way of warning her friends to back off, but she should know better by now. That was not how this trio rolled. They tended to be all over one another's problems. Like Taylor and Jade had been all over Darby's since *The Noah Joplin Show*.

Jade's face shifted from fun friend to concerned mother. Darby hoped Jade remembered Taylor wasn't always keen on those maternal instincts being directed at her. Taylor's mother had ended up in prison when Taylor was young. After that, Taylor had lived with her grandfather, who had taught her all about building things and avoiding her feelings. Which, Darby supposed, explained her grouchy old man attitude. No doubt she'd learned that from the man who'd raised her.

Darby lapped up Jade's maternal affection like a dehydrated puppy. Taylor, however, tended to put up barbed wire barricades and haul out her stash of emotional grenades, which she tossed without thinking about the consequences. Whenever emotions hit too close to home for her, she withdrew and put up barriers.

While she had gotten better over the last year about accepting affection and praise from her friends, and even to offer those to others, Taylor had to be in the right place for those things to happen. At that moment, she didn't seem to be in the right place. She looked like she'd jump and run if pushed too hard.

"Come on. You look completely unsettled," Jade said, gently prodding for information. "Did something happen?"

Taylor sank back in her chair, and defeat washed over her as she wiped her hands on a napkin. Darby's heart sank like a Thanksgiving Day Parade float with a hole in it. Taylor was tough, even when she didn't have to be. Seeing her look so...vulnerable...nearly brought tears to Darby's eyes.

Fear enveloped her. The last week had been one disaster after another. She didn't think she could handle one more. Hadn't the three of them been going through enough?

"I lost another bid," Taylor said quietly. She looked at her pizza and then pushed her plate away as if she'd suddenly lost her appetite. "That's three this month." She shrugged as she continued to stare out over the water. "I think it's time to throw in the towel, guys. I'm not cut out for running my own business."

"That is absolutely not true," Jade stated.

Taylor crossed her arms and jutted her chin out with all the defiance of a teenage rebel. She pulled the change off like a pro and used it often. This was an unspoken warning that Jade should back off. She went from seeming like the weight of the world had crushed down on her to not giving a damn about anything in the blink of an eye. The next warning would be a snappy comment. If that warning wasn't heeded, Taylor would excuse herself and leave.

Darby held her breath and waited, hoping this didn't escalate to that point.

"It is true, Jade," she barked. Warning number two.

"People won't give me a chance. Nobody wants a female contractor. It's ridiculous."

"I agree," Jade said, and in an instant, Taylor's defenses eased and Darby relaxed some.

Rather than storming off, sadness filled Taylor's eyes, and it nearly made Darby sob. This was too much for her already heavy heart to handle. Taylor's company meant the world to her. Her grandfather had been so proud of her for going to business school so she could learn how to run a contracting company. When he'd died, he'd left her what little money he had and all his tools so she could make her own business. He'd told her he didn't want her working for other people all her life. According to him, she was too smart for that and deserved to have her own company rather than be a minion. He'd done everything he could to give her a solid starting point for O'Shea Construction.

Unfortunately for Taylor, she'd gotten caught up with the wrong guy while mourning for her grandpa. They'd gotten married, but their union hadn't lasted long. When they split up, the scumbag stole all the tools her grandfather had given to her and the judge had let him get away with it.

Taylor lost almost everything she had left from her grandfather in her divorce. Seeing her company failing wasn't a simple business issue. This really *was* personal to her. She wanted to do something her grandfather could be proud of.

The idea of her giving that up was soul crushing.

Darby looked at Jade. This was definitely Jade's area of expertise. She was the fixer. However, Jade was looking out at the cove as Taylor had done.

Darby's stomach tightened like a Venus flytrap with a

mosquito inside. *No.* Jade couldn't possibly be thinking that Taylor should quit?

"You're a female in a male-dominated field," Jade finally said.

"Yeah," Taylor said. "I'm aware."

"But I don't think that's really the issue," Jade said tentatively, as if she wasn't sure she wanted to say what she was thinking.

"So what's the issue?" Darby asked when Taylor didn't press.

Jade took a sip of her cranberry juice before saying, "The people who are reaching out to you are looking for someone different. Someone…"

Taylor lifted her brows at Jade. "*What*?"

"It's not fair; it's not right," Jade said as she looked across the table at Taylor, "but I think people are expecting you to be…softer."

"Softer?" Taylor asked.

Jade nodded. "They're looking to hire a female contractor, but they're really getting…"

"Me?"

Darby let out a slow breath. Taylor had been raised on construction sites. She was one of the guys, really. And when she got around a crew, she tended to act that way. "Oh. I see what you're saying."

Taylor seemed to need a few more seconds before she caught on. "They want a powder puff."

"Not a powder puff…exactly," Jade said. "But maybe someone who isn't so…"

Taylor shoved half a breadstick in her mouth as she slouched and started chewing with her mouth open.

"Someone who isn't like this?" she asked around the half-chewed food.

Jade and Darby laughed at Taylor's exaggerated display. The moment had gotten tense, and Taylor's obvious attempt at lightening the mood worked, but that didn't change the fact that Jade was likely on to a truth that Taylor didn't want to hear.

"Something like that," Jade said.

"So what?" Taylor asked as she straightened her back. "I should start wearing skirts to work?"

Jade shook her head. "No. You shouldn't change anything. That's not going to make you happy. You're going to have to keep pushing. That's the only way to break through."

"I know," Taylor said. "But I don't know how much longer I can make it."

Darby sighed and put her plate on the table.

"I'm sorry," Taylor said. "This dinner was supposed to cheer you up. Not drag you into my problems."

"Your problems *are* my problems," Darby said. "Just like mine are yours. That's what friends are for. Right?"

"Right," Jade said.

Taylor nodded a few seconds later. "Right. But let's not talk about this anymore right now. We need something uplifting to discuss. Like Jade's sex life."

Jade gasped and shook her head as Taylor and Darby laughed. "You two are terrible."

"That's why you love us," Darby said and picked up her pizza again. As she took another bite, Taylor lobbed another Liam joke Jade's way.

This was yet another perfect example of why Darby loved her friends so much. She was so thankful for them in that moment. No matter what else was tossed her way, Darby knew she would make it through. As long as she had Taylor and Jade, she'd make it through anything.

Though Darby was certain Jade and Taylor had other things they should have been doing, they spent the afternoon sitting on the beach together, and she loved them for it. Not only did she need them to keep her mind off her problems, but she wanted to finish smoothing over any residual hurt feelings left over from their disagreements.

Usually they would spend days like that on one of the main beaches watching people swim and play in the water. Today, they'd stuck to the cove. Not only were there less distractions, but there was no chance someone would recognize Darby and say something to her. Which meant less chance that Darby would have a breakdown and Taylor would end up in jail trying to defend her—though no one spoke of those reasons, Darby was certain they all silently agreed on them.

After relaxing on the cove's little stretch of beach for several hours, they'd decided to grill out for dinner. The day had been normal. So completely and wonderfully normal. And perfectly boring.

Despite the calm that her friends had created for her, Darby's mind kept sneaking back to relive the confrontation with Jennifer. She hadn't told Jade and Taylor about the grocery store battle yet. She didn't like keeping secrets from them, but she was still processing all that had happened. All that had been said. More specifically, the way Jennifer's words continued to eat at Darby's soul.

What you're doing is mean-spirited. More than mean-spirited. It's cruel.

Cruel.

That was what Jennifer had said. Those were the words that had hit Darby right in the heart. For some reason, Darby couldn't form the words to share that. Maybe because she feared her friends would agree. Maybe she thought they wouldn't defend her.

And maybe that was because she was beginning to see they couldn't. They couldn't tell Darby that Jennifer was wrong. They couldn't debate if she should or shouldn't have said so.

Jennifer was right, and she was right to call Darby out on it.

She *was* being cruel to her former clients.

Taylor cooked chicken on the grill, and Jade disappeared inside her cabin to make a few side dishes. Meanwhile, Darby sat staring out over the cove, finding it difficult to think about anything other than the growing feeling that she'd been wrong from the start of this mess and it had been nothing more than her out-of-control ego that hadn't let her see that.

When had she become so prideful? When had she allowed saving face to become more important than other people? That wasn't like her. She had a kinder heart than that. Somehow she'd gotten swept up in the excitement and lost touch with herself.

She'd let the positive comments on Un-Do go to her head. Noah Joplin's laughter had filled her eyes with stars, and she'd been drunk on a high that led her astray. She'd clung to those affirmations and discounted everyone who disagreed.

Darby couldn't live with herself if she really thought she'd hurt someone. She'd been hurt far too much in her life to be that person. She'd been such an outcast in school that living in her own skin hurt. She wished she'd reached out to Jennifer then. Or at least someone like her.

If she'd been braver, maybe the band of "losers" could have worked together to thwart the bullies. They could have become their own group and shown the popular kids that they weren't losers. That treating people the way they had didn't say a damn thing about the so-called geeks but spoke volumes about the more popular kids.

Darby would never know now if they could have stood up against power and popularity, but she wanted to think that they would have. And she wanted to think that if she was ever in a place where she was bullying someone, they would stand up to her.

She had to consider that was what Jennifer had helped Sue do. Sue felt betrayed and hurt. She felt humiliated. And she'd used Jennifer's podcast to openly call Darby on it.

Even more than admitting she was wrong, that was the part Darby thought had made her stand her ground so firmly. Rather than admit she'd done something wrong, it was easier to point the finger at Sue for putting a name to the story Darby had told and at Jennifer for giving Sue a platform.

Rather than owning up, she'd deflected. But the time had come. She had to face the consequences of her actions and stop pretending they were going to magically fade away. The last week had been hell. And she'd deserved it.

There was only one way to put an end to it.

Accept responsibility for her mistakes, as Jade and Taylor had been telling her, and do what she could to set things right.

When Jade returned, Darby swallowed hard. "I think... I think it's time to change my site," she said.

Jade and Taylor stopped moving to look at her, but it was Jade who spoke. "Okay. Do you want help?"

Biting her lip, Darby tried to hold back her tears. "Maybe just a little support."

Jade was almost instantly at her side and taking Darby's hand. "Okay. Come on."

Darby let Jade lead her inside and dropped heavily onto her sofa. The weight of what she'd done had become almost too much to carry. As they sat close together like that, Darby opened each dress description and deleted the stories about the cancelled weddings.

A big tear fell down her cheek as she pressed the button to update her site. "I didn't want to hurt anyone."

"I know," Jade reassured her.

"Do you think... Should I post an apology on the site?"

After a moment, Jade nodded. "I think that would be nice."

"Would you help me write it?"

"Of course."

Darby sighed as the idea made her stomach twist into knots. "What if they don't forgive me? What if people are still mean to me?"

Jade gave her a half hug and pressed her cheek to

Darby's. "Honey, we can't stop people from being mean, but maybe we can get some of your old clients who aren't upset to do testimonials for you. Then you can try to regain any ground lost this week. Posting an apology is a great first step."

Darby considered her words for a few minutes. "I think I might close it down."

"I think you should post your apology and give it some time. See what happens."

"But it's not fun anymore," Darby said. "I don't want to do this if it isn't fun."

"But you also can't run away. You have to stick around long enough to try to make this right. Look, you don't have to turn the commenting section back on," Jade said. "And if you want, Taylor and I can weed through your email inbox until all the dust settles. We won't let any bullshit comments make it to you."

Darby's heart melted. "You'd do that?"

"Of course. I don't want you to give up, Darbs, but I understand how difficult this is. Let us make it easier for you."

With a lump in her throat and a knot in her stomach, Darby wrote out an apology. She admitted she'd been insensitive. When she tried to say that it hadn't been on purpose, Jade made her erase it. She said Darby had to apologize, not make excuses. Darby wanted to argue that it wasn't an excuse, but Jade simply shook her head.

"A straight-up apology, Darby. That's what you need here. Recognition that you made a mistake and a promise to do better in the future. That's it."

Frowning, Darby did as instructed and apologized specifically to Sue Berdynski for sharing her story on Noah

Joplin's show. Then, as Jade had told her, she made a promise to take a good, hard look at herself so that she wouldn't make this mistake again in the future.

With Jade's encouragement, Darby posted the apology at the top of her website. As soon as the site was updated, she felt better. Her stress eased. Not all of it, but enough that she felt like she could breathe without being restrained. The weight that had been sitting on her chest was lighter.

"I'm so proud of you," Jade said softly.

Darby sniffled and nodded. "Thanks."

"Come on," Jade said. "Let's do what we can to forget about this for the rest of the day." As she'd done when she'd led Darby inside, Jade took her hand and led her back out to the table. She sat her down and poured a drink from the pitcher.

Sinking back in her chair, Darby sipped and glanced at Taylor. She smiled and gave Darby a nod, which in Taylor speak was the equivalent of a high five. *Good job*, she'd said in her own way.

Darby smiled her thanks as Jade went back to setting the table. Warmth filled Darby's heart, filling in some of the cracks the last few days had left. "Look at us," Darby said. "We're like the best little family. I love it."

"Me too," Jade said.

"It's nice to be getting back to normal."

"We're not there yet," Jade said and eyed Darby.

Darby furrowed her brow. "What do you mean?"

"You are *not* back to yourself," Taylor said. "Look at you. You still look like Wednesday Addams trying to fit in at a church potluck."

Running her fingers over her black strands, Darby

glanced down at her black shorts and light-blue T-shirt. "I do miss my red hair."

"So do I," Taylor said. "I never thought I'd say that. I never thought I'd miss your wacky clothes, but for God's sake, will you please stop looking so normal?"

Darby and Jade laughed.

Darby's smile fell quickly, though. "Actually, I don't think so. I think you have to get used to this version of me. At least for a while longer."

"Why?" Jade asked.

Warmth settled over Darby's cheeks as embarrassment and insecurity flared in her chest. "It might sound silly to you guys, but all this stuff with Jennifer brought up a lot of bad feelings."

"Feelings are gross," Taylor said. "Don't have those."

Darby tried to smile but couldn't. "For once, we agree. I need to sort through some things before I can feel comfortable standing out again. I need to blend for a while."

Jade sat next to her with her concerned mama face on. "Don't hide yourself, Darby. That won't help."

"I'm not hiding as much as..."

"You're hiding," Jade said when Darby couldn't explain what she was feeling.

"Healing," Darby said after a minute. "I need a little bit more time to heal."

"Okay," Jade said softly, "but don't take too long. We really do miss you."

EIGHT

ONE OF DARBY'S favorite things to do with Taylor and Jade were spontaneous road trips. They always had so much fun on their little adventures, finding new places to explore and restaurants to try. It was a great way for them all to break away from the stresses of running their own businesses.

In the past they'd gone to polo matches, explored caves, and tried new and strange foods to eat. Darby could now say that she'd seen bats in real life. She wasn't a fan. She could also say that she'd eaten shark. Not a fan of that either. But she'd tried it, and that was a badge of honor she never would have had if she and her friends hadn't taken time away from their lives to actually experience things.

Darby needed the distraction and suggested they go on a trip to leave the stress of Un-Do behind them, at least for a few hours. So the following day, they climbed into Jade's car and hit the road.

Since it was Taylor's turn to pick where they were headed, they ended up at some lighthouse looking over the Atlantic Ocean a little over an hour's drive from Chammont Point.

Darby didn't mind. The long drive had been good for them. Singing loudly and mocking one another's inability to carry a tune had made the day feel perfectly normal. Without the weight of her mistake lingering over her, Darby was able to actually enjoy the ride.

Looking at old buildings was one of the few activities that allowed Taylor's tough exterior to slip. The excitement she felt examining the structures overshadowed her unconscious need to protect herself. She was like the proverbial kid in a candy store whenever she got to look at crumbling architecture. Seeing her focus on architecture without the usual personal distance she kept around her was refreshing.

As they headed down a path toward the structure, Taylor talked about brick and masonry and some other shit Darby didn't understand. She didn't think Jade understood it either, but she was great at asking questions and seeming like she was actually interested. She did that with Darby too. No doubt Jade had no idea about, or interest in, French seams or ladder stitching, but she always listened when Darby rambled as they sat together by the cove at the end of the day. That was one of the things that made Jade such a good friend. She listened.

That was something Darby needed to work on. She tended to get swept up in her own overblown problems and dramas. The habit was likely because she'd spent so much time alone through her formative years. She'd had no one but herself to help her resolve problems.

That wasn't the case any longer, and she needed to learn from Jade and Taylor. They needed to learn from one another so they could all grow and heal from the traumas that had damaged them. Wasn't that what friendship was really about?

Though the three of them tended to get off-balance from time to time, the foundation of their friendship was strong. Like the lighthouse. They weathered their fair share of storms and kept standing. Whether that was Jade's divorce, Taylor's insecurities, or Darby's...everything, they were strong enough to keep going.

Darby needed that kind of security in her life. She needed that kind of resilient and ongoing love that she'd found in her friends. Most of her family was still in Mexico City. Without her mom, Darby had been on her own for too long. She needed Jade and Taylor and their bond like she needed air and fashionable clothing.

"Do you see how the astragals create a pattern?" Taylor asked with her head rolled back and a hand pressed above her eyes to shield them from the sun.

"The what?" Darby asked.

Dropping her hand, Taylor eyed Darby. "The... See the pretty panes of glass?"

Turning her focus to the big room at the top of the lighthouse, Darby nodded. "Neat."

"Neat?" Taylor asked. "Do you have any idea the time that must have gone into framing and placing the panes? How much thought had to go into the structural integrity?"

"Uh. No." Darby shrugged. "I really don't know, and I'm not so sure I care."

Taylor looked offended for a split second before huffing and rolling her eyes. "Whatever. Come on. You'll appreciate it once we get to the top."

"Remember when we went to Mount Vernon?" Jade

asked as Taylor rushed them along the path leading to the tall red and white structure.

"Give me a break," Taylor said, but the smile on her lips let them know she wasn't offended.

Darby put her hand to her heart. "It was like Christmas morning for her," she said with a wistful grin like a proud mama reliving one of her favorite memories. "She didn't know what to gawk at first—the cup of cola or the view from the pizza."

Taylor laughed loudly. "You wanna try saying that again?"

"You know what I mean," Darby said with a wink, happy that her intentional mispronunciations had given them another moment of normalcy. She had a habit of playing dumb to get laughs from her friends. The truth was, she lived for fancy design and extravagance. She knew exactly what she meant—the cupola and the piazza had been her favorites too. "You were the one drooling over them."

"She's not wrong," Jade chimed in. "I was afraid you might get arrested, the way you were fawning over George Washington's Central Passage."

Darby giggled. "That was nothing compared to the way she was eying his Lower Garden."

"All right," Taylor said before any more bad puns could be made. "So I'm an architectural and history nerd. Like you guys aren't weird in your own ways. And you call me a jerk."

Laughter filled the air for a few moments before quiet fell over them as they walked, slightly faster than usual, toward the lighthouse. The silence between them was companionable as they listened to the birds chirping and the wind rustling the trees. This was a peaceful kind of quiet.

They all seemed to be contemplating something. Jade

was likely considering her relationship with Liam, Taylor was probably thinking about her business struggles, and Darby's mind was racing round and round about all that had happened to her since opening The Un-Do Wedding Boutique.

Who knew one business decision could turn someone's life on its head so damn quickly?

And not just her life. Her entire perception of herself had shifted so quickly, she was still feeling the aftershocks. The confidence she'd worked so hard to find had been far too easily shattered. Meaning, it hadn't been real. None of what Darby had come to believe about herself was real.

Even though she'd apologized and changed the site, she still felt lost and confused about what she'd done and why. Worse than that, she felt uncertain about who she really was.

Jennifer had called her a fake, as had so many people in the posts on Un-Do's website. Darby couldn't shake the feeling they were right. She'd been using her retro style to force herself into a station in life where she hadn't belonged, and she'd been caught.

She felt like the kid trying to sit at the grown-up table. The nerd trying to join the cheerleading team. The outcast trying to fit in where she never would. None of those things felt good, but they all felt far too familiar. She wished she had some kind of fairy godmother who could come down and guide her through this mess—*this mess* being her life.

Darby was more than halfway through her thirties. Shouldn't she have a better grasp on life by now? Shouldn't she have a clearer idea of who she wanted to be and how to actually become that person?

Other people her age had careers, families, schedules

that held them accountable. Darby had two slightly dysfunctional best friends and a disaster of an online business.

Damn it. Her life was a joke.

She was a joke.

All those people, including Jennifer Williams, had been right. And that stung.

"What are you thinking?" Jade asked, disrupting Darby's ugly spiral into self-loathing.

Darby looked up at the azure sky. A few puffy white clouds slowly drifted inland, and the incessant squawking from seagulls grew louder as they neared the lighthouse.

The scene should have been picturesque. Perfect.

But Darby felt like crap all the way down to her soul. "It was all fake," she said softly.

"What?"

"The hair, the clothes, the no-fucks-to-give attitude. It was all a facade that I put on to hide what a loser I am. And now it's falling apart."

Jade strolled quietly next to her before finally heaving a sigh. "First thing, you absolutely are not a loser, Darby. You're amazingly kind and considerate. And you're fun. You are so much fun. I don't think I've ever laughed as much as I have in the year since I met you. Which says a lot because I didn't have a lot to laugh about a year ago. Second thing, everybody's outer layer is a facade. Whether it's bright red hair, bold and colorful fashion, or a fuck-it-all attitude. We're all faking it to an extent, but that doesn't mean it *is* fake."

While Jade was easily the smartest person Darby knew, in that moment, she wasn't making much sense. "Isn't that exactly what it means?"

"No," Jade said. She nodded toward Taylor, who had moved quite a bit ahead of them as her excitement grew. "Look at her. Do you see how happy she is when we go on these little road trips? How...unguarded she is when she's taking it all in? That's Taylor. The *real* Taylor. That's the reason we tolerate her tough act when she gets triggered by her past. Because we know beneath her attitude, she's an excited little kid who can't wait to touch old, crumbling bricks and tell us all about how they were made, even if we don't care. I spent decades building a career that ultimately destroyed my marriage because of my need to present myself as successful to the world. I needed people to see me as someone who had made a good life for herself. That was my facade, Darby. But underneath the calm, cool, and collected executive act, I was terrified of failing. Your facade is so carefree because inside all you want is to be accepted. We all wear masks to protect ourselves. But the people we care about, the ones who really matter, they get to see what's behind them. You're not fake, Darby. You're protecting a precious part of yourself, and that's okay. You're allowed to decide who you let into your life based on how they treat the person you present to them."

"But you're doing so much better," Darby said, surprised by the swell of emotion that hit her.

"Am I?" Jade asked with a slight laugh. "I have a wonderful man standing right in front of me waiting to embrace him, and I'm too scared to have my heart broken again to let him in. That doesn't seem so great to me."

"At least you have a man," Darby said with a scoff. "I haven't dated in years. And now that I'm a social pariah, I doubt that will ever happen again."

Jade ran a soothing hand down Darby's back. "Honey, this won't last forever. I know it seems that way, but it won't."

"I guess," she said and heaved a sigh. "Having people hate me without even knowing me is the story of my life. I'd hoped to have outgrown that bad habit by now."

"Darby," Jade said with her understanding mama tone, "there will always be people who choose to not like you. No matter what you do or how hard you try, you cannot please everyone. None of us can. Please don't take that personally. Sometimes people simply don't mesh. Sometimes they don't want to. That's not your problem to solve. You have to be happy with yourself and live a life that makes you happy. As long as you aren't intentionally hurting someone else, that's really all you owe anyone. Don't get caught up in this misconception that everyone has to like or agree with you. That will never happen."

"I know," Darby said with a frown. "I have a hard time remembering, that's all."

"Nobody is good at remembering that," Jade said with a sweet smile. "That's why we have friends to remind us as needed."

"Come on," Taylor called as she opened the door to the lighthouse. "You guys are so slow!"

Darby moaned miserably. "She really is going to make us climb to the top, isn't she?"

"Yep."

And they did, step by agonizing step, until they reached the top and could view the world through the lantern pane. The glass-enclosed space made Darby feel like she was in a fishbowl. Rather than being a part of the world around her, she felt trapped, seeing the world from afar. Another feeling she knew all too well.

As much as her instinct was telling her to hide, to blend in and not be seen, her heart was telling her that wasn't the way. She had to face the storm brewing outside her proverbial lighthouse. She had to face her mistakes or her fears would win. Darby wasn't going to let that happen.

As she looked out at the world below them, watching the trees sway and the birds pivot toward the cresting waves, another feeling came over her. Guilt and shame for the role she'd played in hurting people.

Darby had posted her apology online, but that wasn't enough. Not really. She needed to offer Sue a face-to-face apology for dragging her story onto *The Noah Joplin Show*.

Darby had always been better at hiding in the shadows and running when accountability came into play. She'd never been great at owning up when she should, and she certainly hadn't ever mastered the art of facing her demons. But Sue deserved the chance to tell Darby to her face what she thought of her.

That wouldn't be easy or comfortable, but this was a pivotal moment for Darby, and as much as she wanted to, she couldn't run from it. Just like she'd had to accept the hits and acknowledge her mistakes after Noah's show, she had to face the heartache she'd caused for Sue Berdynski—even if Darby hadn't done so maliciously.

Time to grow up, Darbs, she said to herself. *Time to face the music and be an adult. Yuck.*

"Guys," Darby said quietly since they were all standing in the same small glass room. She considered her words for a few seconds before turning from the glass panes and the astragals that had so captivated Taylor. After eying both her friends, she swallowed hard and then said, "I need your help."

Darby grinned when, later that evening, Taylor held a peach bridesmaid dress to her chest and winced.

"Who would choose this color for a wedding?" Taylor asked.

"What was your wedding like?" Darby asked. Taylor had only ever mentioned her marriage a handful of times, but Darby was curious. Mostly because she couldn't picture Taylor as anybody's wife. She was too set in her ways.

Taylor tossed the dress aside. "Too much whiskey and a lot of bad decisions."

As she carefully added tissue paper to the box she was packing, Darby pictured Taylor as a happy bride. The image didn't fit, but neither did Taylor jumping into marriage on a drunken whim. "I'm serious."

"Me too."

"Taylor," she pressed.

Sinking onto Darby's couch, Taylor shrugged. "We got married at the courthouse. Nothing fancy. We couldn't afford fancy."

"What'd you wear?"

"Jeans and a blouse."

Darby stopped moving. "You wore jeans to your wedding?"

"What else would I wear? Shit like that?" Taylor gestured

toward the dresses they were packing to ship. "You wouldn't catch me dead in ruffles and sequins."

"What'd you wear to your prom?"

A big eye roll told Darby the answer before Taylor spoke. "I didn't go to prom. I barely went to school. The only reason I did was because the principal called Grandpa one day and told him if I skipped one more time, I was going to be expelled."

Darby smiled, mostly because she wasn't at all surprised that Taylor hadn't wanted to go to school. "You skipped a lot, then?"

"Almost every day. I'm pretty sure the only reason I graduated was because they didn't want to hold me back and deal with me one more year."

"Well, you went on to college, so it couldn't have been that bad."

"Community college," Taylor said. "And I did that for my grandpa. He needed to think I was going to make something out of my life. What about you? Did you go to prom?"

"Nah," Darby said, closing the box. "Nobody asked me."

"You could have gone on your own. You don't have to have a date for those things. The requirement of an escort is a lie society has been telling women for centuries."

"Right. That's what every high school girl wants to do. Go to prom alone. Besides, Mom couldn't afford a dress, and I would have been laughed out of the gym if I'd made something on my own. I wasn't that great at sewing back then. People could tell I stitched my own clothes."

Taylor taped the box shut as Darby held the flaps in place. "Sounds like that old Molly Ringwald movie. I'm pretty sure that worked out for her."

"I was never as cool as Molly Ringwald," Darby said.

"Molly Ringwald was cool?" Taylor asked and then smiled.

Darby grabbed the last dress she needed to send—the peach bridesmaid dress—and carefully folded it. "Even if I'd been able to buy a dress, I wouldn't have gone without a date. That would have been embarrassing back then. Nowadays, I'd never let that stop me from having a good time."

"So you didn't date much in high school?"

Shaking her head, Darby thought back on those miserable years. "I didn't have my first date until I was in my twenties. But I was still awkward and weird. We dated for a little while, but he was even more awkward and weird than I was, if you can believe it. I didn't start really dating until I transformed from Wallflower Darby to Rockabilly Darby. Rockabilly Darby is so much more fun."

Taylor tilted her head. "Don't label yourself like that, Darbs. Wallflower Darby is as much you as this version. You always had this fun side. It just took some time to find it. That's all."

"When are you going to find your fun side?" Darby deadpanned and then laughed when Taylor threw a makeup brush at her.

"Screw off," Taylor said. "When are you going to go back to your other boutique?"

"I don't know," Darby said, putting the dress inside a box. "I am waiting to see if my apology is accepted and people forgive me."

"I'm sure they will, but you have to give it some time. Don't you?"

"I guess. If they continue trying to cancel me, I might have to find something new altogether."

"Cancel you?" Taylor asked.

Despite the heaviness in her heart, Darby chuckled. "You really do have to start paying attention to the world around you, Tay. Cancel culture is a thing, and I fear it's coming for me."

Taylor held the box top closed so Darby could run a long bit of tape across it. "Yeah, you have to fill me in on this because I don't know what you're talking about."

"Cancel culture is when the world finds a target and dumps on them until they're blasted into oblivion. Bullying, blacklisting, threats... It's sadistic and ugly, and I'm ninety percent certain that's what's about to happen to me if people don't understand that I really am sorry for the pain I caused."

Taylor was quiet as she watched Darby stack boxes next to her door to take to the post office. "Was your apology sincere?"

Darby smiled slightly. "Yes. I didn't... I didn't tell you this before, but I ran into Jennifer at the store yesterday. We got into it a little bit in the cosmetics aisle."

Dropping onto her couch, Taylor watched Darby intently. "And?"

"She accused me of being cruel to Sue and the other brides. That really... That hurt because... Well, you know."

"I know."

Shame curled its way up Darby's spine and settled over her heart. "I made Sue Berdynski cry because I shared her story. I embarrassed her to the point that she was crying. I didn't want that, Taylor."

"I know you didn't."

"I didn't think it would matter because I didn't say her name, and I guess once I realized it did matter, I wasn't ready to admit that I'd done something so incredibly wrong. I don't want to be like that."

"You're not like that," Taylor assured her. "You made a mistake, but that doesn't define you, Darby."

"I hope not."

"I know not," Taylor insisted. "You're a good person. You screwed up. You'll make it right."

Darby gave her a weak grin and nodded. "Yeah. I'm going to try." She swallowed hard before voicing a concern she'd had all afternoon. "What if Sue doesn't forgive me? What if... What if I make things worse?"

Taylor shifted for a moment before exhaling slowly. "If she agrees to meet you, do you want us to go with you? Jade can negotiate if it comes to that and I can...kick her ass if she gets too mean."

Darby smirked. Taylor was always threatening violence, but Darby knew she'd never hurt anyone. Like Darby, Taylor had been scarred but hadn't turned hard. She liked to pretend she was tougher than she really was. Like Darby liked to pretend she was more carefree than she was. "I'd like that," Darby said softly. "I think that would help me."

"Okay. We'll go, then."

"You guys really are the best."

Taylor smiled. "Yeah. I know. Come on. Let's go make sure Jade can go."

As they stood, a familiar and annoyingly happy giggle filtered through Darby's window.

"Ugh," she moaned. "Liam's here."

Taylor scrunched up her face. "God, she sounds like a

high school cheerleader trying to hook up with the quarterback." She peered out the living room window at the cove where Jade and Liam were paddling to shore as the sun set in the background.

"I know." Darby joined Taylor in peeking outside. "It's gross. Before long, they'll be splashing each other and screaming. Then Liam will swoop her up and she'll scream, and..." She sighed. "It's sweet, really, but I'm tired of hearing it."

As Darby had predicted, Liam rushed up and threw his arms around Jade's waist as she reached the shore.

"Here we go with the squealing," Darby warned.

This time, however, Liam didn't lift Jade into the air and spin her around playfully. He spun her right then and there where she stood. Darby and Taylor gasped dramatically. Even from across the beach, Darby could feel the intensity flare between Jade and Liam. Their sexual tension washed over the cove like a tropical heat wave.

"He's going to kiss her," Taylor whispered as if they might be overheard.

"Oh my God." Darby gripped Taylor's arm, enthralled by what they were seeing. "He is. He *finally* is."

"We shouldn't watch," Taylor said, but neither made a move to turn away as Liam cupped Jade's face in his hands.

"This is better than my telenovela," Darby said.

Liam leaned in, and Darby held her breath. She wanted to jump up and down and cheer her friend on, but then Jade turned her face to the side and Liam stopped short of kissing her.

"Wait...what?" Darby asked with a voice several octaves higher than usual. "What happened?"

A moment later, Jade shook her head, said something, and then pulled away. Liam dropped his hands and said something back.

"*No*," Darby said with disappointment. "What are you doing, Jade?"

Liam ran his hand over his shaggy brown hair, and Jade stepped around him.

"She turned him down," Taylor said with disbelief. "She *actually* turned him down."

As they watched, stunned, Jade headed toward Darby's cabin. Liam watched her walk away for several long moments before pushing his kayak back into the water and climbing in. Jade didn't look back until he'd already started paddling away.

"Oh, no," Darby said, putting her hand to her heart. "Why did she do that?"

"Is she playing hard to get?" Taylor asked.

As Jade neared the cabin, Darby saw the distress on her face. "No, I don't think so. She looks sad."

Jade reached the top of the stairs. Darby knew the moment she caught them watching her. In an instant, she went from looking pained to looking shocked. "Oh my God!"

"Busted," Taylor muttered and slowly backed away.

Jade threw the front door open and gawked accusingly at her friends. "Were you spying on me?"

"No," Darby insisted. "We were looking out my window. You happened to be there...with Liam."

Widening her eyes, Jade stared her down. "I would expect this out of you," she said to Darby. "But *you*?"

Taylor simply shrugged. "If you don't want your private

life out there, don't do it in the cove. I mean, you're right there. For everyone to see."

"For everyone..." Jade huffed and shook her head. "I can't believe you two."

"What happened?" Darby asked softly, dismissing Jade's chastisement. "Why didn't you kiss him?"

Gaping at her, Jade didn't speak. Didn't move. Didn't do much of anything until her bottom lip quivered and tears filled her eyes. "I don't know. I like him. I do. *A lot*. I don't know why I keep pushing him away."

Darby offered her a sympathetic look. "Maybe it's because—"

"No," Jade stated firmly. "We're not talking about this."

Frustration lit in Darby. They'd been talking about her issues for over a week now. But Jade didn't want to talk about hers? That wasn't fair.

As Jade snagged a tissue from the chartreuse box on Darby's end table, she asked, "What were you guys doing?"

"Nothing as interesting as you," Taylor muttered.

Jade offered her a playful glare and then focused on Darby.

"Taylor offered to go with me when I go to talk to Sue...if she'll talk to me. Can you come too?"

Jade glanced at Taylor. "We're not interfering."

"Not unless needed," Taylor agreed.

"It would help me so much if you guys were close by," Darby said. She stuck her lip out ever so slightly in the pout that usually won Jade over.

"Okay," Jade said, caving in. "But we're only going for moral support." That statement was made toward Taylor, a warning of sorts. "Not to interact on Darby's behalf. This is her issue to resolve."

"And if we want our issues to be resolved," Darby said gently, "we should talk about them. With our best friends so they can help us move forward and help us get our lives straightened out so we could maybe...date a cutie pie guy, if we wanted to." She eyed Taylor in a silent plea for backup.

"Right," Taylor said. "I mean, look at me. I've been one ongoing issue for as long as I can remember. I wouldn't get shit done if I waited for this mess"—she gestured toward herself like a game show hostess—"to be resolved. You know, I had to start working on it, and you guys have helped a lot."

Looking from Taylor to Darby, Jade sighed. "I'm sure. But we've talked about my problems all I intend to. I mean, if we're going to try to fix someone, we're not lacking options in this room."

When Darby and Jade turned to Taylor, she threw her hands up. "Hell no. We are *not* talking about me."

Darby held up her hands when Jade and Taylor looked at her. "Nope. We're not saying another word about the fire I'm about to walk into by reaching out to Sue." The smile on Darby's face faded when she noticed Jade looking at her with concern in her eyes. "What?"

"I found her number. Are you ready to give her a call?"

Darby felt like she could melt into the floor. "You found her already?"

"Your stalking skills are terrifying," Taylor said to Jade.

Jade held up her phone. "I put it in a text to you. All I have to do is hit Send."

Glancing from Jade to Taylor, Darby clutched her hands together. Holding her breath, she counted to ten, and then she nodded. Jade fiddled with her phone for a few seconds, and then Darby's dinged to let her know she had a new message.

She stared at the device for several long seconds before opening the text. There were the digits needed to call Sue and hopefully put all this mess behind her. Her fingers trembled as she hovered over it. "What do I say?" she asked, barely above a whisper.

"Tell her that you're calling because you'd like to apologize, and if she's willing, you'd like to do that in person," Jade said.

Darby's mouth suddenly ran dry, but she closed her eyes and tapped the screen. The phone rang for several seconds before Sue Berdynski's voice mail picked up. Thank the heavens for voice mail. Darby listened to the message, and as soon as the beep filled her ear, she swallowed again.

"Sue," she said far faster than she'd normally speak, "this is Darby Zamora, and I... I was hoping we could meet somewhere. Sometime soon." Shit, she was starting to stumble already.

Jade put her hand on Darby's and gave her a soft smile.

Darby cleared her throat. "I, um, I'd like to apologize to you for...for sharing your story. I was hoping I could do that in person. If you're willing. Please call me or text me back at this number, and...I understand if you don't want to see me, but I do want you to know that I am incredibly sorry."

She pulled the phone from her ear and ended the call. Her eyes were wide when she looked at Jade again. Okay. She'd just done that. Even if Sue never called her back, she'd apologized to her...well, to her voice mail. And that felt damn good.

NINE

THE NEXT AFTERNOON, Darby sat in a little cafe in Richmond with her hands wrapped around a mug. If she were there for any other reason, she'd be thrilled by the aesthetic that reminded her of a television show her mom used to watch. The waitresses weren't quite so sassy and the décor wasn't as dated, but the feel of the little cafe was familiar in a way that seemed like a warm hug from her past and brought her some comfort. Well, as much comfort as she could get while waiting for someone to come and tell her to her face that she was a horrible person.

She had barely hung up from her voice mail to Sue the night before when she'd received a text telling her they could meet at this place, this time. Sue had followed up with directions and a declaration that she was eager to chat.

"Eager to chat" didn't sound as much like "looking forward to putting this behind us" as Darby had hoped.

The scents in the air—greasy burgers and onion rings—would usually make her crave a huge helping of unhealthy food, but she felt far too sick to her stomach to even consider eating. She was certain if her waitress brought her anything fried, Darby would lose all the contents of her stomach then and there. Though that wouldn't be much because she hadn't been able to eat anything for breakfast either. Her nerves were wound too tight and her entire body was on alert— ready to run on a second's notice.

The pounding of her heart echoed in her ears, drowning out the old Buddy Holly and the Crickets tune. As with the décor, if this were any other day, this scene would fill her with joy. Any other day, Darby would be bopping her head and doing a little dance in her booth to the song filtering from the speaker. But she could barely breathe. Dancing and enjoying one of her favorite songs wasn't an option at the moment. Not with her stomach sitting like a boulder and her pulse beating faster than the melody coming from a speaker above her.

She tried to force her anxiety to go down a notch or two. If she didn't find a way to calm down just a touch, she was going to stammer and stumble and ruin any chance she had at earning Sue's forgiveness.

Darby looked at the table next to her. Taylor and Jade would be inconspicuous to anyone else, but to her they were like a rainbow poking through a dark cloud. If she was lucky, Sue wouldn't show, and she could call them to join her at her table and her stomach would settle enough that she could order a slice of pie from the display case they'd passed on the way in. While waiting to be seated, she'd distracted herself by looking over the various types of fruit nestled between layers of golden, flaky crust.

If the universe was on her side, she'd be eating a slice with tart apples and saying "well, I tried" in no time. None of that hope was because she didn't want to apologize—she did. She simply didn't want to face Sue's wrath in person. Even if her wrath was deserved.

When Darby glanced at her friends again, Taylor offered her a slight smile and a reassuring nod before sucking hard on the straw stuck in her thick chocolate milkshake. Again, Darby wished she had an appetite, but anything more than the hot tea in her mug would probably make her vomit.

"What the hell am I doing?" Darby muttered and looked fearfully at the glass double doors, debating if she should make a run for it. The knots in her stomach were so tight, they were turning in on each other, and the weight on her chest made inhaling even more difficult. She couldn't remember the last time she'd been this terrified—so scared that she'd do about anything to put an end to it.

Time slowed to a turtle's pace as Darby sat waiting for Sue to join her, knowing a confrontation was inevitable. Knowing she was going to have to look the woman in the eye while she said nasty things. Sitting there alone, fearing some kind of trouble was about to begin, was once again taking her back to high school. Only this time, rather than ducking her head and trying to hide, Darby had willingly put herself in this situation.

"If she says one ugly thing…" Taylor had said several times during the drive from Chammont Point to Richmond, only to be reminded that the woman was about to confront someone who humiliated her in front of half of the state of Virginia. She probably wasn't going to be overly polite.

Darby appreciated Taylor's protectiveness, but in this instance, Taylor's need to defend her was misplaced. If anyone had the right to treat Darby with less respect than most, it was Sue Berdynski. She hoped Sue would listen, but if she only agreed to meet Darby to lash out and speak her mind, then that was what would happen. Darby would listen and do her best to be humble and honest in her apology. But she understood that didn't mean Sue would accept it.

Darby had barely been able to breathe since walking into the cafe. No. She hadn't been able to breathe since she'd made the call. But when the door opened and Sue walked in, the gut punch that Darby felt caused her entire body to tense. Filling her lungs wasn't even an option. However, emptying her stomach became much more likely.

Oh, God, she thought. *This is going to be so bad.*

"She's here," Darby said loud enough for the people at the table next to her to hear.

"You got this," Jade said.

"I have a milkshake ready to dump if need be," Taylor added.

Darby wished she could find the comment as amusing as she was certain Taylor intended, but she simply couldn't. She couldn't stop staring at the door, wishing she could run out and pretend none of this had ever happened.

Sue scanned the dining area before locking on Darby. She didn't smile. In fact, the scowl on her face deepened, and Darby had the distinct feeling of elephants wrestling in her stomach. Sue shoved her sunglasses on the top of her head so they rested on the short brunette strands. The woman's eyes were dark but angry. And tired.

Though she couldn't be much older than her midtwenties, Sue looked like she'd lived a hard life without nearly enough self-care or downtime. She looked like she needed a vacation. An honest to God, no responsibilities vacation.

Darby felt bad for her. She felt responsible. No doubt much of the exhaustion so plainly displayed on Sue's face was the stress of the last nine days...ever since Darby sat in Noah Joplin's studio and told the world about a groom, two bridesmaids, and an unscrupulous trip the trio made somewhere on Chammont Lake.

Sue narrowed her eyes as she glared at Darby. The hard look in her eyes didn't ease as she slid into the booth. "Well," she barked harshly, "what the hell do you want?"

Darby fought to swallow again. She glanced at the table next to her, this time to Jade who gave that maternal you-can-do-it smile. As she took a long, slow inhale, Darby returned her attention to Sue. "I-I wanted to tell you how sorry I am."

Sue stared, clearly unmoved.

"I didn't mean—"

"To make money by telling the world my ex screwed my two best friends in my canoe?" Sue asked with all the fury and accusation of a woman who'd been cheated on. The vein in her forehead bulged and her nostrils flared, as if she was about to jump up and tear her shirt in half and scream out a battle cry.

Darby put her hand to her heart, fearing it might explode in her chest. Her head spun—either from lack of oxygen or her spiking blood pressure. She hadn't expected this to be easy, but part of her hoped she could get through this without their meeting turning into a brawl in a dinky, greasy diner.

"I didn't think that I was hurting anyone."

"Are you stupid?" Sue asked flatly. The anger and outright

hatred in her eyes were undeniable. She despised Darby. Or at least had an incredibly strong dislike for her.

Darby saw Taylor start to stand and Jade stop her. After another forced swallow, Darby worked up the courage to give her the obvious answer, "No. But I should have thought about how my actions would impact you and the other brides. I didn't do that, and I'm sorry."

Sue did smile then, but nothing about the way she was baring her teeth was friendly. The glint in her eye was wicked, like she knew what she was about to say was going to inflict pain and she was going to enjoy it. Her smirk spread right before she spat, "So you aren't stupid. You're simply insensitive and vicious."

Yup. That was an arrow that hit the target. Darby had always gone out of her way to not be seen like that because she'd been on the receiving end far too many times. "I'm sure it seems that way," Darby said softly as her shoulders slumped under the weight of Sue's statement.

She lowered her eyes and fought the tears that wanted to surface. She wasn't there to cry and wallow in her hurt feelings. She was there to give Sue the apology she deserved so hopefully she could heal and put the pain Darby had caused behind her. As much as Darby wanted to scream and yell and stomp her foot until Sue heard how sorry she was, she knew that not only would that not help, but she certainly didn't have the right to demand anything from this woman.

When Darby lifted her gaze again, blinking back her tears, Sue's shitty smirk had spread. She sat a bit taller, clearly proud that her comment had hurt Darby's feelings.

"It *is* that way," Sue stated, refusing to consider that Darby wasn't simply being vicious for the sake of making some sales. Leaning on the table, the loathing and resentment Sue felt shone bright for Darby to see.

That old saying "if looks could kill" ran through Darby's mind, because she would have died under Sue's hateful stare. Darby wanted to look to the table beside her for reinforcements, for a little support, but she kept her gaze locked on Sue's. If she saw the fury on Taylor's face or the sympathy on Jade's, she'd probably crack.

"You think I believe this bullshit excuse?" Sue asked through clenched teeth and thin lips. "The only reason you're apologizing to me is because people are calling you out for being a bloodthirsty bitch."

Darby lifted her brows. *Ouch.* She wasn't startled at Sue's merciless behavior as much as the implication that Darby wasn't being genuine. If she considered Sue's position, she could probably understand why she didn't believe Darby, but she wasn't even giving her an honest chance to apologize.

Sue was on a roll and didn't seem interested in hearing anything Darby might have to say. "If you were actually sorry, if you actually wanted to repent for your transgressions against me and the rest of the women you kicked in the face to make a buck, you would have shut your site down by now."

Darby simply stared. "But...that's my livelihood."

"Your livelihood? It was my *life* that you were making fun of there. *My* broken engagement. *My* humiliation." Sue scoffed and shook her head almost imperceptibly. "I saw that lame little apology note you posted online and how you deleted your *cute* little stories. As if that changes anything. It doesn't. In case you were wondering. None of that changes anything. That apology was as fake as this one."

Again, Darby shot her brows toward the tiled ceiling. She again needed a moment to sort out what Sue was saying. All the times she'd been called fake in the last week, all the times she thought that accusation hurt, those were nothing compared to this one. She wasn't being fake. Her soul was bleeding shame from what she'd done. The expectation that Sue may not accept her apology had done nothing to prepare her for being told her apology wasn't sincere.

"You don't care about hurting others. Not really, do you?" Sue asked with shades of disbelief coloring her words. "All you care about is getting a few sales. Making a little money." The last words practically dripped of the venom of her accusation.

Falling back in the cracked vinyl–covered booth, Darby stared with wide eyes, recalling how she'd told Jade and Taylor that she was making sales so what she'd done couldn't have been all bad. But she'd come to realize she was wrong. She understood now. "I apologized online because I realized I was wrong. I asked to meet you because I realized I was wrong."

Sue stared as if she didn't understand the point Darby was making. "Apologies mean nothing if you don't change your actions."

"I took the stories down."

"After what? Ten days? Ten days of feeding off other people's pain? Ten days of getting hits and sales and upping your leverage for advertising? That's not repentance, Darby. That's not a real apology. That's doing what needs to be done to save yourself."

"No—"

"*Yes*. People are turning on you because the novelty has

worn off already. People are starting to see how mean it is to laugh at other people's shattered dreams. And you're apologizing because they're making you look bad online. Not because you're actually sorry. If you were," Sue said, "you'd take the damn site down."

Darby held the oxygen in her lungs for a few moments. "I changed the site. I'm not using those stories anymore. I posted an apology. A *sincere* apology."

"That's *not* enough."

Pressing her lips together, Darby shook her head. "Sue, I'm sorry that I hurt you, but what happened, the story I shared, that happened years ago."

"Why does it matter if it happened years ago or a week ago? You had no right to tell that story. *My* story."

After swallowing hard, Darby said, "I didn't mean..." A long exhale left her as she put her words together. "I only mean that had I known you were still suffering from what happened, I wouldn't have dreamed of sharing your story. I got caught up in the moment with Noah Joplin, and I said more than I should have. I see that now. I see that it was wrong."

Sue stared at her for several long, drawn-out seconds. "Did you get caught up in the moment when you put your website together too?"

Darby nodded slightly. "In a way, yes. I was getting responses, and that made me think it was okay. I shouldn't have let it go that far. I should have recognized sooner that I was causing pain for my former clients."

"Yes," Sue stated flatly, "you should have. You should have recognized that much sooner." Pressing her hand to her chest, tears glittered in her eyes and her voice cracked as she spoke. "I lost the man that I loved. The man I thought I was going to spend the rest of my life with. I lost my closest friends. They betrayed me in the worst possible way. And you know what, Darby? They apologized too. They said they didn't mean for things to happen. Didn't intend to go so far. They weren't trying to hurt me."

Darby blinked back her tears. "I *am* sorry."

"You told the world about the most painful moment of my life."

"But...the only reason anyone knew it was you was because you went on Jennifer Williams's show and told them."

Sue scoffed, and she stared for a long time. "You can't be this dense, Darby. Chammont Point isn't that big of a town. You think I relocated to Richmond for shits and giggles?"

Another punch in the gut hit Darby. "I don't know why you moved."

"Because my broken engagement was the talk of half the damn town and I had to get away. I had to leave because of what they'd done. And here you go, dredging it up all over again."

Another layer of guilt fell on Darby's shoulders. "I can't imagine how much that hurt."

Sue wiped her cheeks when tears fell. "No, you can't." After drying her hands on a napkin from the dispenser on the table, she wadded it up and carelessly tossed it aside. "What kind of friends sleep with your fiancé days before your wedding? In your canoe? And what kind of wedding dress seamstress uses that painful memory to sell the dress you were supposed to get married in?"

Put like that, Darby couldn't find the words to defend

what she'd done. She realized the true depth of her mistake. "I can't take back what I did," Darby whispered. "All I can do is tell you how very sorry I am."

"But you aren't going to take your website down," Sue said. "You aren't going to stop profiting off those dresses, are you? Because you aren't sorry, at least not enough to stop. You truly are heartless," Sue said coolly. Pushing herself up, she exhaled with an audible sigh. "I ran into one of my old friends not too long ago—one of the ones from *your* story. She apologized again and said the hardest thing she had to do most days was look at her reflection and know she'd caused me so much pain. I hope to God you have a hard time looking at yourself too."

With that, she turned and walked out of the cafe.

Darby's heart lodged in her throat as she looked at the table next to hers.

"You okay?" Jade asked.

Darby shook her head. She'd known that was going to be brutal, but she'd hoped Sue would accept her apology. That hadn't happened. From the sounds of it, that would never happen. She was determined not to break down in the cafe, but a choking sob left her.

"Oh, baby," Jade said as she sank into the booth beside Darby.

Darby leaned over and let Jade hug her close as she cried. Of all the horrible things Sue had said to her, the one that had stuck the most was questioning what kind of seamstress would use a bride's broken heart to sell the dress she'd intended to marry in. That one had hurt.

That question had more than hit the mark; it'd gone straight through, and Darby's soul was bleeding out. It was that comment that had really made Darby see how callous her jokes had been. Her stomach clenched, and she thought she might be sick. She probably would have been if Jade wasn't gently rubbing her back and offering soothing words of support.

Darby closed her eyes tight so she couldn't see Taylor cycling through emotions. She didn't seem to know what to do. She seemed torn between running after Sue and telling Darby she'd been warned her actions were as terrible as Sue had said.

The fact that she'd been warned, even if it'd been gentle nudges from Taylor and Jade, made the feeling so much worse. Darby couldn't stop chastising herself. Why hadn't she just listened? Why hadn't she stopped for one moment, like Sue had said, to consider what she was doing?

The shame filling her chest grew, and she leaned deeper into Jade's hug as she cried harder.

Instead of making things right with Sue and easing some of the guilt she'd been carrying around for days, Darby had made things worse. Even though she had tried to explain her mistake and all but insisted she hadn't meant to embarrass anyone, Sue hadn't given the forgiveness Darby had been seeking. In fact, Darby felt sadder than ever before.

As soon as Jade and Taylor led her from the diner, she sank into the back seat of Jade's sedan and sniffled to herself the entire ride back to Chammont Point. Jade and Taylor had tried to cheer her up with encouraging words and jokes that might have been funny any other time, but their efforts were no use.

Darby felt like crap. And rightfully so.

Sue had been brutal in her honesty, ripping away any rose coloring Darby had tried to paint over her decision to use the so-called funny anecdotes on Un-Do's website. And then to reiterate them on *The Noah Joplin Show.*

Sue had lost her would-have-been husband and two of her best friends. And Darby had used that to make a few bucks. The shame Sue had piled onto Darby for those actions was well-deserved and didn't feel like it'd be going away anytime soon.

When they got back to Chammont Point, Darby had wanted to curl under a blanket and let the world pass her by. Her friends wouldn't allow it. They made her sit on the water's edge of the cove, and though there wasn't much conversation, they hadn't left her alone.

She loved them for that, even if she'd rather be burrowed on her couch and dwelling on what a loser she was. As appealing as that sounded, she'd known—as had they—that she needed to be surrounded by people who loved her and weren't judging her nearly as harshly as Sue had.

Since Taylor and Jade refused to leave her alone, she told them they had to cook dinner. She wasn't up for it. They had gladly agreed, and any other day, their routine of Taylor grilling and Jade tossing together sides would have felt normal.

Nothing felt normal on this day.

Darby sat back as Jade put a bowl filled with fresh-cut salad onto the table. Even this was normal because on nights when Darby was supposed to be hosting dinner, Jade tended to do most of the cooking. Darby would flutter about setting dishes and utensils and Taylor would ramble about her day, which hadn't consisted of much lately since she'd lost yet another bid for a project and didn't have anything else lined up.

This was how dinner always went, even when it was Darby's turn to cook. While she loved making finger foods and fun appetizers, she never quite knew what to do about creating an entire meal. Trying to get all the food done at the same time was more than she could manage. Her dinners tended to be a hodgepodge of things until Jade had not-so subtly started giving more direction.

Darby was glad for that, but as she sat at the table watching her friends easily fill the roles they'd taken in their friendship, the feeling that the world was off its axis grew.

Self-pity had sunk in before they'd even left the cafe, and Darby's mood had done little to improve since. Watching her friends take care of her, she felt like this wasn't where they wanted to be or what they should be doing with their time.

While Darby could make the table pretty and fix any mixed beverage they could think of, that didn't feel like nearly enough to balance the scales of what they did for her. While she was quick-witted and able to crack Taylor's serious exterior or Jade's tendency to overwork, she didn't feel like that was enough. Because on some level, she had always been convinced that *she* wasn't enough. That feeling was boiling over after the ten days.

As if sensing where her mind was going, Jade pulled her into conversation. Though Jade was perfectly happy to drink her juice straight, she asked what kinds of drinks—nonalcoholic of course—Darby could make. Something with cranberry juice. Jade drank cranberry juice like fish drank water.

Though she saw through the deliberate distraction, Darby was thankful to think about something other than the disaster she'd created. She skimmed Jade's fridge and gave her a few ideas. Though nothing she came up with was out of the ordinary, Jade acted like Darby had been brilliant to suggest a cranberry and pineapple juice blend.

Darby's spirits did lift a little, she had to admit. Jade's praise always made her feel a bit warmer inside. She truly was a good person, and while she tended to sugarcoat, she didn't lie. She wouldn't be Darby's friend if she hadn't seen something in her. And Taylor wouldn't be nice just for the sake of being nice. If she hadn't truly cared about Darby, she wouldn't stick around. Though she lost sight of those truths when the ugly voices in her head toyed with her emotions, she could always find a way to come back to them.

Jade and Taylor really had become like Darby's family and did wonders to keep her grounded and focused on the better parts of life when the darkness wanted to creep in and take over her mind. Had they not come into her life, she likely would have moved away from Chammont Point by now. She had a way of scurrying from one place to another when she felt those depressive cycles starting. Relocating and starting something new had always helped her cope.

Her hometown always called her back, though. She'd be gone for a year, maybe two, and then she'd come back and find a place to rent. The last time, she'd decided she was making her stay permanent and bought her cabin. Then she'd had the bright idea to buy the one next door when her elderly neighbor was moved to an assisted living facility. She thought she'd gotten a great deal because her neighbor loved her... Turned out she'd been sold a money pit. While that had been a bit of a disaster, she didn't regret it. Her short-lived venture into property management had brought Jade and Taylor into her life.

However, as Darby stirred a can of ginger ale into the cranberry and pineapple juices, she was questioning whether that was enough. She wanted to run away and hide. Far, far away from Chammont Point. Far from where people knew her and had tied her to the Un-Do Wedding Boutique. If she started over somewhere else, she could remake herself into someone no one would ever connect to this disastrous misadventure. Someone who had never opened an online bridal consignment shop.

"Earth to Darby," Jade said as she pulled a bright yellow cob of boiled corn from a pot. She offered a sweet smile. "What's going on in your head?"

"Thinking about running away," she admitted. "I hear New Zealand is nice. I could buy a cottage in the woods, plant a garden, and live off the land forever."

"Good luck," Taylor said as she eased a platter of grilled chicken breasts and veggies onto the counter. "You can't even keep an orchid alive." She added a grin and a wink so Darby would know she was teasing.

"Orchids are tricky," Jade offered. Due to Jade's healthy eating, Darby consumed far more vegetables than she used to, but she still liked to douse them in dressing, so Jade added a bottle of ranch to the table before sitting. "But rather than running away, why don't you stay off the Internet until all this blows over? It's the middle of summer, sweetie. Spend some more time on the beach and less time focused on what's happening online."

Darby looked at the meal Jade and Taylor had cooked but didn't think she could bring herself to eat any of it, even with the ranch dressing Jade kept on hand for her. The elephants were still wrestling in her tummy. "What if it never blows over?"

"It will," Jade stated firmly and filled a plate. "You've posted your apology and explained that you thought the descriptions were funny but you hadn't considered how hurtful they might be to the would-be brides. You explained that you didn't think things through."

"Sue..." Darby's voice creaked like she barely had the strength to speak. Her throat grew tight as her stomach twisted into a knot. She looked at the plate when Jade held it out to her. Forcing herself to continue, she said with a quivering voice, "She said if I were truly sorry, I would close the site." She looked up at Jade for some kind of confirmation or denial. Something. "Do you think..."

"You have to make that decision," Jade said and pushed the plate closer, silently instructing Darby to take it. "Nobody else can do that for you."

Darby sighed as she accepted the dinner, and she wished someone would give her the answers. But then she sighed again because Jade and Taylor *had* given her the answers. Days ago. They'd told her to take the descriptions down *days* ago. They'd told her she might hurt someone.

She hadn't listened then.

But she was listening now, and no one seemed to know the right thing to say. The knot in her stomach turned into a ball of cement, heavy and unforgiving, low in her gut. She couldn't possibly eat.

Closing her eyes, Darby pressed her lips tight so she wouldn't release the sob building in her chest. Of all the times she'd messed up in her life—and there had been plenty—she'd never felt such a sense of shame and regret. She'd never felt so horrified by her own behavior.

She carried her plate to the table and then sat and stared at her food. When Jade and Taylor joined her a minute later, she still hadn't even touched her fork. Her body told her to eat, but she couldn't bring herself to do so. The act that should be so natural felt like a chore she couldn't muster the energy to complete. She knew, just looking at the food, that it would make her stomach feel even heavier.

She'd expected to feel some of this ache in her heart to ease after apologizing to Sue. She hadn't anticipated that somehow the weight would press down harder.

If she closed her site, she wouldn't have a means of income. She would still have dresses she'd be taking a loss on. And she'd have to come up with another way to pay her bills...pronto.

But if she didn't, Sue would never believe she was sincere.

As much as Darby wanted an easy, straightforward answer, she was starting to see there wasn't one. She could either continue to appear like a callous, money-hungry bitch, or she could take a loss and scramble to find a new venture to bring in some cash.

Neither of those sounded appealing.

"Let it rest for today," Taylor suggested with an unusually gentle tone. "You've done all you can do for today."

The words nearly broke the last thread of strength Darby

had been clinging to. Taylor's show of support and concern usually came gift-wrapped in brutal honesty or sarcasm. Neither were present now. She looked worried. She sounded worried. And that nearly did Darby in.

For what must have been the thousandth time in the last few days, tears filled Darby's eyes and settled on her bottom lids.

Jade frowned and covered her hand, squeezing tight. "Is there anything we can do?"

Darby shook her head. "You've done more than enough."

She didn't miss the worried glance that her friends shared, but Darby couldn't find the strength to reassure them.

She pushed her plate away and smiled weakly. "I know you're worried, but I'll be okay. I think I need to be alone for a while."

"Darby," Taylor said.

Darby stood and grabbed her purse, ignoring their concerned looks. She'd find the energy to reassure them tomorrow, but she just couldn't tonight. "I'll see you guys tomorrow," she said as she headed for the door.

She walked, much slower than usual, back to her cabin and kicked off her shoes inside the door. Though she was a stickler for skincare, she tossed herself onto her bed and pulled a blanket over her head, determined to sleep what was left of this day away.

Depression was creeping in, taking hold. She knew the signs. She knew how the overwhelming feelings could suffocate her. But she didn't care enough to fight them. The world was caving in on her, and she didn't have the fortitude to fight it.

She'd just gotten comfortable when someone dropped onto the bed next to her like a champion high diver. Darby bounced and grumbled her discontent. As she was struggling to get the blanket over her head to glare at Taylor—because she couldn't think of anyone else who would body slam her —Jade stretched out on her other side. Her full-sized bed was big enough that they didn't have to be that close, but they had managed to sandwich her in.

"Guys," she complained.

"Did you hear something?" Taylor asked.

"Not a thing," Jade said and shifted to crush Darby even more.

She kissed her head through the blanket and hugged her, which eased Darby's irritation at being disturbed.

A moment later, the TV mounted on Darby's wall clicked on. That was Taylor too. She was on the side where Darby kept her remote. After a few clicks, the distinct sounds of a movie opening started. Darby didn't want to watch a movie. She wanted to be alone. She was on the verge of kicking them out when the opening strands of a familiar song started. She pushed back the blankets enough to peek at the screen.

"*Grease* is my favorite movie," Darby said.

"We know," Jade said.

"I never wanted to be like Sandy. I wanted to be Rizzo."

"We know," Taylor said.

Darby sniffled as she pulled the blanket down farther. "We should have matching pink jackets."

"No," Taylor said simply. "No, we shouldn't."

A smile tugged at Darby's lips as she sat up enough to watch the movie. A moment later, a bag of popcorn appeared under her nose. They must have brought that with them, since Darby definitely would have smelled the popcorn popping. And then, next to the popcorn, they waved a can of soda under her nose. "Yeah," she said. "We totally should." She stuffed her hand into the popcorn and grabbed the drink with the other, already planning time to buy pink satin.

"I'll never wear it," Taylor vowed.

Darby smiled, thinking how fun it would be to pester Taylor until she gave in and put the jacket on, at least long enough to snap a photo of the three of them. Snuggling between her best friends, she chuckled.

Yup. She was making them matching jackets.

TEN

DARBY SAT on her sofa the next morning clutching several tissues from the dispenser on the end table with her laptop open. She'd fallen asleep before the movie had ended the night before, still smooshed between Jade and Taylor, but when she'd awoken, she'd been alone.

The bubble of warmth they'd surrounded her with was gone too, and without it the negative feelings bombarded her again. Almost immediately, her mind filled with Sue's sad eyes and harsh words. Before she even rolled out of bed to shower, she'd replayed the entire scene from the cafe at least three times over.

As she'd gotten ready for the day, she'd debated what she should do. How she should move forward. *If* she could move forward. When she sat on the sofa, rather than opening her site to conduct business, she read and reread the apology Jade had helped her write. The words had been heartfelt, but now they seemed as empty as Sue had accused them of being.

Staring at the screen, Darby let her focus swim as she

thought of all the comments she'd read. Though she had deleted the posts days ago, she could still recall much of what had been said. The harsh words had been burned into her mind.

But she could also still bring to mind the encouraging ones. The ones that told her how funny her site was. The ones that told her how talented she was. So many women had asked if Darby could help them with their wedding dresses because they loved her work. They'd appreciated the unique style Darby provided for the brides. All of her dresses had been personalized to the bride's tastes, color preferences, and wedding themes. Each one had been customized down to the type of stitching used. People loved that about the dresses, especially women looking for gowns for their upcoming weddings.

Not everyone had seen her site as pitiless or vindictive. Not everyone thought she was monopolizing on heartache. But now, she had to admit, to some extent, she'd done just that.

Once again, her mind flashed to Sue's teary eyes and the hurt so plainly on display when she'd told Darby the only way to prove her contrition was to shut her site down. Frowning, Darby scanned the site to see how many dresses she still needed to sell. Enough that shutting down the site could cost her a few thousand dollars in unsold listings. Not to mention the thousands of dollars she could make if she accepted requests for customized dresses that had been coming in prior to turning off her comments.

The Un-Do Wedding Boutique could still be the venture that turned things around for Darby. She could finally have one business that was a success. One venture that actually made it beyond the usual month or two before she screwed it up.

This could be her chance to succeed.

Should she turn her back on that because Sue insisted that was the only way to absolve herself of the mistake she'd made by sharing personal stories?

Darby's internal battle had turned into a nuclear war in her mind when her front door opened.

Taylor spotted her on the couch and offered her a soft smile as she lifted a drink carrier with three beverages tucked inside, including a large iced mocha that was Darby's go-to at the local coffee shop. "I was hoping you'd still be sleeping. What are you doing?"

Darby returned her attention to the computer screen but let her eyes swim out of focus. "Trying to determine if I'm a horrible person."

"Well, I can settle that," Taylor said as she put the drinks onto the coffee table before dropping down beside her. "You're not."

A big, sad-sounding exhale left Darby as she let her shoulders droop. "I was thinking about all the comments I got before turning off the option on the site. Mostly about how most of them were supportive. Not only have I made people laugh, but I've helped women be able to afford one of a kind wedding gowns they wouldn't have been able to without me reselling these dresses. I *have* helped people." Her voice cracked as her emotions swelled again. "And I could help more people. I could make more dresses. Dresses that weren't for someone else and without the bad energy attached to them. I could have a successful bridal shop. I could do this, Tay."

"I know you can," Taylor said.

"I can make this work."

"I know." Taylor wasn't one for doling out affection, but she draped her arm around Darby's shoulder. "This is a hiccup. That's all."

"But it feels like more than that. It feels like there's no way to recover from this. Like the only way to make it end is to disappear. Should one bad decision bury my company?"

Taylor shook her head. "You have to make that decision, Darbs."

"Why?" she asked with the exaggerated pout she usually saved for Jade.

Grinning, Taylor patted Darby's shoulder. "Because it's not my company. Besides"—Taylor untangled her arm from Darby's shoulder and sat forward to grab the iced mocha—"you don't want business advice from me. I stink at this."

Darby accepted the drink as she shook her head. "That's not true."

"That's very true." Taylor sat back with her paper cup between her hands. She took her coffee strong and bold, which Jade and Darby often commented was very fitting for her. "I have one project this week, Darby. *One.*" She lifted up a single finger and waved it to emphasize her point. "And it's so simplistic that I'm pretty sure I was hired out of pity. Or some misguided idea to support a local female business. It'll take me all of two hours to complete and won't even make me enough money to buy groceries for the week." She shook her head slowly, and the hint of a smile faded from her lips. "I'm not going to make it much longer. I'm going to have to find something else to do. I'm running out of money—and time—to make this work."

Darby swallowed hard, but the tears in her eyes fell anyway. Taylor put her heart and soul into her work. Seeing her struggle was heartbreaking.

Hell, everything was heartbreaking for Darby right now. She was like some hormonal teen watching sappy movies on repeat. Her tears never seemed to stop lately.

Wiping her nose with the wad of tissues in her hand, Darby whispered, "I'm so sorry."

Taylor shrugged. "It's okay. It happens, you know."

Before Darby could respond, Jade threw the door open. "Oh, good," she stated as the panic on her face eased. "You're both here." She closed the door and turned and then looked from Darby to Taylor and back again. "Oh, no. What now?"

"Nothing," Taylor said dismissively as she sat forward. She pulled the last drink out of the container and held it up. "What's wrong with you?"

Jade accepted what was likely some sort of tea. She dropped into a chair and sagged as if the weight of the world was on her shoulders. "Liam..."

"What did he do?" Taylor said with a hard tone that implied she was about to go into battle.

Jade stuck her lip out in the way that Darby usually did for attention. "He broke up with me." Her voice quivered and her lips trembled as she sank even deeper into the chair.

Darby sat taller and furrowed her brow. "How could he break up with you? You aren't dating."

"I know." Tears shimmered in Jade's eyes. "He told me he wants to take things to the next level, and I said I wasn't ready. So he..." She choked out a sob. "He told me we need to take a break because he can't wait forever."

"Oh, honey," Darby said softly. "I'm sorry."

"Want me to go punch him in the face?" Taylor asked.

Jade laughed lightly through her tears. "No. I really like his face. How can he..." She roughly wiped away a tear with her palm. "Why can't I..."

Darby huffed out a breath as the furrow in Jade's brow deepened and her lip trembled again. "Look at us," she said with a croaking voice thick with emotion. "How did we get here, guys?"

"Where?" Taylor asked.

"So...broken," Jade whispered.

Taylor grabbed the tissue box of Darby's coffee table and crossed the room to offer a tissue to Jade. "We're not broken."

Darby took a long drink from her coffee before saying, "I think we might be, Tay. My life is a disaster, Liam broke up with Jade when they weren't even a couple, and your business is on the verge of closing. I think it's safe to say we are indeed broken. Or at least incredibly screwed up."

Taylor set the box down and shook her head. "No. We're going through some hard times right now, but we're not broken. We were broken before we found each other." She gestured toward Darby. "You were hiding behind your makeup, Jade was oblivious to how her life was a facade, and I was...sad and angry with no one to help me. We were broken a year ago, but we're not now. We're better now because we have each other. We've stumbled a little. That's all."

Jade blew her nose loudly. "Stumbled a lot, I'd say," she said and then blew again.

"*No*. Look at us," Taylor said with urgency in her voice. "Look at how far we've come."

Darby laughed dryly. "I don't think I've come very far."

"You have a successful business," Taylor said. "Yes, you have hit some...marketing issues..."

"Marketing issues?" Darby asked with disbelief. "Did you see what I did to poor Sue Berdynski? I'm a terrible person."

"No," Jade stated firmly. "You are not."

"And you," Taylor said lifting her hand in Jade's direction. "Sure, your husband dumped you for someone much younger—"

"Not *that* much younger," Jade insisted.

"She's pretty young," Darby offered.

Taylor continued as if they hadn't been debating the issue. "But you have picked yourself up and are living your best damn life. In the last year, you've started your own business, bought a cabin on a beautiful lake, and you're healthy and happy... Well, you know, when Liam isn't dumping you."

Jade scrunched up her nose and twisted her lips together before muttering, "I'm not sure this pep talk is helping."

"And look at me," Taylor continued without missing a beat. "Statistically, given my childhood, I should be in prison by now, but I've never even been arrested. Okay," she said, lifting her hands, "there was one time after a bar fight, but once they confirmed that I had nothing to do with it, I was released. But overall, that is a win, you guys. A *huge* win. And Darby, you..." Taylor held her hand out, but her words faded as if she didn't know where to begin...or couldn't find something positive to say.

"Made a mess out of everything," Darby finished.

"You have grown *so* much," Taylor said, as if that had been the point she'd intended to make all along.

Darby slowly shook her head. "I don't think so. But thanks for trying."

"You have grown," Jade said. "If you hadn't, you wouldn't have found the courage to talk to Sue face-to-face. That was difficult, but you did it. We're proud of you for that."

Darby sank back into the sofa and sucked on her straw, frowning when it slurped with the telltale signs of an empty cup. She shook it, rattling the ice, and then slurped again to confirm she had downed her entire drink already. Her frown grew as she set the cup aside. While she appreciated Taylor's words of encouragement, Darby actually felt worse. Mostly because Taylor was right. Jade had picked herself up. Taylor was persisting with her company, trying everything she could to succeed.

And then there was Darby.

Sure, she was doing better financially than she had been in a long time, but her heart was torn and she had no idea what she should do. She had trampled all over people's feelings without even taking a moment to consider what she was doing. She'd shattered Sue's heart all over again by making her relive a past better left alone.

And that was just one would-have-been bride who had come forward. No doubt there were others who hadn't had the courage to come forward and share how hurt they were by Darby's actions. The idea that there could be up to a dozen brokenhearted and humiliated women reliving their pain because of The Un-Do Wedding Boutique made the guilt in Darby's stomach grow.

Damn it.

She didn't know if she had the courage to apologize to each and every one of them, but in that moment she realized she really had to. She had to make the effort to make amends for her bad decision. They deserved to hear that straight from her, as Sue had.

While she didn't know if Sue was right about closing down Un-Do, Darby realized that her lame attempt of an apology posted on the site wasn't enough. At least not for those who had been directly impacted by the stories she'd posted online.

Those women deserved a sincere, heartfelt apology. And, as Sue had gotten, a chance to put Darby firmly in her place for what she'd done.

The idea of hearing over and over how much pain and humiliation she'd caused someone else became too much in that moment. In her mind, she pictured herself sitting in that greasy cafe as a line of bitter would-have-been brides formed, one behind the other, waiting for a chance to sit across from Darby and call her all the things Sue had tossed her way.

"You guys," she said flatly, "I need to make a list of all the women I have to apologize to. And then I have to... I have to actually apologize to them. Sue was the only one to confront me, but...the others need to hear how sorry I am too."

Silence hung in the cabin. Jade and Taylor were likely coming to the same realization that Darby had—that was a lot of apologies and a lot of fire to walk through.

"Oh," Jade finally said softly. "Yes. I suppose you should."

"Shit," Taylor whispered.

Darby swallowed hard as her stomach tightened around the coffee there. Though it was early yet, she checked her watch and confirmed that Harper's would be opening soon. As the misery of what lay before her sank in, Darby did what she always did when she was feeling at her lowest point. "Ice cream?" she suggested.

"Damn straight," Jade said, standing up.

Taylor pulled her keys from her pocket. "I'll drive."

It was well after ten in the evening when Darby noticed a fire in the pit that sat near the water's edge. Peering out the window, she saw Jade sitting and staring into the flames. Knowing her friend was still upset about Liam's decision to put space between them, Darby put on a pot of water for tea. When the water was hot, she poured it over a tea bag she kept at her house for Jade and filled a wineglass with a rosé for herself.

She didn't know if Jade would want company or not, but she had to at least try to be there and support her. Heavens knew Jade had done more than her share of propping up Darby over the last few days. If it hadn't been for Jade's kindness and ongoing support, Darby would have crumpled under the weight of Un-Do, Jennifer Williams, and Sue Berdynski even more than she already had.

After having ice cream at Harper's, Jade and Taylor had sat with Darby as she made a list of all the would-have-been brides that she needed to apologize to. Then, with the list tucked into her pocket, Jade said she'd do what she could to find each and every one so Darby could personally reach out to each one and express her remorse for sharing whatever had caused their weddings to blow up. The knowledge of what was coming sat like a boulder on Darby's chest all day.

When Jade and Taylor said they planned to go kayaking, Darby had excused herself.

Instead of going out on the water, she'd gone home and had done her best to not think about the gauntlet she'd soon be facing. The evening had dragged on, however, and her depression had grown with each passing moment. The idea of sitting with Jade by the fire soothed her—and not only because she wanted to check on her friend but because being with someone else for a while would likely help Darby as well.

With the mug of tea in one hand and a wineglass in the other, Darby walked to where Jade had been sitting. The fire she'd built was roaring as the stars twinkled in a clear sky above them. Bugs chirped and the occasional sound of a fish snagging a snack filtered to Darby as she eased down the rocky path.

"May I join you?" she asked when she reached the area they shared.

Jade subtly wiped a tear from her cheek. "Of course."

Darby's heart lurched in her chest, knowing that her friend was hurting so much. She would do anything to help Jade and Liam work through whatever was going on with them. Poor Jade deserved to be happy, not crying alone by a fire in the middle of summer.

Holding out the tea, she offered a soft smile. "I made this for you."

"Thanks." Jade accepted the mug but didn't drink.

Darby took her seat and sipped her wine before asking, "How are you doing?"

Jade shrugged one shoulder as she returned her gaze to

the flames. "Honestly, I don't know. I feel terrible for pushing Liam away. I didn't even realize I was doing it until it was too late. No," she immediately conceded, "that's not true. I did realize I was doing it, but I couldn't stop myself." She blew out a long, heavy sigh. "I was debating texting him, but I don't know what to say. He's right. We do need to take this time apart. But I miss him already," she added, her voice cracking.

Darby gave another soft smile. "Give it a day or two, Jade. Let him think about things too. You guys will work this out. I know you will. You're too perfect together to let this keep you apart."

A hint of a smile tugged at Jade's lips but faded quickly. "I hope you're right."

"I'm so sorry you're going through this."

"Thanks," Jade said. Finally, she looked at Darby. "I don't want to agree with you that we're all falling apart. I'd much rather believe Taylor's unusually optimistic approach that we're growing, but it kind of feels like everything is going to hell in a burning handbasket, doesn't it?"

Darby swallowed hard. "A little. I wish I could go back in time and put the toothpaste back in the bottle." She knew she got the saying wrong, but she hoped to see Jade smile. Jade always smiled before gently correcting her when she misspoke.

However, Jade didn't appear at all amused. She simply stared blankly as another big tear rolled down her cheek.

"Jade," Darby practically begged, "things with Liam will work out. He cares about you so much. Everyone knows that."

Jade's chin quivered as she nodded. "I know. I know we'll be okay."

"So why are you sitting here beating yourself up like this?"

"Because I thought I was doing better than this about dealing with my divorce. I *was* doing better, but then Liam started pushing, and I got scared. Things have been awkward since he tried to kiss me the other day. I knew this was coming. I mean...I told him I needed time and he told me he couldn't wait. And here we are. Over before we began."

"You're allowed to take time," Darby said. "Don't feel guilty about needing more time to get your footing."

"Darby, I've had this wonderful man standing in front of me, waiting for me to take the next steps with him, and I keep looking back at the disaster I left behind. My ex has moved on. He's remarried, for God's sake, and here I am... clinging to the pain instead of letting it go and moving on. And that really *is* pathetic."

"No, it isn't," Darby said, almost desperately.

Finally, Jade gave a soft laugh. "I don't want to talk about this anymore. Like you said, this will work out. How are you?"

Darby wanted to push, but she bit her tongue. This was Jade's heartache, and Darby couldn't force her to deal with it if she wasn't ready. Instead, Darby bit her lip hard as she considered how to answer that. "I'm torn. I've tried to make things right with Un-Do, and I know the next logical step is apologizing to the rest of the women I might have hurt, but I don't know... Maybe Sue's right. Maybe that isn't enough. I *want* it to be enough, but...maybe it isn't. Maybe the only way I can fix this *is* to walk away from it all and start something that hasn't been tainted."

Jade sat quietly for several heartbeats. "Do you understand why Sue is hurting?"

Yet another layer of shame washed over Darby as she again imagined how difficult it must have been for Sue to have had her nose rubbed in something that she undoubtedly had worked so hard to put behind her. "Yes. I do."

"Did you mean it when you apologized to her?"

"Down to my soul."

"Sometimes that has to be enough," Jade offered. "She may never forgive you, Darby. And that's her right. It's her decision to hang on to that anger. You can't make that go away. All you can do is move forward."

"I guess that's the problem. I don't know how."

"You've taken the right steps. You've altered the website to post an apology to your customers and you've stated your intent to apologize to the rest of the brides who may have felt hurt by your site. That's more than a lot of people would have done."

She knew that to be true. She could have very easily ignored the nasty comments, let Jennifer Williams's video add to the hits on her website, and kept going as she was. She hadn't done that. As soon as she'd realized how offtrack she'd gotten, Darby had taken steps to correct the course. And that really was more than many would do. "I guess I'm still undecided on whether that's enough or not."

After sipping from the mug Darby had brought out, Jade asked, "Are you wondering if that's enough because you feel bad or because you worry about what people are thinking about you?"

Darby slouched as she was reminded that the weight that

had fallen onto her shoulders wasn't only because she'd caused pain but because people were intentionally inflicting pain on her in response. "A lot of both, I guess. I understand why people want to say ugly things about me, but I wish they'd stop to consider they don't have to. I'm sad enough without that. I hurt myself too. And I'm already embarrassed enough without them mocking me."

"Why are you embarrassed?"

Darby shifted in her chair. "You know, I never even dated until my midtwenties. I was too awkward and weird. Mark Penn, the one I kind of vanished on, he was a loser, Jade. He was never going to do anything with his life, and I was smart enough to know he would have dragged me down with him. Not that I had a hell of a lot of potential back then."

"Don't cut yourself down."

"I'm not. It's true," Darby said. "Back then, I was still hiding in the shadows because I didn't want to be seen. That worked out really well with Mark because he didn't want to put in the work of acknowledging me. But even as big of a loser as I was, I knew I deserved better than some beer-guzzling slob who refused to grow up. Maybe I didn't handle breaking up with him well, but ending our relationship was the best thing I could have done. Nobody even got my side of the story. They listened to his fake sob story and decided I was the bad one."

"But that doesn't matter," Jade insisted. "Not really. Does it?"

"I don't want people thinking bad things about me. Especially when they aren't true." Darby frowned. "I've always hidden myself away, but now... For the first time in my life, I was comfortable in my skin. I liked who I was. I actually wanted people to see me."

"But you've said the clothes and the hair were your armor. They weren't seeing you. They were seeing your protective layers."

She laughed dryly. "Yeah, because I know what people are like. I know how they can be. Look at the comments on my website," she said as if that proved all she was saying. "That's exactly why I've always been careful who sees the *real* me. But I was ready, Jade. I was ready to put myself out there and be me and...and then this happened. Maybe I shouldn't care, but I do. I don't want to be seen in the light that Jennifer presented me in, but I don't know how to change it. If the apologies aren't enough, then all that's left is walking away."

After staring into the fire for several moments, Jade blinked and then met Darby's gaze. "People are going to see you how they choose to see you. Some will look at your style and see you as brave for being true to yourself. Some will see you as seeking attention. Others are going to see you as sad and broken and putting on a show. But you're the one who has to live with who you really are. You're the only one who can decide when you've done all you need to do to make this right."

"I know."

"But the fact that you're concerned is growth," Jade said. "I mean, you spent most of the last year tossing your cares to the wind. Taylor's right when she says you've changed and grown. I wish you could see how much you've changed. You've really come a long way."

"So have you," Darby said with a weak smile. "Don't give

up on Liam," she said around the lump in her throat. "Please, Jade. Not when he makes you so happy."

Jade sipped her tea. "This is going to blow over someday, you know? My problems, yours, and Taylor's. They'll blow over and will be a part of the past. We'll move beyond this, and life will feel normal again. I'm sure of that."

"I hope so," Darby said. "This feels like..."

"What?" Jade pressed when Darby let her words fade.

Darby swirled her wine, watching the firelight dance in the pale liquid. "When I was growing up, there weren't a lot of other Hispanic kids in Chammont Point. Mom worked hard, but we were poor. My clothes were used and ratty. I couldn't afford makeup or hair products. By the time I was in high school, I was overweight and had acne and frizzy hair I couldn't tame. I was an easy target."

After taking a gulp from her glass, Darby continued, "I know what it's like to be bullied, Jade. I would never want to do that to someone, but I did. Not knowing that was what I was doing isn't a good enough excuse, and I see that now. I should have thought about what I was doing from someone else's point of view instead of wanting something funny to get hits on my page. I spent years trying to find a way to love myself after I was torn down to the core in school," Darby said. "I finally did, and then I did something stupid, and all those old insecurities are coming to the surface. All of a sudden, I feel like Darby Pigmora again."

"Did you say Darby *Pig*mora?" Jade asked softly.

Darby frowned. "That was my nickname."

"Oh, honey," Jade said. "I'm sorry for that."

"I told you I was an easy target." Darby took another

drink of her wine. "I never thought I'd be on the giving side of this kind of treatment. I'm so disappointed in myself."

"Darby," Jade pressed, "I know this is hard, but I really want you to take a minute to recognize your growth and the steps you've taken to make this right. I realize it doesn't feel like enough, but you have done so much, and you deserve credit for that."

"I—" Darby started after a moment.

"Stop," Jade insisted. "Look at me."

Sitting taller to clearly see Jade over the flames, Darby stared into her eyes.

"You have taken the appropriate steps to correct your mistake. You have done what you can to make amends to someone you unintentionally caused pain. You are a wonderful person."

Though it was slower to fill her heart than usual, Jade's kind words finally chipped away some of the self-loathing that had been oozing from Darby's soul. "Thank you. But now I have to decide if that is enough. If that is all I can and should do. And then," she said and frowned, "I have to decide the right thing to do with my boutique. Once I do that, I have to work up the courage to do it."

She gulped the rest of her wine because she suspected that was going to be even harder.

ELEVEN

DARBY WATCHED CURIOUSLY as Jade slipped into her kayak and paddled out of the cove early the next morning. Jade spent every morning, weather permitting, out on the lake. This was her morning routine. The curious part was that Liam wasn't sitting at the mouth of the larger body of water waiting for her.

Jade lacked her usual fervor as she cut through the water and disappeared into the distance. Her movements were slower, less enthusiastic. Her posture wasn't as erect and her movements not as confident as they normally would be. It was clear that Jade was still feeling depressed about her relationship with Liam.

Darby hated seeing her friend so sad. She wished she could do something for her, but she understood her need to have some time while dealing with her feelings. Her divorce had done a number on her, and she deserved to take the time to heal. But Darby also understood Liam's side of things. He clearly wanted to be with Jade, and he'd been waiting so long. Darby could see why he was ready to take the next steps.

Why the hell did everything have to be so complicated all the damn time?

Why couldn't Jade simply recognize that Liam was a great guy and let go of her fears? Why couldn't Sue see that Darby really was sorry and forgive her? And why the hell wouldn't people take the time to recognize that Taylor was an amazing contractor and hire her to do their projects? Darby knew from experience that Taylor put so much into her work and wouldn't stop until the job was perfect.

She deserved a chance. They all deserved a chance. Every one of them.

Frowning, she considered how much things had changed since Jade and Taylor had come into her life.

Last summer had been the best summer Darby could remember. They'd gone on adventures and spent so much time sitting around the fire pit talking that she'd feared they'd run out of topics. Everything was fun and exciting, and now...now everything felt like one disaster snowballing into the next until they were all buried under an avalanche of problems.

She wanted things to go back to how they were. Back before her boutique took over her life, Taylor's job insecurities ruled her mind, and before Jade and Liam started dancing around their feelings for each other.

And definitely back before Darby ran her damn mouth about other people's personal lives when she shouldn't have.

The weight of the world settled over Darby. Her role wasn't usually the one of fixer, but as she stood there watching Jade paddle away, she wished she could make Jade see that Liam wasn't like her ex. She wished she could make Taylor see how valuable she was as a friend and a contractor. More than anything, Darby wished she could take back the hurt she'd caused so many people.

Tears pricked Darby's eyes, and her lip trembled as she sank down to sit on her stairs.

She was distracted from her looping thoughts when a door slammed. Turning enough to see Taylor walking away from her truck, Darby wiped her cheeks dry and took a few deep breaths. In true Taylor fashion, she was bringing coffees and a green tea for Jade to try to start their day on the right foot. Which seemed impossible lately.

"She's already out on the lake," Darby said as Taylor started up the stairs.

"It's early," Taylor said as she on one step below Darby. "Why is she out so early?"

Darby smiled weakly. She didn't have the strength to debate that not everyone considered nine a.m. early. "Why are you here? I thought you'd be working. Didn't you say you had a project?"

"I finished it already. But I was offered another job... replacing a board. Like, *literally* replacing *one* board on this lady's deck. I told her the board doesn't need replacing, she just needed a nail and she could hammer it back into place herself. She doesn't need to pay me for that, and even if she did, how the hell do I charge someone for that? It'd take me like five minutes. That's not worth my time or her money. It's like I've become a pet project to the elderly women in this town. Like they had a meeting, and in between baking cookies and knitting baby booties, they elected me as their charity of the month. I can't stand it. I never get real work, just pity projects. I'm about to scream." She sipped her coffee and then glanced at Darby. "Never mind all that. I wanted to check on Jade."

"I haven't talked to her yet. She went right out onto the lake." She let out a long exhale. "I'm worried about her, though. I think Liam asking for a break has really shaken her. She didn't see it coming."

"I don't think any of us did. What about you?" Taylor gently nudged Darby's knee. "You've had a rough couple of days too."

Darby grinned. "Look at you, acting like the mama bear you pretend you aren't."

Taylor chuckled. "You two are falling apart. Someone has to check on you."

After taking a long drink from her iced coffee, Darby looked out over the water. "I'm doing okay, I guess."

"For real?"

Shrugging, she said, "I still feel like the world is crashing down on me. All because of one stupid mistake."

"You would change it if you could," Taylor offered.

Darby nodded. "But I can't. So I keep struggling with how I make this better. Do I really put an end to my only source of income? Or do I accept that I've made changes and keep building on the foundation that I've made, even if that foundation has a few cracks?"

"I don't know," Taylor said. "It's easy for me to tell you what to do because I'm not the one impacted. Jade and I can roll through the options with you a hundred times, but you have to make that decision yourself."

"I know." Darby took another long drink from her coffee. "It should be easy, I guess. I can find something else. But I've actually found a business that's successful. Revamping it should be enough. Shouldn't it?"

Taylor paused as she looked at Darby. "There are companies that have made much bigger missteps and survived. You *can* turn this around, Darby, but you have to decide if you want to."

"What will I do for money?" Darby asked.

"Budget your expenses," Taylor suggested, causing Darby to frown. Taylor was always trying to tell Darby she was too extravagant. That she spent too much on nonessentials. However, Darby had completely different ideas of what was essential than Taylor.

"There's more to this than money and having a successful business," Taylor said. "You have to think of the long-term impact this might have on you. All of the negativity around Un-Do could drag you down further before it gets better. It might never get better. There may always be people who are going to remind you that you started your business with a bad marketing scheme. If you want to continue with the boutique, you have to know that and be willing to push through."

Darby made an exaggerated frown. "People suck sometimes."

"I agree," Taylor said. "What you have to do now is recognize that you made a mistake. It happens. You're human. We all make mistakes sometimes."

"Yeah. Trust me, I've made more than my share of mistakes in my life, but this..."

"But you also have to recognize that you're trying to fix it, and that counts for something. This will get better, Darby."

Darby offered Taylor a soft smile. "Jade said that last

night. I think I am starting to feel better about what I need to do. The thing that really irks me though..." She looked out over the water, debating if she even wanted to voice the thing that was boiling low in her belly. "I know I hurt people, and I know saying that wasn't my intent doesn't excuse what I've done, but what Jennifer did—editing that video to make it seem like I said things I hadn't—that was intentional. That's worse, isn't it?"

"Yeah, on some level it is," Taylor said. "But those were Jennifer's actions, and you can't control what other people do. You can only react to them."

Darby watched Jade reappear at the mouth of the cove. "This all feels so unfair. She should be called out too."

"Well," Taylor said, "life isn't meant to be fair."

"No. It's meant to be survived like some kind of war game," Darby muttered.

Taylor chuckled. "Sometimes."

"What are you going to do about your company?" Darby asked, changing the subject.

Shrugging, Taylor looked out over the water too. "I don't know. I'll figure it out. Jade's back."

"I saw that. She wasn't out long."

That might not have seemed like a big deal to some, but Jade's time on the water was what others might have considered meditation. She found her peace out there. That was where she got her head around things. Being on the water helped her make sense of the world. She hadn't been out nearly long enough to do that, which seemed like a bad sign.

"Come on," Taylor said, standing. "Let's see how she's doing."

By the time she pulled her kayak onto shore, Darby and Taylor were at the table, pulling chairs out to finish their drinks.

"That was fast," Darby pointed out when Jade approached them.

Jade sat heavily and accepted the tea Taylor offered her. "I couldn't stop thinking about..."

"A certain handsome guy," Taylor suggested.

Nodding, Jade pulled her phone from the waterproof pouch she always took out with her. "I'm going to text him."

"And say what?" Taylor asked.

"That he's an asshole for pressuring me and I don't appreciate it."

Taylor put her hand on Jade's. "Maybe reconsider how to phrase that."

Jade scowled as she looked up, but then her face sagged. "Am I wrong to ask for more time?"

Darby twisted her lips. "No. Not if that's what you need."

"I was thinking about how far you've come in the last few days," Jade said to Darby. "How you went from standing your ground to recognizing you needed to make amends, and I...I wish I could be like you."

Darby sat taller. "Like *me*?"

"You're being so strong."

Shaking her head, Darby disagreed. "I'm a mess. I'm a freaking disaster."

"But you're pushing ahead anyway," Jade said.

Taylor nodded. "You're going to apologize to all those women. That isn't going to be easy."

"You recognized where things went wrong, and you're taking the steps to make it right," Jade said. "That is amazing.

And I... I need to do that with Liam, but I... I don't know how."

Taylor shrugged. "Maybe calling him an asshole isn't the best step."

Jade rolled her eyes. "But he was an asshole."

"Maybe," Darby said, "you should tell him that you understand where he's coming from and you need him to recognize that you're nervous about starting something new."

Jade stared at her screen. "Fine. But in my mind I'm still calling him an asshole." She pecked away. After several seconds of looking like she could be sick, she pushed her phone to the center of the table and closed her eyes. "Someone else hit Send."

Darby tapped the button. "Sent."

Jade moaned miserably before muttering, "Asshole."

Taylor pulled her phone from her pocket. "My turn. I'm not taking any more of these sympathy projects I'm not really needed for." She tapped out a message and set her phone next to Jade's. "There. I'm kindly refusing to replace that lady's board. Someone send it."

Jade pressed the button, and they both looked at Darby.

"Well," Taylor said. "What about you? Do you have anything you need to send that you've been putting off?"

"You mean besides about a dozen apologies?" Darby let her smile fall and swallowed hard. "If I'm going to sort through all this mess, I have to... I have to know why Jennifer did what she did. Why did she target me like that? Why did she twist my words around and make me look so horrible?" She looked at her phone for several seconds before scrolling through her received calls and finding the call she still regretted taking. She used the number to start a new text, typed out a message. and set her phone in the center.

However, before Taylor could push the button to request Jennifer meet with her, Darby pressed it herself and then swallowed the lump that formed in her throat.

Later that evening, Darby sat nervously at a table at La Cocina. Generally, this was her happy place. This was where she and her friends sat and laughed and ate endless chips and salsa and went through more margaritas than was advisable. Luckily for them, Jade didn't drink, so they always had a designated driver, which was almost always needed.

She wasn't here for the margaritas or salsa this time. This time she was here to meet Hallie Mitchell—the bride from the other story she'd shared on *The Noah Joplin Show*. Hallie had been surprised to hear from Darby but hadn't been cold on the phone like Sue had. That gave Darby hope that this apology would go better. But that hope was slim.

This feeling was the exact same that she'd felt at the diner in Richmond. Her nerves were lit like a forest fire burning her alive under her skin. The urge to run was almost undeniable. When a waitress approached the table, she offered Darby a friendly smile.

"Margarita?" she asked, because Darby always had Lo Cocina's margaritas. Like her, they used fresh limes instead of a mix. They were nearly impossible to resist, but this time, she did.

With a shake of her head, she said, "Water, please."

The woman's smile faltered before nodding and walking

away. Once Darby was alone, she gnawed at her lip and scanned the restaurant. She wasn't sure if she'd been wise to agree to meet Hallie in this sacred place. Either the feeling that this was a home away from home with really delicious food would be shattered because Hallie trashed her there, or the feeling that this was a safe place would be reinforced.

Darby's chest nearly caved in on itself when the door opened and Hallie walked in. Like Sue had done, she scanned the room before locking eyes on Darby. But unlike Sue, Hallie didn't immediately scowl and shoot a death glare Darby's way.

Okay, Darby thought. *This might not be too bad.*

Hallie dropped an oversized tote purse into the booth and slid in. She smiled slightly, not overly friendly, but it was better than Darby had gotten from the last woman she'd had to bare her soul to.

"How are you?" Darby asked with a tense voice.

"I'm fine." She leaned on the table and heaved a sigh. "I'm guessing this about your website."

Darby nodded much too quickly. Tightening her hands into fists, she reminded herself to stay calm. "I feel so bad about sharing your story."

Hallie shrugged. "I didn't even know about it, honestly. Someone saw it and asked if you were the one who'd made my wedding dress. We went on your site to check it out."

Biting her lip, Darby swallowed hard. "Did you know that I shared your story on Noah Joplin's show?"

Lifting a brow, Hallie seemed to process this. "Did you use my name?"

"*No*," Darby stated firmly. "No, I *never* used anyone's name."

Hallie glanced around for several seconds. "Did you sell my dress?"

Darby's guilt grew. "Yeah. I did."

Hallie reached into the bowl of chips and pulled one out. "Good. I always felt bad that I didn't pay you for that."

As she watched Hallie eat the chip, Darby put her hand to her chest. "But I didn't charge you, so you couldn't have paid me."

"I know, but that felt wrong." Hallie brushed her hands together. "Are you apologizing because that other bride threw you under the bus?"

Shrugging slightly, Darby said, "She was upset and had every right to be."

"But is that why you're apologizing to me?"

"I didn't think about how you would feel when I posted the story of your cancelled wedding on my website. I should have put myself in your shoes before I did that. I was wrong, and that's why I'm apologizing. I did not mean to embarrass you. I would never want to do that."

Sitting back in the booth, Hallie scoffed. "Why would I be embarrassed? I didn't cheat with my sister. That was all on him."

"Even so, I shouldn't have just put that out there like I did."

When the waitress approached the table, Hallie smiled but didn't order anything. "I'm not staying, but thank you." When they were alone again, she looked at Darby. "Look, I get why some of the brides are upset. But nobody knows the person you were talking about is me. It doesn't feel great to have my problems used for a marketing ploy, but it isn't going to destroy me. I appreciate your apology, I do, but it's not necessary, Darby. I'm glad you finally got paid for the dress."

The weight that had settled on Darby's shoulders the moment she'd walked into the restaurant lifted. Tears bit at the back of her eyes, but she blinked them back. "I want you to know that I really regret using your pain to further my business. I hadn't considered that was what I was doing, but I do see it now and I'll do better in the future."

Hallie offered her that soft smile again. "That's all any of us can do, right? Learn and grow." She held up her fingers in a peace sign before grabbing her bag and sliding from the booth. "I'm glad you reached out to me. I appreciate it, but really, let this go and move on. It's done."

"So you accept my apology?" Darby asked, not sure she was understanding Hallie's chill attitude.

"Yeah. I mean, you'll think things through next time, right?"

"Right."

"Cool. I'll see you around." She walked away, and that seemed to be the end of that.

Darby sat still, almost unable to believe what had just happened. Hallie had been nice—a million times nicer than Sue Berdynski. As soon as Hallie had answered Darby's call and agreed to meet her, Darby had been bracing herself for another horrific showdown. She'd walked into La Cocina with her heart in her throat and her hands trembling. But as she fell back against the seat, she exhaled with relief.

That was one down. She still had another to go. She glanced at her watch and confirmed that her chat with Hallie had taken much less time than she'd expected and she had plenty of time before her next potential confrontation. This time when the waitress came to the table, Darby ordered a small margarita to celebrate her small but profound win with Hallie and a lunch combo that would give her two of her favorites—a beef enchilada and a hard-shell taco.

When her drink arrived, she toasted herself and took a sip, enjoying the high of earning forgiveness from at least one of the people she had wronged. As she waited for her food to be delivered, she texted an update to Jade and Taylor, and her mood lifted even higher as they both responded with congratulations that her meeting had gone well.

Her good mood eased some of the stress she'd felt about facing the next person who would be sitting across from her. However, as she finished eating her lunch and time neared for the next meeting to start, her stress returned.

When her plate was taken away, she was tempted to order another margarita but had her water glass refilled instead. She needed to have her wits about her. She needed to be able to defend herself if the discussion came to that, and she expected it would.

As her stress spiked again, Darby pressed her palms to the table and took a big breath to ground herself. She had chosen this place for a reason. It really was a sacred place for her.

She loved the scents of La Cocina. Though this wasn't the restaurant where her mom had worked, the happy atmosphere reminded Darby of where she'd spent so much of her childhood. Day after day, she'd sat tucked at a corner table doing her homework while her mom worked her shift in the kitchen. The owners of that restaurant brought her food and sodas and always said how proud her mom was of her for working so hard at her schooling.

Those were some of her favorite memories now, but she'd resented spending most of her life in a booth back then. She wished she could go back and thank them and her mom for always trying to encourage her. Sadly, when the owners of that restaurant were ready to retire, they closed down and moved away.

Darby hadn't seen them since.

She was pulled from her thoughts when Jennifer dropped down into the booth across from her. Darby's heart, which had been filled with hope, thumped at the unenthusiastic look on Jennifer's face.

Jennifer didn't seem nearly as pleased that Darby had invited her to lunch as Hallie had been.

"First one who storms out pays for lunch," Jennifer said as she dug into the basket of chips.

"I'm not planning to storm out this time," Darby said. "I'm here to tell you that you were right."

Jennifer stopped lifting a chip to her mouth. "Seriously?" She ate the chip in one bite and then immediately started digging for another. "What made you see the light?"

"Sue Berdynski is miserable," Darby said. "Even if I didn't mean to, I definitely had a hand in that. I was wrong."

Jennifer smirked. "Yeah, I know. I told you that."

Rather than acknowledge her I-told-you-so, Darby said, "I tried to apologize to her, but she didn't accept."

Jennifer smiled up at the waitress and ordered a diet soda before returning her attention to Darby. "Some wounds take longer to heal. What she went through was devastating. Not just embarrassing or unfortunate. Being betrayed by her fiancé and best friends like she had been was *devastating*."

Darby frowned as she considered Jennifer's statement. "I

know. I didn't consider that I was pouring gasoline on smoldering embers. I really didn't."

"Okay," Jennifer said after a few moments. "So what are you going to do about it?"

Though she was full from her lunch, Darby needed a distraction. She reached into the chips, looking for one big enough to scoop the chunky salsa onto as she considered what to say. "Sue says if I was really sorry, I'd close my store. I've been considering that."

"That's one way to prove you're repentant," Jennifer said. "I saw you posted an apology and took the stories down. That's another way. But clearly you're still struggling with the guilt. Otherwise you wouldn't look like someone pissed all over your breakfast."

Darby scowled at her. "Hey, I'm not here to be judged by you. I made mistakes, but so did you." She scoffed. "You know damn well what you did in that video you posted."

Jennifer sat back and glanced around the dining room before nodding. "Yeah, I did. I pulled your comments together and made you look like a bigger ass than you already were."

"*Why*?"

Meeting Darby's gaze, Jennifer blinked unrepentantly. "Sue's my cousin. Did you know that?"

Darby jolted. "Wait. What?"

Jennifer shrugged and went back to digging in the chip bowl. "She heard you on *The Noah Joplin Show* and called me, crying. She was horrified and couldn't believe you'd betrayed her like that. She didn't know what to do."

"And you decided to trash me by splicing an interview together?"

When the waitress set Jennifer's drink down, Jennifer immediately took a sip from the straw and then used it to slowly stir the drink as she thoughtfully stared at the ice cubes. "We watched the interview a few times. At first I was trying to tell her it was no big deal. Like what you said, you didn't tell anyone her name. But then her social media blew up with people asking if that was her. The knife kept twisting, and every time, she started crying again."

Darby had to blink away her shame as she processed how much that must have hurt. "I didn't think something like that would happen."

"Nobody does, do they?" Jennifer asked softly. "Nobody thinks about how the ripple effects could turn into giant waves. They just throw the rock. Anyway, seeing my cousin hurt like that, I knew I had to step in and do something. So..."

"What?" Darby demanded as she widened her eyes. "You decided to lie about my intentions?"

At that, Jennifer scoffed. "So I called you and set up that interview, and then I went right to Sue's house and showed her the footage. She was furious. She thought you didn't care how much you were hurting her."

"Why didn't you tell me? I could have tried to make this better without you making this so much uglier than it already was."

"Because I was angry. And because I agreed with Sue. You didn't seem too concerned about hurting anyone. You seemed pretty content to rake in the money coming in from their broken lives." Jennifer shrugged. "Karma finds you every time, you know. And that was what I chalked it up to.

You hurt my cousin on a podcast. I had the means to use my podcast to hurt you back."

Darby pushed her empty water glass aside and tapped her nails on the table. "So how did you find my ex-boyfriends?"

Jennifer laughed lightly. "Like everybody else finds stuff out. I went through your old social media content. How else would I find them?"

"And you just happened to pick the two that had the worst things to say about me?"

After taking another drink from her glass, Jennifer looked away as if she was struggling to answer. "I just happened to use the footage of the two who had the worst things to say about you."

"What does that mean?"

Jennifer dug back into the chips as she cast a glance toward Darby. "Not everyone had such bad things to say. Actually, most of them said you were very sweet, that things simply didn't work out."

Darby narrowed her eyes at Jennifer. "You manipulated that footage as well."

"Maybe. But does it matter?"

"Of course it matters. You made me look *terrible*."

"Oh, man," Jennifer chuckled. "I'm going to remind you, one more time, you used my cousin's broken engagement and cancelled wedding to earn a few bucks. You're not some innocent in this, Darby. I didn't wake up one morning and decide to retaliate for nothing."

After a moment, Darby nodded. "Okay. So we both did things that hurt other people. I think you can step down off that high horse you've been riding and acknowledge that what you did wasn't any better."

Jennifer pressed her lips together and looked away instead of agreeing.

"So now what?" Darby pressed. "I've apologized. I've changed my site. What are you going to do about your mistake?"

Rolling her eyes, Jennifer faced her again. "Now I guess you finish what you started. You've apologized to Sue and you took down the descriptions. But she's told you what you need to do to make it up to her. Now you decide. Are you sorry that you hurt her because it's caused you pain? Or do you finally understand what you did was wrong and want to make the necessary changes to fix it? Because there's a difference, Darby."

"Un-Do is my income. It's my business. So the only way to prove I'm really sorry is to lose my income? That's what you're saying?"

Jennifer shrugged. "Sue is the one who was hurt."

"Okay, well, I was hurt by your video, so you need to stop doing your podcast."

Rather than agree or disagree, Jennifer stared like she didn't understand the words that had come from Darby's mouth.

"By your logic," Darby pressed, "if I made a mistake and hurt someone, I should have to shut down my business. I'm telling you, right here to your face, that you manipulated that video, and that hurt me. So shut down your podcast."

Scoffing, Jennifer looked away but her smile faded. "No."

"Why not?"

"Because..."

"That's how you make a living," Darby finished.

Jennifer shifted in her seat and chewed on the nail of her pointer finger for a moment. "The circumstances are completely different."

"Yeah," Darby said, "I didn't realize I was hurting someone. You did it on purpose. To retaliate. Rather than just telling me, you threw me under a big ol' bus to get even. That doesn't make you better than me."

"I never said I was," Jennifer said softly. Leaning forward, she clutched her hands together on the table and stared at them for a few seconds. "For the first day or so, it was funny to see what people were saying to you—about you. But then it started feeling like..."

"Like you were the bully instead of the geek?"

"Yeah," she said on a breath. She glanced at Darby with what appeared to be shame in her eyes. "I didn't like that feeling. I didn't want to be that person. I remember being on the receiving end of comments like that, and I didn't want to be the reason someone was going through that—even you."

Darby nodded. "Yeah, I've been thinking about high school a lot. How mean the kids could be. How funny they thought it was to pick on the defenseless."

"You're right, we were both wrong to do what we did."

"Yeah. So...what do we do about it?"

When their waitress returned, Jennifer sighed. "Have a drink?"

Darby nodded and then ordered another margarita, and since she'd already eaten lunch, she asked for sopapillas—her favorite dessert.

TWELVE

THOUGH THEIR FRIENDIVERSARY dinner didn't end up being the big fancy event Darby had hoped it would be, she wouldn't change a single minute of it. She, Jade, and Taylor had crowded into Darby's cabin and stumbled around one another as they prepared dinner with Johnny Cash singing quietly from the record player.

As always, Taylor manned the grill, Jade tossed together some sides, and Darby mixed drinks and set the table. They sat and ate, as they would any other night. Darby's heart was much lighter as they laughed and shared stories. The cloud that had been hovering over her for weeks was fading. This night, however, when the meal ended, Darby made them sit and wait while she presented them with their surprises.

First, she pulled from the freezer an ice cream cake that she'd brought from Harper's earlier in the day. Across the layers of various flavored ice cream, written in fancy font with red icing, were the words "Happy Friendiversary, Jadartay!"

"What the hell does that say?" Taylor asked as Jade creased her brow.

"Jadartay," Darby said with a laugh. "Come on. That's our names meshed together like they do for Hollywood couples. Please don't tell me you've never heard of people doing that, Taylor. I couldn't live with you if you'd never heard of couple nicknames."

"Yes, I've heard of it. For movie stars." Taylor laughed.

Jade shrugged. "It's kinda cute. That was clever, Darby."

"Thank you," she said and grabbed a knife. However, when she tried to cut the cake, it was too hard. They laughed at the way Darby struggled.

Taylor shooed her away, insisting she could cut through the frozen layers. Her efforts were as futile as Darby's had been.

"Okay," Taylor said, "this beast has to thaw for a few minutes before we dig in."

"That's okay," Darby sang out, "because..."

"Uh-oh," Jade muttered, causing Taylor to giggle.

"Do *not* be rude, ladies." Darby pulled out three small gift bags from a cabinet and dangled them as she walked back to the table. "I got us pressies!"

"No," Taylor groaned. "I didn't do anything."

"You bought the steaks," Jade reminded her. "I'm the one who didn't do anything."

"You made a salad, sweetie," Darby said and laughed when Jade rolled her eyes. "Okay, I got these because you two have been my anchors the last couple of weeks. My life was falling apart, and you could have walked away and let me face it alone, but you didn't."

"Because we love you," Jade said.

Darby put a bag in front of each of her friends and then sat with one in front of her. "On the count of three, okay? One…"

"Three," Taylor and Jade said at the same time, just like they did when they raced across the lake.

This was a race Darby could actually take part in, though. She giggled as they all tore into their bags and pulled out the little boxes. Jade was the first to lift the top off, but Taylor was right behind. Darby had stopped digging because she knew what was inside. She was more interested in seeing their reactions to make sure they loved her gifts. She was pretty sure Jade would, but Taylor was iffy.

Jade gasped and put her hand to her chest as she looked at Darby. "Oh, honey, this is adorable."

"This is cool, Darbs. Thanks." Though she lacked the enthusiasm Jade shared, Darby saw how touched she was. She was quiet and thoughtful, and her comment was soft rather than sarcastic. Darby couldn't have asked for a better reaction.

Jade lifted the necklace from the box in her hand and let it hang so she could admire the three entwined hearts. They were small because Darby knew Taylor would never wear something flashy, but they said so much about how she felt about her two best friends. They were tied together, forever, in a way she'd never been tied to anyone before, and she hoped they felt the bond as strongly as she did. She was certain they did, but voicing it made her feel insecure.

"It might be a little overly sentimental," Darby said softly, "but when I saw these, I thought of us. Three hearts, locked together."

"I love it," Jade stated and went to work on putting the necklace on.

Darby glanced at Taylor to gauge her response.

Taylor smiled. "I love it too," she said. "Thank you." She smiled and then put hers on as well. She ran her fingers over the silver chain and small trio of hearts. "I haven't worn a necklace since I was like...twelve."

"Well," Darby stated, opening her box, "you're never allowed to take this one off. It's a forever necklace for forever friendship."

Taylor touched the hearts and then stood up. "Okay, this is getting too heavy. I'm taking a chainsaw to this damn cake."

While Taylor attacked the cake, alternating between cursing and muttering to herself, Jade and Darby cleaned up dinner. As they did, Darby couldn't help but chuckle as she recalled the first time she had met Jade. Darby had owned the cabin next door and used it as a rental. Jade had booked the place for a week. However, as Darby had been walking over to greet her, she'd watched the porch banister give way and Jade flew through the air, landing face-first in the patchy grass. Luckily, Jade hadn't been seriously hurt.

"I can't believe it's been one year since I almost killed you, Jade," Darby said.

"Good thing I'm resilient," Jade told her with a smile.

"I'll have to try harder next time," Darby teased with a wink before blowing her friend a kiss.

Laughter filled the cabin again, and Darby had never been so happy to hear a sound. At one point, when everything felt like it was falling apart and the old feeling of not belonging threatened to consume her, she thought she might lose this. She had actually thought that they wouldn't want to be her friends any longer and would find a way to remove her from their group.

What a foolish thing. They were family in all the ways that really mattered. They couldn't walk away from one another, and they had proven time and time again that they wouldn't turn their backs on one another. Her fears had been insecurities pulling at her, but her friends had helped her overcome them.

These women had become part of Darby's heart and soul. Their friendship was the gravity that kept her grounded...as grounded as she could be. She could finally put her fears to rest—this was the one place in the world where she didn't have to question if she belonged.

Jade's smile faltered as she looked at Darby. "Hey," she said with concern in her voice, "what's wrong?"

Darby blinked and then forced her emotions back as she grinned. "Nothing."

"Darby?" Taylor pressed.

"I'm really glad I have you guys. I mean it when I say you got me through this stuff with Un-Do and having to step back and reassess my actions. I wouldn't have made it through without you. I want you to know, I have learned some things in the last two weeks. The biggest one being that..." She swallowed before saying, "I think I should see a doctor about my depression. I always find ways to avoid dealing with it, but I hit some pretty scary lows over the last couple of weeks. I don't want to feel like that. I have to learn how to cope better with the things life throws at me. Avoidance isn't healthy, but that's always been my go-to. I have to find better ways to get through tough times."

"No," Jade said tenderly, "it isn't. I'm glad you see that and are willing to take the steps to get help. We're here if you need anything."

Taylor nodded her agreement. Once again, the topic was probably getting into territory that was a bit too icky for her to take part in, but Darby appreciated her keeping that to herself. Admitting she needed help was challenging enough. Getting teased, even good-naturedly, would have stung.

"Good for you," Taylor said.

Darby inhaled deeply. She hadn't realized she was concerned about how they would respond until the wave of relief washed over her. She didn't know why she'd been so worried. If anyone would support her struggles with mental health, it would be her best friends. Even so, the fear she'd felt was as real as any other sensation that had overcome in her the last couple of weeks.

Shaking her head to free her brain from any negativity that was trying to take hold, she announced it was time to make margaritas and get some of that cake she'd bought, effectively ending any further discussion of the things that had been a constant point of conversation lately.

Darby smiled as she swayed her hips to the old tune coming from her speakers. She cut limes and squeezed them for freshly made margaritas while Jade made herself cranberry juice, straight with ice. While the blender was going, Taylor finally managed to cut three slices of cake from the block of ice cream on the counter.

"I'm not sure how margaritas are going to go with that cake," Jade muttered.

"Margaritas go with everything," Darby justified.

"Probably not chocolate ice cream," Taylor countered.

She served them up on plates and then turned toward the living room, carefully balancing all three plates and spoons.

They hadn't had movie night in a few weeks, and Darby was so excited to get back to the tradition. Sitting on the couch, overeating, and having random conversations was the best.

She'd picked a cheesy B movie with a nerd turned superhero. Though Darby thought the plot was somewhat fitting considering she'd been such a weakling and finally managed to stand on her own, Taylor was going to hate every minute of the bad movie. That, however, was part of the fun for Darby when she picked movies. The more dramatic the reaction she could get from Taylor, the better. Their good-hearted tormenting of one another was one of the best parts of their friendship. They were like sisters who could pick at one another but never doubt their bond, even though they hadn't grown up together.

Taylor always got her revenge, though. As much as Taylor hated bad movies, Darby hated slasher films, and Taylor always chose one of those when it was her turn to pick. If Darby never had to see another witless camper get decapitated with a machete ever again, it would still be too soon.

However, she welcomed horror movies with open arms over the brainiac biopics and mushy romantic comedies that Jade liked. Though they never could agree on which genre of film to watch, movie night was the perfect way to wrap up their friendiversary celebration, so whatever was flashing across the screen didn't matter, not in the long run.

"Jade," Taylor called as she walked through the living

room toward the window overlooking the cove. "Were you expecting Liam?"

"No," she said from the kitchen.

Taylor turned and smirked. "He's climbing out of his kayak with flowers and...if I'm not mistaken, a bottle of... juice." She laughed and shook her head. "Only you could be wooed with juice."

"I don't drink alcohol," Jade reminded them as she peered through the window. "What is he doing with all that stuff?"

"Really?" Darby asked.

"Well, you see..." Taylor stared. "When a boy likes a girl—"

"Stop," Jade muttered. She focused outside. "He's just... standing there."

"He's nervous," Darby whispered as if Liam might hear. "Go on."

Jade shook her head. "No, I can't."

"It's time," Taylor told her. "We know you're scared to get hurt again, but it's time, Jade."

Jade looked at Darby with a plea in her eyes. "What if it isn't time?"

"It is." Darby put her hand on Jade's shoulder. "It's time. Go get that man."

"But..."

"Go," Taylor said.

Jade closed her eyes and took a few deep breaths before she rolled her shoulders back. She nodded. "Okay," she said but didn't move. "Okay. I'm going."

"I can tell," Darby said flatly.

"I am. I need one more minute to—"

222

"Hey, Liam," Taylor shouted through the window.

Jade grabbed Taylor's arm as Liam stopped walking toward Jade's cabin and looked around. "*No*," Jade all but begged. "Guys."

Taylor laughed before she again yelled, "Hang on a minute. Jade is on her way."

Pressing her hands to her face, Jade moaned miserably. "I hate you sometimes."

"You love us," Darby said and laughed. "*Go*."

"Okay. I'm going." With that, she rubbed her palms together as if to muster up the courage to walk out of Darby's cabin.

"I'll fucking carry you," Taylor said.

"I'm going," Jade spat, and then she marched toward the door. Turning back, she gave them one last look. "If this turns into a nightmare, I'm blaming you two." Then she disappeared through the door.

Darby and Taylor peered back out the window at Jade walking down the stairs toward Liam. As Jade reached the shore, Liam held the flowers and juice out. He said something, and Jade nodded. And then, without warning, she jumped into his arms and kissed him full on the mouth. Liam dropped the juice and flowers as he wrapped his arms around her and pulled her close.

"*Whoa*," Taylor said, rearing back.

Darby blinked in surprise. "She just…" Lifting her hands like claws, Darby mimicked Jade's attack. "*Rawr*. She's on it. Jade's getting her man."

"She's getting something," Taylor muttered when Liam lifted Jade, who wrapped her legs around his waist. They continued their steamy kiss.

After a few moments, Taylor said, "Maybe we shouldn't—"

"Shh." Darby waved a hand to hush her. "This is like a living romance movie. Don't ruin it."

Liam eased Jade down to her feet, and Darby smiled, expecting more talking or hand-holding or something equally sweet. She certainly wasn't expecting the way the couple crumpled onto the beach with Liam on top and Jade wrapped around him like an alien in one of those other terrible movies Taylor had made them watch.

"Oh." Darby blinked several times when Liam leaned back enough to tear his T-shirt off. "Whoa. They're... I mean... Are they going to... Right there. On the beach. Where we hang out."

"Leave it to Liam to ruin a perfectly good beach." Taylor closed the window and then dropped the blinds. "I don't want to know how far they're willing to go right there on the cove, and we aren't going to find out. Do not ask for details about this in front of me. Got it?"

Darby turned wide-eyed to gawk at her. "I'm not sure I want details either, but as her neighbor and a half owner of that beach, I'm going to have to set some rules. We spend far too much time out there to have...*that* become a regular occurrence."

Taylor chuckled as she left the window, still carrying three slices of cake. "What shit movie do you have for us to watch?"

The next morning, Darby carried her phone with her as she rushed down the well-worn path that ran between her cabin and Jade's. She pushed the door open and walked in without hesitation. "Jade? Are you up?"

Almost instantly, Jade walked out of her bedroom wrapped in a robe and her hair amiss. She pressed her finger to her lips in a silent motion to hush Darby. Gasping, Darby glanced out toward the cove and noticed Liam's kayak was still on the beach.

She stared with wide eyes as she came to a realization. He'd spent the night! At Jade's cabin! *With* Jade!

Only then did Darby realize her days of barging in unannounced were probably over. The last thing she wanted was to accidentally walk in on something. "Oh, no," she whispered. "Were you and Liam...doing *naughty* things?"

Jade smiled brightly, and her gray eyes danced with a kind of happiness Darby hadn't seen in a long time. "Nope. He's still sleeping. Apparently I wore him out."

Darby winced with all the dramatics of a grossed-out teenager. "Ick. No. Don't tell me that." She laughed softly. "I'm happy for you, but I don't want to hear this. I have to be able to look Liam in the eye."

Jade giggled, but her cheeks turned bright red, implying she was at least somewhat embarrassed by her confession.

"Seriously, though," Darby said more gently. "I'm so happy for you. I'm glad you were able to move forward with him."

"Me too." Jade's smile softened. "What's up? What had you running in so excited?"

"You have to see this." Darby woke up her phone and pressed Play on the video she'd already watched five times. Holding her breath, she waited, half convinced she'd imagined everything she'd heard. However, as Jade stood next to her, the video started. A few seconds later, Jennifer Williams appeared without a lick of makeup and her hair pulled back in a messy bun.

"Guys," she said pathetically, like she was announcing to the world that her favorite pet had passed away, "I made a mistake, and I need to apologize to you all. But mostly, I need to apologize to Darby Zamora, the owner of The Un-Do Wedding Boutique."

Jade gasped and turned her wide eyes to Darby. "What?"

"It gets better," Darby said. "Watch."

Silently, they watched Jennifer explain how she had edited Darby's story together to make the episode more dramatic. She even admitted that after interviewing several of Darby's ex-boyfriends, she picked out the two who made her sound the worst, rather than sharing that several other of her exes had really nice things to say about her.

That was wrong, Jennifer admitted, and she had come to realize that. Though she didn't confess the reason she'd done the edits was out of some misguided attempt at retaliation for her cousin, she did admit that she and Darby had a long conversation and they both recognized the missteps they'd taken on their websites.

"I'm sorry," Jennifer said. "To you, my followers, for letting you down, and to Darby for misrepresenting her. I hope you'll forgive me." And with that, the video ended.

"That's...unexpected." Jade walked to the fridge and pulled out her cranberry juice. Getting a glass from the cabinet—she didn't bother offering one to Darby, who hadn't been shy about telling Jade she thought straight juice was gross—she asked, "Do you forgive her?"

Darby considered the question. "Yeah. I think I forgave her before she apologized on-air. When we had lunch yesterday, we both admitted to the mistakes we made and what led us to them. She really was sorry. So am I."

"I know you." Jade sipped her juice before grinning at her. "You're all grown up now. I'm so proud."

"Thanks," Darby said. "My biggest worry has been that the rest of the world saw me as the jerk she painted me out to be. That was all I cared about. Now that she's cleared that up, I can rest easy."

"I hope so," Jade said.

Darby tapped to exit Jennifer's site and locked her phone. "So this is over, right? My life is going to go back to normal now?"

Leaning against the counter, Jade shrugged. "Honestly, it might take a bit longer for things to blow over, but this should go a long way in restoring your image. I really am proud of you, Darby. I hope you know that. This has been hard on you, but you stayed strong."

Darby's heart warmed. "That's nice to hear. I'm not sure I agree with the strong part."

"You're stronger than you realize."

"Thank you, Jade. I don't think I would have made it through this without you."

Jade accepted the hug Darby gave her. "You're welcome. I knew you'd make it through this."

"I wish I could get to a point where what other people

thought didn't bother me, but I'm not there yet. But look at you. You look happy," Darby whispered.

"I am."

"So you and Liam are...together. Obviously."

Jade nodded. "Yeah. We're together. We stayed up late last night—"

"Nope," Darby stated firmly and playfully pressed her fingers to her ears.

"Talking," Jade finished. "We stayed up late talking. We talked about a lot of things we should have said weeks ago. He knows I'm...terrified."

"I'm glad. He's a good guy. He's not going to hurt you."

Jade nodded her agreement. "I feel like we've turned the corner. All of us."

"I'm glad. I'd be lost with you."

"I feel the same."

"Okay." Darby grabbed her phone as she said, "I'm going to get out of here so you can get back to...whatever you were doing."

"Hey," Jade called when Darby started out the door.

Darby turned and lifted her brows in question.

"You are a really good friend, Darby Zamora. Don't forget that."

A smile broke across Darby's face. "Thanks. So are you, Jade Kelly. I'm glad we found each other."

"Me too."

Darby left, phone in hand, and had to giggle at how the urge to skip in the sunshine washed over her. Things were looking up. Yes, they'd all had a bit of a rough patch, but things were definitely looking up.

After taking a deep, cleansing breath, Darby looked out over the cove. The quiet of the morning matched the peace in her heart. For the first time in weeks, she felt calm. She felt whole.

She felt like she was finally getting her shit together.

When she walked into her cabin, Darby stopped and looked around. Like Jade said, they'd turned the corner. Things were shifting. Darby felt that down into her soul. Changes were happening, not only around them but within them. They were growing in different ways, but in many ways, their growth was entwined with one another.

Grabbing her purse, Darby dug her keys out and then walked to her car. Rather than jamming to her favorite tunes like she usually would, she turned off the radio and sat in silence as she drove to the lookout point over the lake where she always ended up when she needed to connect with memories of her mom.

Though it was morning and there were no stars to be seen, Darby looked up to the sky. She may not have been able to see them, but they were there. Always. Like her mom.

As she sat in the quiet of her car, she did her best to connect with memories of advice she'd been given while growing up. What would her mom say to her now? What advice would she give to Darby as she faced this crossroads that had been pulling her for the last two weeks?

Yes, she'd started down the road to healing, not just herself but the women she'd hurt with her actions. Yes, she'd proven a point to Jennifer, that she was just as wrong as Darby had been. And yes, Darby had grown as Jade and Taylor told her.

But there was still something sitting on her shoulders.

There was still something nagging at her. Something wasn't quite right yet.

Closing her eyes, Darby listened to the silence. In her mind, she heard Sue telling her that if she was repentant, she'd shut down the website. She'd stop making money on the pain she'd caused.

Though the idea of shutting down the one successful venture she'd had terrified her, when she considered the option, she felt a wave of peace wash over her. Darby might not like it, but Sue was right. She couldn't continue to monopolize off the pain and stress that the last couple of weeks had caused so many people.

She had to walk away. She needed to wipe the slate clean and move forward without the guilt and shame hanging over her.

"Okay, Mama," she whispered. "I hear you."

Before heading back to her cabin, she texted Taylor that she was grabbing coffee and heading home. She needed Taylor's help right away.

On her way home, she went through the drive-through of their favorite coffee shop and got their usual order, less Jade's hot tea since she was otherwise occupied, and rushed home. Taylor was sitting on her couch when she got there.

Looking up, Taylor looked suspicious. "What's up?"

Darby walked to the coffee table and eased the drink carrier down. "I figured it out. I know exactly what I need to do. Well. Kind of. I mean... I know step one of what I need to do. Step two is a bit of a question right now."

"Okay," Taylor said hesitantly. "What's step one?"

After taking her drink from the carrier, she stood tall and

took two big gulps before exhaling. "I'm closing The Un-Do Wedding Boutique and donating what's left of the dresses."

"Okay. This is a great idea, Darby, but I don't know why you need me."

Darby's smile faded and her shoulders slumped slightly. "Because I'm awesome at coming up with ideas, but I suck at the execution. I need to drag what's left of the dresses to the thrift store. Help me?" she asked with a slight pout.

Taylor chuckled. "There can't be that many dresses left."

"There aren't, but if I don't have a grown-up supervising me, they're never going to leave this house. I swear. It'll be on my to-do list for like a month."

Instead of arguing, Taylor nodded once in firm agreement. "Okay. So we'll do that after we have coffee. But... are you sure about this?"

"Yes," she stated, "I definitely don't want to be the type of person who'll step on someone else to get ahead. I've decided what I need to do," she announced. "I'm going to donate the dresses I have left and close The Un-Do Wedding Boutique." After stating it a second time, the decision still felt right. "This is the right thing to do. For me and everyone else who has been impacted by this. I want to put Un-Do, Sue Berdynski, and Jennifer Williams behind me. I don't ever want to think about this mess again."

Taylor chuckled. "Okay, but let's shut down the site first. I need more coffee in my system before I touch all that sequin and lace."

Darby laughed as she opened her laptop and waited for it to boot up. "So, someone spent the night with Jade."

Taylor sighed. "I think we're going to be seeing significantly more of that guy, huh?"

"Yeah, but it's good," Darby said. "It's good for Jade."

"It is," Taylor agreed. She watched Darby log in to the admin page of Un-Do. "Okay," she said. "Are you ready?"

"Ready." Darby went through the process of deleting the site and all the archived posts. When the final warning came up telling her she wouldn't be able to retrieve her site if she clicked Okay, she glanced at Taylor.

"On the count of three," Taylor said. "One..."

"Three." Darby pushed the button, and the site was erased. Forever.

An unexpected weight lifted off her chest. She could breathe again.

"Okay," Taylor said. "Nice work. Now what?"

"What do you mean?"

Taylor shrugged. "You said this was step one. What's step two? The slightly foggy one."

"Oh." Darby bit her straw for a moment before taking a drink and swallowing hard. After a few seconds, she looked at Taylor. "Step two is figuring out what I do next." A few seconds passed before she shrugged. "I still have the Mistress of Ceremonies website."

"Don't you dare," Taylor muttered, causing Darby's laughter to fill the cabin.

THIRTEEN

DARBY WRAPPED a light sweater around her shoulders as Taylor added a few logs to the fire pit. Though summer was still alive and kicking, a front had moved through and brought cooler temperatures with it. The evening felt more like early autumn with a hint of crispness to the air.

Darby never grew tired of evenings like this. Sitting around with her best friends was the absolute best feeling in the world. Now that she had apologized to Sue, Jennifer had admitted her mistakes, and Darby had started the negotiations to sell The Un-Do Wedding Boutique to some designer who was hoping to capitalize on the scandal, the amount of stress she'd been under was finally easing.

At least, it was until she saw the sadness on Taylor's face as she stared into the fire. Her brow was tightly knitted and her mouth dipped into a deep frown as if the weight of the world had left Darby's shoulders and settled on Taylor's.

"What is it?" Darby asked. "What's wrong?"

Jade looked at their friend and concern filled her face too. "Uh-oh. That looks serious. I hate when you look like that."

Taylor scrunched her nose up. "You hate when I look like me?"

"I hate when you get quiet and stare off into the distance," Jade clarified. "Nothing good comes from that look."

Taylor shrugged. "I lost another bid today. I'm..." She focused on Darby. "I'm getting concerned. I don't think my business can keep going like this."

Darby's heart sank. "Jade can help. Jade's a marketing goddess. Right?"

"She's tried," Taylor said. "It's not the marketing, Darbs. It's me."

"No," Darby stated. "I refuse to believe that."

"Okay," Taylor corrected, "it's this." She gestured to her body. "People don't want to give me a chance. As soon as they figure out Taylor O'Shea is a woman, they decide to go with a so-called *real* contractor. I don't think I can keep fighting for this."

"We can try some other marketing, Tay," Jade offered.

Taylor shook her head. "It's time to accept that this isn't going to work."

"What are you going to do?" Darby asked. "You can't give up."

"I'm not giving up, but I am thinking that maybe I need to switch directions. I need a new line of work. That's all. I've been thinking about that a lot." Taylor opened her phone and tapped on the screen. "Remember how I lectured you for being irresponsible with your rental property last year, Darby?"

"Yeah." Darby hadn't been a fan of Taylor's lectures, even if she had been right. Had Darby realized how much work went into owning a rental property, she never would have tried it.

Taylor handed her phone to Darby, and Jade scooted closer to take a look.

"You're buying a house?" Jade asked.

"I was thinking, maybe I'm not cut out to do the business end of contracting, being all *female* and everything. Maybe I'm better suited at being a property manager. I have the skills to do the repairs, I won't have to deal with people in person much, and I'm not afraid to evict someone if they act up. In fact, I'd probably enjoy it."

Darby pictured Taylor tossing someone's belongings out onto the street while telling them to get the fuck off her property. The image suited her much more than smiling as she tried to prove she was the best contractor for a job. "Yeah, I think you would."

"You know how to do the rental end, right?" Taylor asked Darby. "You can teach me how to list the houses on all those vacation house sites. Most of the business end is online, isn't it?"

"Yeah," Darby said. Her spirits lifted as she realized Taylor was asking her for help...like *genuinely* needed her help. Excitement filled her veins, and she beamed brightly. "You wouldn't have to even see the renters if you didn't want to. Actually, that's how it's supposed to be. I only introduced myself to my renters because I couldn't stand not knowing who was staying beside me. You're not as social as me, so that probably won't be a thing for you."

Taylor widened her eyes. "No. Probably not something I'm going to do."

"I can help with advertising," Jade said. "You don't have to rely on those sites to show your rentals. You can run ads too."

"See?" Taylor laughed as she focused on the stars coming out above them.

Darby smiled. *The answers are in the stars*, her mom always said.

Taylor returned her gaze to Darby. "I need to change direction. This is perfect, don't you think?"

"Could be." Darby flipped through the photos. "What about your company? O'Shea Construction is so important to you."

"You started that company to honor your grandpa," Jade reminded her. "You shouldn't give up because people in this town are scared of hiring you."

Taylor frowned. "I can still do projects, I guess, but this would probably be my main income. Then I don't have to stress about not getting bids. I mean, let's face it, the small projects I do land aren't going to be enough to keep me going. The last big project I had was your remodel, Jade."

"Which is amazing," Jade said.

"Amazing doesn't pay the bills." Taylor accepted her phone back. "I can do this."

"Would you live in one of these?" she asked. "I'd visit you more if I wasn't so scared of your neighbors."

Taylor didn't try to defend the neighborhood where she lived. Located in the outer edges of Chammont Point, the area was mostly forgotten as the tourist industry grew and people wanted to be closer and closer to the lake. The houses weren't well-kept, and the residents were a bit more sketchy than in other areas of town. Taylor insisted she liked the neighborhood because people kept to themselves. "I guess I could. If I found a decent place, I could live there while I fixed it up and then sell it for profit or something."

Darby gasped in the way she always did when a firecracker of an idea went off in her head. All her boutiques started with that little spark that grew and grew. She lived for that spark and the excitement of starting something new.

Even Jade moaned. "Oh boy."

"No," Taylor said before Darby could speak. "Whatever you're thinking, no."

Darby sat forward in her chair. "Listen—"

"*No.*"

Darby clutched her hands to her chest. "Taylor," she begged, "listen to me. This is brilliant."

"No."

Darby focused on Jade. "Seriously, you guys. We could be like Chip and Joanna Gaines."

Taylor sat back and creased her brow. "Who?"

Darby rolled her eyes as she wondered how Taylor lived so out of the loop of everything but decided this wasn't the time to educate her. "We buy a house. You do the repairs. I do the décor. Jade lists it to sell *by owner* so we don't have to pay some agent. Then we move on to the next one, making a big pile of money along the way."

"House flipping?" Taylor asked flatly.

Her tone implied she wasn't nearly as excited as Darby, but that was nothing new. Taylor rarely got excited about anything. She turned to Jade, who was looking equally skeptical.

"Yes," Darby said. "House flipping. We can do this. The three of us. We would be unstoppable. We would rule this town." She sat up and acted like she was placing a crown on her head. "Jennifer who? I don't know who that is. I'm queen around here."

"Darby." Taylor chuckled and shook her head. "That sounds great when you're watching a TV show, but the reality is not so glamorous."

"I have to agree," Jade said. "They don't show the really ugly side of house flipping on those shows."

"What side?"

"Losing your ass financially if you can't sell the property," Jade said.

Taylor nodded. "Or buying a property that's beyond repair and has to be torn down. Those people make money by being on TV."

"We would make money solely based on resell profits," Jade said. "It's risky."

"But it would be really cool remodeling run-down houses," Darby teased. "We could knock down walls and yank out cabinets. And...you know...sledgehammer stuff."

Taylor smiled slightly, which was saying a lot. In fact, that little smile said all Darby needed to know. Taylor was tempted. She liked the idea, even if she didn't want to admit it out loud. Which meant she needed Jade to agree so Taylor wouldn't be able to refuse.

Clasping her hands under her chin, Darby batted her eyes at Jade. That approach rarely worked, but she had to try. "Come on, Jade. It would be so much fun. *We* would have so much fun. We would be working together all the time."

"Oh," Taylor said, "in that case, I'm out. No way."

"Hey," Darby yelled. "That's rude!"

"What about your online store, Darbs?" Jade asked.

Darby waved her hand to dismiss the notion. "Un-Do is

all but sold." She gasped. "Oh my God! I really would be like Joanna!"

"That sounds like a lot of work," Jade said.

Darby knew that was more of a warning than an observation. Okay, she never did enjoy the laboring part of working, but this...this would be different. "This would be so much more exciting than running an online site. Don't you think?"

Taylor laughed lightly. "Maybe."

"It would be," Darby insisted. "And you know it."

"You couldn't do crazy décor, though," Jade stated seriously. "If you're staging a house to sell, you have to use neutral tones and normal furniture. Things that appeal to the masses."

"I can appeal to the masses."

"Right," Taylor said with a snort. "Okay, look, some states have restrictions. We'll have to check the laws and determine cost and how all this would fall into place. I'm not going to agree to anything without proper research. I'm not...*you*."

Darby grabbed her phone and tapped on the screen until a search engine revealed the answer to her question. "There are no state laws prohibiting flipping," she read, "but your mortgage holder may have rules on how soon a title can be changed." Beaming, Darby eyed Taylor as she used a cheerful, singsong voice. "We can totally do this."

"It takes money, Darby. We'd have to buy a house and pay for supplies with the hopes of making a profit. Just to be clear, what I'm saying is that we have to have *money* to *buy* a house and *pay* for supplies *before* we can even *try* to make a profit."

"Once *you* pick a house," Darby said, mocking the way

Taylor emphasized so many words, "tell *us* how much *we* need and *we'll* get the money."

Taylor rolled her eyes to her. "Darby, it's not that easy."

"Actually, it is. I'm about to sell Un-Do for way more than is reasonable. This guy really wants the site. He's an up-and-coming designer, and this is the perfect starting point for him." Earning money had never been a problem for Darby. She'd always found a way to earn a buck when she needed one...or several. Her problem was that once she had the money, she invested in the wrong things. Like the cabin that Jade had to buy from her so the repairs didn't swallow her up. Or that time she let a co-worker at a bar convince her to give him the money to create a company based on this brilliant idea he had to create a coffee soft drink. She later realized he'd stolen that from a well-established brand that had failed, despite investing millions compared to her measly deposit. By the time she called him on it, he'd already spent her money "testing the product."

Because she'd handed over cash, Darby had no way to prove she'd given him a dime, and she'd lost all the money she'd been saving up to move to California. Not that she would have stayed out there long anyway.

No, it was better if Darby used her good luck to make the money and let Taylor decide where to invest it. That way, they'd make their money back. And she could trust Taylor not to disappear with her investment.

"I don't mind making an initial investment," Jade said. "So long as Taylor is on board to do the repairs."

Darby gasped. "Did you hear that? We can do this, Taylor. We can *so* do this."

Taylor hesitated. "There's no guarantee we would make our money back. It really is risky."

"Okay," Darby said with a rarely used practical voice, "so we'll buy a house we can rent during the summer. If we can't sell it, we have a rental that will pay for itself over time. People pay out the ass for vacation rentals."

Taylor chuckled before nodding. "Okay, I'll think about it."

Squealing, Darby bounced in her chair. "This is going to be awesome!"

Darby put her hand under her nose as she stepped into the living area of the house she, Jade, and Taylor were viewing. The avocado shag carpet looked original to the place. The previous owner must have never moved the furniture. Walkways had been worn in, but where the couch, a coffee table, and what seemed to be a spot for a box TV in one of those big wooden consoles were, the carpet was as thick and green as if brand-new.

The scent of cheap beer and stale cigarette smoke overwhelmed the space. If she were blindfolded, Darby might have thought they'd walked into a bar that hadn't been cleaned for weeks. However, the little house wasn't large enough to have hosted more than a handful of people. At least not comfortably.

The entryway had a set of four carved floor-to-ceiling wood poles that Darby was certain didn't serve any purpose other than being what used to be stylish. The dark cherry stain on the outermost pole had been worn away from years of someone running a hand over the same spot time and time again.

She smiled slightly, despite the stench, as she pictured some stranger she'd never met running her hand over that spot as she aged. Or maybe the culprit was a child who had grown up in this home and was constantly chastised for touching the pole but hadn't been able to resist for so long, leaving a permanent mark that his parents had eventually grown to cherish.

Her heart grew heavy for a moment, wishing her mom had lived long enough to cherish all of Darby's quirks. There certainly had been plenty of them. When Darby was at some of her lowest points in high school, her mom seemed to sense that she was struggling. She'd always seemed to know when Darby had needed a walk on the beach or a long car ride listening to loud music to make her feel better. Of course Darby's taste in music compared to her mom's had been night and day, but her mom would usually let her listen to whatever she wanted.

Her mom had even learned the words to some of the more popular songs that Darby had listened to over and over. She'd drive along the scenic routes surrounding Chammont Lake doing her best to mimic Britney Spears and Christina Aguilera. But then she usually followed up with a reminder to Darby that pop music wasn't the best influence on her and that she should really consider sticking to more traditional music like Johnny Cash or Dolly Parton.

Darby's mom loved a good classic country song. A lump formed in Darby's throat as she ran her fingers over the pole again. She'd give about anything to have her mom there to take her on a car ride. She'd even let her listen to country music.

And she'd sing along.

"Holy shit," Taylor muttered, drawing Darby's attention to her.

Taylor and Jade now stood in the middle of the room looking over the sage-colored textured wallpaper. As she dared to run her fingers over the wallpaper, Darby gawked at the window trim that someone had painted an odd shade of lime.

"Oh, Taylor," Jade said. "What is this place?"

"Why is there so much green?" Darby asked. "I mean, I like green and all, but...*why*?"

"Well," the real estate agent said as he joined her at the window, "you can see why it's still on the market."

"This is going to be a lot of work." Taylor joined them and peered between the dusty vertical blinds toward the street.

Darby didn't need to look outside to recall how the little ranch reminded her of the set of a horror film. The front yard needed a lot of tough love from a landscaper. The bushes had been left to run wild, and the grass looked like no one had mowed the yard since the previous summer. The weeds were so overgrown, they seemed to be an intentional part of the abandoned home aesthetic this place had going on.

Darby had been hesitant to even get out of the car and walk to the front door. Honestly, if Taylor and Jade hadn't been with her, she probably would have driven right by, kept going without slowing down.

The house practically screamed *Come on in if you'd like to be brutally murdered and buried in the backyard with the others.*

The thought made Darby skim the old carpet for

bloodstains and body parts. "I think a serial killer lived here. Or at least someone who aspired to be one."

The real estate agent chuckled. "Well, at the very least, they murdered every fashionable trend that ever entered here."

Jade eyed him, but Darby laughed.

When he turned away, Taylor elbowed Darby and shook her head.

"What?" Darby whispered. "He's funny."

"He's trying to charm us into buying a house from him," Jade said.

"By being funny?"

"Yes. Stop responding to his cheesy jokes," Taylor warned and rolled her head back. After looking at the ceiling for several long seconds, she frowned. "This place needs so much work."

"Most things worth the time and money do," he said and then offered Darby a wink.

Darby started to smile but remembered Taylor's advice and simply shrugged. "I guess."

As Taylor and Jade moved farther into the house, Darby followed behind, almost afraid of what she might see next. Like the living area, everything in the kitchen was outdated and green—even the cabinets.

"What is with this color palette?" Darby asked. "Olive on top of avocado on top of sage." She trembled dramatically. "What kind of monster did this?"

The real estate agent chuckled. "Believe it or not, this was quite the setup in the seventies. I bet this was a happening place to be." He smiled and winked at Darby again.

Her breath caught a touch. The man had a killer smile,

and that wink... He was adorable. But then she spotted Taylor glaring at her. Darby looked away. She *wasn't* going to flirt with him. She *wasn't* going to flirt with him. She wasn't... Not much, anyway. And only because she needed Taylor to focus on the house rather than Darby's behavior.

Before Taylor would commit to anything, she wanted to find a house and estimate the cost of the purchase and repairs. Darby was trying to respect Taylor's logical approach, but she was dying a little inside. They'd been talking about this business idea for days. Taylor had a long list of *if this* and *if that* and *what if*, but Darby was ready to jump. Jade fell somewhere in the middle. She wanted to be cautious, but she also understood whatever they bought was going to need a certain amount of work. But she seemed ready to make a decision.

Taylor, on the other hand, was dragging her feet and doing calculations and...being *Taylor*. How many times did they have to go round and round about if they needed the money first or the price first? How many times could they possibly debate if they could or should or would? Taylor was driving Darby to the point of insanity. She was ready to scream from frustration. Shaking her head, Darby walked away so she wouldn't smile and bat her eyes at the agent. As much as she wanted to, that would distract Taylor from her internal cat and mouse chase, which would add more time to Taylor making a freaking commitment to their business idea.

While the real estate agent tried to break through Taylor's resistance using potential income and possible corners to cut on repairs, Darby opened a door and backed up three steps. "Oh, Lord. There's carpet on the bathroom floor. *Ladies*." She spun with her hand covering her heart as shock and horror rolled through her. "There's carpet in the bathroom."

"Gross," Jade muttered but didn't get any closer.

"It happens," Taylor said, moving to peek in. She scrunched up her face as she confirmed the same green shag from the living room was on the bathroom floor as well. "I bet the floorboards are shot from years of moisture being trapped against them."

A full-body shiver ran through Darby. "All kinds of moisture."

"Ew," Taylor said and visibly cringed. She skimmed the walls, painted the same lime green as the window trim in the living room, up to the cracked ceiling. "I don't know about this one, guys. There could be serious structural issues here. I think this might be too much work."

"You've said that about every house we've looked at," Darby said.

"Because I'm the one who's going to be doing the work," Taylor countered. "Your job is to make it pretty. My job is to make it habitable. That's going to be a big challenge in this place."

"The price is right," the agent offered from behind them, keeping plenty of distance between himself and the icky bathroom. "The owner passed away, and her son wants out from under it. We're three blocks from the beach, ladies," he added. "That's going to up the price quite a bit once you've completed renovations. Whether you resell or do a seasonal rental, you're going to make your money back. *Easy.*"

"Easy, he says." Darby nudged Taylor, who rolled her eyes and turned away. Darby looked to Jade, who shook her head. Clearly she wasn't sold on this house either.

"If it was easy," Taylor muttered, "he'd buy this dump and make the money himself."

Taylor was probably right. The project was going to be a lot more work than that cutie pie real estate agent was letting on, but she wasn't scared of the work. She had seen what Taylor could do. Taylor could take this place and make it a freaking palace in a matter of weeks. Okay, it might take longer than that, but she could do it. She could turn this lump of coal into a diamond. And Darby could make that diamond shine. They could resell this house and make a profit.

The rest of the house wasn't much better, however; one bedroom was decked out in blues. That must have been where the woman's son had slept. The one sanctuary from the inexplicable love of green. After exploring the inside, they moved to the overgrown backyard. The fenced-in space was larger than many yards this close to Chammont Lake. The city had squeezed as many houses into the vicinity as they could. This lot had been owned long enough that the boundaries hadn't been broken up when others were split. That would also add value to the resale price.

Darby's heart fluttered. Okay, so this place needed work, but even Taylor had to see the underlying value. However, Darby's hopes faded when Taylor began a speed round of asking how old things were, when stuff was updated, and other things Darby didn't care about. What Darby cared about was digging in and making this old house beautiful.

She wanted to pick paints and flooring. She wanted to choose decorations. She wanted to make something lovely. And this house was about to become a blank canvas. Yeah, Taylor was responsible for the bigger part of the project, but she had to see how awesome this place could be. This would be a great home for someone or a perfect rental property if they went that route. Darby looked to Jade, but she was too hard to read.

Darby could practically see how the little house would look with mostly neutral coloring. *Mostly*, because no matter what Taylor said, people did like pops of color, and if Darby knew anything, she knew how to bring color together. She could already imagine little turquoise and orange accents mixed with off-white walls and light blue furniture. Tame but colorful. Not boring but still within the confines of what most would see as normal.

Excitement filled her, and she nearly squealed out loud. She could hardly wait to start buying paint and décor and knickknacks. "Guys, this is going to be amazing," she whispered.

"Shh." Taylor hushed her and urged her toward the door.

"We'll talk about the pros and cons and get back to you," Jade said to the real estate agent.

She'd said that about every house they'd viewed because Taylor was still being a Debbie Downer about the entire thing.

Darby was certain as soon as they got into Taylor's truck, she'd say no. She'd list off all the reasons the house wasn't worth investing in and start the process over. No way. That wasn't happening this time. And Jade would be wishy-washy, and they would want to look at one more house, and then the cycle would start all over again. They were driving her crazy!

Darby was going to dig her heels in this time. For once she was going to push Taylor to jump into something and drag Jade along. She was going to strong-arm some spontaneity out of her friends if the effort killed her.

"We're doing it," Darby said as she buckled up. She sat back, waiting for Taylor's excuses to start rolling. The wait was short, only a few quiet seconds.

"I have to price—"

"We're doing it." Darby wasn't going to take no for an answer. She wasn't going to sit by and wait for Taylor to worm her way out of something she clearly was excited about. If she'd learned anything about her friends in the last year, it was that Taylor would do about anything to not try something new and Jade would be passive and indecisive until she was ready in her own time. Darby wasn't going to let them back out, not on their new business. "This is the one. The location is perfect. You heard the real estate agent. Even if we can't sell the house for a profit, we can rent it to cover the cost. We're doing this."

Taylor shoved her key into the ignition and turned until the engine kicked to life. Another long silence drew out before she continued her list of reasons why she might back out. "I have to price the supplies, Darby."

"We need an inspection," Jade added.

"Taylor," Darby stated in an unusually calm tone, "even if we have to replace the carpet, paint the walls, and clean up the landscaping, we can sell this place for more than it's listed. You know we can."

"Darby," Taylor said in an annoyingly mocking, calm tone, "if we buy this house and don't bring the electric, plumbing, and *everything* else up to code, we can't sell anything. We can't even try."

"Okay, if we find out the house is that bad, we have the

structure torn down and sell the lot."

Jade chuckled. "I admire your ambition, Darbs, but we're not buying anything until we know exactly what we're getting ourselves into."

Darby sank back in her seat.

"Since I'm already pissing on your parade," Taylor said, "let me remind you about the rules we set about mixing business and pleasure."

After blowing out a long raspberry, Darby shook her head. "He's cute, but...I have a date with Noah Joplin next week." She jolted and sat taller. "I can't believe I said that. I have a date. With Noah Joplin."

Jade laughed. "Oh, good! You guys are going to have a great time."

"Boys are gross," Taylor said. "I don't know why you want to date one."

"Sex," Jade and Darby said in unison.

Taylor shrugged. "Yeah. There's that. But...how are you going to have time to help me remodel a house if you have your head up some man's ass?"

"I absolutely will not have my—" Darby gasped as she looked at Taylor. "Are we doing this?"

Taylor turned in her seat to look at Jade. "What do you think?"

After one more glance toward the green house, she shrugged. "Yeah, let's do it."

"I guess we're doing it," Taylor said.

Darby clapped her hands and bounced. "Yes! This is going to be amazing!"

The End

ACKNOWLEDGMENTS

Thank you to Shelly Stinchcomb for all the hard work you have put in behind the scenes. Your efforts are very much appreciated.

COMING SOON

The Breaking Point

Book #3 of Chammont Point Series

ALSO BY MARCI BOLDEN

The Women of Hearts Series:

Hidden Hearts

Burning Hearts

Stolen Hearts

Secret Hearts

Other Titles:

California Can Wait

Seducing Kate

The Rebound

ABOUT THE AUTHOR

As a teen, Marci Bolden skipped over young adult books and jumped right into reading romance novels. She never left.

Marci lives in the Midwest with her husband, kiddos, and numerous rescue pets. If she had an ounce of willpower, Marci would embrace healthy living, but until cupcakes and wine are no longer available at the local market, she will appease her guilt by reading self-help books and promising to join a gym "soon."

Visit her here:
www.marcibolden.com

facebook.com/MarciBoldenAuthor
twitter.com/BoldenMarci
instagram.com/marciboldenauthor

9 781950 348657